A woman kidnapped . . .

She picked herself up from the roughhewn deck and rubbed her bruises. "It will take more, much more than that to make me cry," she said proudly.

"But it also takes much less," he commented with a grin, "to make you moan and thrash around with love."

Her color heightened. She was ashamed he could chide her for that. "Only a heathen devil would mistake disgust for love," Maida responded hotly.

She could hear the sounds of the women captives in the other ships. Some wept; others moaned. Like herself, no doubt, they had been ravaged and then put aboard the ships to be taken to Gottland. She crossed herself and silently prayed to the Blessed Virgin to succor her and all the other women who had fallen into the hands of the Vikings.

THRALL OF LOVE

Riva Carles

A BERKLEY MEDALLION BOOK
published by
BERKLEY PUBLISHING CORPORATION

I

TODAY WAS THE second most important day of her life; the first had been the day of her birth and the third would come when she would bear her first child, hopefully in nine months, or at the very least by next year at this time. Impatiently, Maida twisted away from the two serving women who were trying to bathe her and looked out of the narrow window.

Huddled nearby were the thatched stone houses of the villagers; some fifty in all, according to her marriage contract with Algar, the ealdorman of the shire, who held no less of a title than her father, a duke. In addition to carefully detailing the item of her dowry, the marriage contract gave her six more servants than she had in her father's castle, a horse of her own, and the right to build a chapel for herself should she desire one. These gifts were given by Algar to show his generosity and gain her love.

To the east, beyond the village itself, lay a small cove, protected from the violent surge of the sea, by a narrow strip of barren land bent like an arm around it, that even on this warm September day, was topped with sea mist, showing where the huge waves were torn asunder by the rocks.

She had already been told that during the winter, when the wind blows off of the sea, the thunder of the waves sounded like the beat of a mighty drum that engulfs everything, even the ringing of the church bells. Though she could not see them from the window, the fields of barley,

1

wheat and millet stretched from the edge of the village westward, to the distant rolling hills and southward to the river. And all of it belonged to the man whose wife she would that day be.

Maida placed her hands on either side of the narrow opening and standing on her tiptoes attempted to catch a glimpse of the commotion that suddenly errupted in the courtyard below.

She was a small woman of seventeen years, with firm, round breasts; a flat stomach and hips that would give ample support to a man and the children she would carry. Her dark complexion betrayed the strain of Roman blood in her mother's line, from which she also had been given her raven hair and glowing black eyes, fringed with thick ebony lashes.

"Fie, girl, to stand at the window with your breasts bare on your wedding day," Paige, the elder of the two women, scolded. "That sight is for your lord."

"That and much more," Glenna said with a lascivious laugh. "You can be sure he'll want to see more than just your breasts and do much more than just—"

"Hush up!" Paige exclaimed. "A husband has his rights. He does what God says he should do."

"Aye . . . But if that's God's work," Glenna responded between spurts of laughter, "I'd rather it be less demanding."

"Not so my pet," Paige said, now addressing her young mistress. "Your lord will only ask that he find satisfaction in you and for you to give him that requires no effort . . . It is your Christian duty to do it."

"Posh!" the other exclaimed derisively. "For her to just lie there like a slab of beef and let him have his way with her is a sure way to make him look for a wench who will add some sport to God's work."

Used to their constant chatter, Maida hardly heard them, though Paige had been more like a mother to her than any of the other women in her father's castle.

Paige and Glenna were slaves. They had been taken captive in a raid by her father. For awhile, Paige had even shared his bed. But after Maida's mother had died from the coughing sickness, he gave the woman to her. And years later, when her monthly blood had begun to flow, he presented her with Glenna.

Of the two women, Glenna cared much less about the delights of heaven than she did about the pleasure of life; and from her, Maida had heard the most delicious accounts of what happens between a man and a woman in bed, or any other place where they might couple.

Long before Glenna had told her anything about the sweet ecstasy that someday she would experience, Maida had seen the men and women of her father's court perform the rites of love in the dimness of the castle's great hall where everyone slept. And she had also heard the sighs of delight, the groans and grunts of deep satisfaction, and the moans of pleasure for a long time before she became curious enough to ask what caused them.

Glenna had vividly explained all: from the desire of the man to fondle a woman's breasts, even suck at the nipples like a child taking milk from its mother's teat, to the insertion of his tool into the place provided for it by the Devil in her body, to how the man will ride her until they become delirious with pleasure and finally how his fluid will gush into her at the moment when her body quakes with pleasure . . .

Though these were not Maida's precise thoughts, they hovered in her brain the way brightly colored butterflies dally over a field of summer flowers. And when the noise in the courtyard caught her attention, she was certain that

3

she heard the voice of her future husband, Algar. In that instant, those butterfly thoughts of future sensual delight rose up and quickened her breathing.

Maida strained to catch a glimpse of the man who would make all of Glenna's stories of passion and pleasure come true. She had seen him all but too briefly the previous night at supper; before then never. In the wavering yellowish-red light of the torches, he looked nothing like she had imagined he would. She had fancied him to be younger, and he was older, leaner, and he was thickset with broad shoulders and large hands. She had pictured him to be handsome—and though not ugly, he was considerably less than the image she had conjured for herself.

He had been dutifully courteous to her, asking about the health of her father, the pleasantness of the journey from her father's domain to his, and if she were pleased with the room he had provided for her and her two women.

After she had answered his questions, he had turned his full attention to devouring all the food that had been set before him, talking to his men in the local dialect that she could not understand, and drinking a great deal of mead.

The first meeting with Algar had left Maida if not disappointed, then most certainly confused. She had expected something more, some gesture from him that would have indicated he was pleased with her. But he seemed oblivious to her youth and beauty, though she had purposely worn a green gown cut low over the voluptuous swell of her breasts.

Now that she heard Algar's voice, Maida wanted to have another look at him in the full blaze of sunlight.

"Come away," Paige called.

"Soon," Maida answered. "I am certain I hear Algar."

"And well you should," Paige answered, "since it was he and his men who captured these devils from across the

4

sea just before we came down the road from the hills."

"Vikings?" Maida asked in a frightened whisper, turning to look at the woman.

"Twelve of them," Glenna said. "The others were routed and took to their ships."

As if she were suddenly touched by a chilling wind, Maida shuddered. Prickles rose on her skin and her nipples hardened with fear.

"Killed half as many as they took," Glenna told her. "It all happened in the early afternoon, where the road from the mountains follows the shore."

"I remember it," Maida answered, crossing her arms over her bare breasts to alleviate the chill that seized her.

She realized now why Algar had paid more attention to his men than to her. After such a bloody encounter, they needed his praise, his reassurance, and, most of all, his ability to make even the most difficult situation appear to be no more than some trivial matter. She had seen her father do the same thing many, many times. For Algar to have done anything less would have lessened him in the eyes of his men and in her eyes, too. When the opportunity presented itself, she would tell him how proud of him she was. Perhaps after the wedding feast, or when they were in bed before he took her? But she wanted to know more about what had happened.

Anticipating her mistress's next question, Paige said, "I was told about the skirmish this morning by one of the castle servants when I went to fetch water for your bath. She also told me that all of those captured would probably be killed and their heads stuck up on poles along the beach to serve as warning to others of their kind."

"And I was told last night by one of Algar's men," Glenna informed them, "that one of those taken captive is a chieftain, the kinsmen of a jarl."

"Not one full day here, and you have already lain with

one of Algar's men,'' Paige commented critically.

Glenna shrugged. "He told me Algar intends to make a slave of the chieftain."

"Christ save us all from such slaves," Paige responded, crossing herself.

Still naked, Maida turned back to the window and strained to see more of what was happening below her in the courtyard.

II

THE EIGHT CAPTIVES were fettered to one another with a stout rope looped around each of their necks and a second one coiled around their bare waists. Their hands were tied securely on yokes of wood laid across their shoulders. Several of them were streaked with dull red stains of dried blood. Two were gray with age, and all, even those whose wounds would soon kill them, stood still and silent in the blazing sun.

Algar paced back and forth in front of his prisoners. In his right hand be carried a switch of oak and every so often, he laid it hard across the callused palm of his left hand and then with a swift backhand motion, he sent it slashing down on the captive nearest him. Before long, everyone of them felt the searing pain of the switch but none uttered a sound or made any attempt to dodge the lash.

"When I tire of this," he told them loudly, "the reeve can beat you and when he tires, my sergeant can do it. You will be beaten until I find out which of you is Geir, your chieftain . . . I know he's here . . . I know his name. In the fray yesterday I heard it called several times."

Algar stopped pacing and waited for one of the captives to speak, but when none did, he went straight to one of the old men and beat him until blood streamed from his shoulders and chest. The old man cowered under the lashing and finally dropped to his knees.

Suddenly one of the captives shouted, "Enough!"

7

Algar stayed the movement of the switch. His brow was beaded with sweat and his eyes glazed with fury. He looked toward the man who spoke. He was the last man in the line of captives.

"I am Geir," he said.

An angry murmur came from the people in the court yard who had come to see their ealdorman mete out punishment to the marauders. All of them knew who Geir was. By telling them they would be left for Geir and his men, mothers sometimes frightened their wayward children into behaving. In truth, during several of the past summers, Geir and his men swept down on some unsuspecting hamlet or town to plunder and rape, and carried off many of the children into slavery. Geir and the Devil were one and the same.

"Leave the old man be," Geir said. "I'm the one you seek."

With a swift movement of his arm, Algar wiped the sweat from his brow. Geir was younger than he would have thought . . . Perhaps only twenty or so? He was tall, slender, not as broad-shouldered as himself, but no less muscular. His face, that portion of it revealed above his blond beard, was weathered to the color of old leather. His eyes were light blue and his long hair was flaxen.

Algar summoned the reeve and handing the switch to him, he said, "Continue to beat the old man until I tell you to stop."

Geir suddenly shouted something in his native tongue. In an instant, the two ends of line came together, encircling the reeve in their midst. "We'll stomp him to death," Geir shouted.

The reeve screamed for help.

Algar ordered his men to free the king's agent. They broke through the circle of bound men and flung them to the ground.

8

The reeve was dragged to safety, but blood poured from his nose, his jaw was smashed, and most of his ribs were stove in.

The tumult ended as abruptly as it began. The captives were sprawled in the dust.

"Viking!" Algar shouted at Geir. "Save you, all of them will die."

Geir struggled to his feet. His men followed his example and stood up.

"Cut him away from the rest of them," Algar ordered, pointing to the Viking chieftain.

Several of the castle's men ran forward. In a few moments, they cut the two ropes that bound Geir to the other Vikings.

"Bring him here," Algar ordered.

Geir was roughly herded to where the duke stood.

"On your knees, Viking!" Algar commanded.

"I bow to no man."

"Then you will learn. Teach him to bow."

The next instant, the duke's man threw Geir to the ground.

"You will be my slave, Viking," Algar told him. "You will wear a rope around your neck and walk like a dog at my side. If you disobey me, I will beat you, as I would any dog. You will be taught tricks by our jester and if you do not learn them, you will be beaten. I will make you wish you were dead. What have you to say to that?

Geir remained silent.

"Answer me when I ask a question!" Algar fumed.

Gathering a wad of spittle in his mouth, Geir lifted his face and spat. Algar grabbed hold of Geir's hair. He wrenched his head back, and he said, "I will not let you provoke me into killing you, Viking. . . . I want you to live and suffer."

Geir's eyes became mere slits. Many times in the past

9

he had raided this part of the English coast and had fought against Algar and his men. Twice they had even exchanged sword thrusts, but Algar had always broken off the fight and run. But yesterday the duke came upon them just as they were beaching their ships. The fight that followed was swift. Geir and his men fought a holding action and though he had signaled to Bjorn, his cousin, to join the fight, Bjorn had not come.

"Others from Lid's stronghold on the other side of the sea will take warning from what I do to you and your men," Algar said. "And they will think twice before they come here to plunder."

Some distance beyond the dark mass of Algar's shoulders, where there was an opening in the gray stone of the castle wall, Geir caught sight of a woman. She was peering down into the courtyard. In the bright sunlight her hair was as black as a raven's feathers. Her shoulders were bare, and when she strained to see more of what was happening, he could see the white slope of her breasts.

"Viking," Algar thundered, "I will teach you how to bark like a dog. Unless you bark to my satisfaction, you will not be fed." He let go of Geir's hair and said, "Kill the others and have their chieftain put each of their heads on poles."

"Kill me too!" Geir exclaimed, struggling to his feet.

Algar delivered another blow that sent the Viking sprawling in the dust.

Geir made a third attempt. This time he was successful, and before the duke could knock him to the ground again, he ran toward his men.

Algar went after him, and grabbing hold of the end of the rope around Geir's neck, he pulled hard.

The Viking stumbled and went down headfirst.

"Kill them," Algar ordered, waving his men toward the captives. They rushed at them with drawn swords, and in a matter of minutes, all of the Vikings were dead. They died willingly, shouting the name of their god, Odin, as they ran to meet the sword thrusts. The brown dust of the courtyard where they lay was stained red with blood. When the killing was done, the heads were chopped away from the bodies.

Algar pulled Geir to his feet, and pointing to the dead men, he said, "See that you plant their heads so they look out toward the open sea, toward your land."

Geir said nothing. His neck and shoulders ached with more pain than he had known even after having labored at the oars for three days and three nights without a moment's respite. Flies were already bloating themselves on the fresh blood of the dead men, and overhead the crows were gathering to feast on the bodies.

Geir turned his eyes up toward the wheeling birds and he remembered that Kar, the old soothsayer, had said the gods were against the raid, that many of those who would go with him would become carrion for the crows, and that he himself would be no less than a dog—his hands stained with the blood of his kinsmen. . . . His eyes followed the flight of the birds, and as they passed over the tower, he saw the woman again. For an instant, she looked straight at him. Then she vanished, leaving the space empty and filled with yellow light of the sun.

Algar beckoned to his sergeant. "When Geir is finished putting the heads on the poles, bring him back to me. I want to show him to Maida. Perhaps when he is trained, she might take pleasure in leading him around." And handing the end of the rope to his man, he added, "If he tries to escape, beat him senseless. But I do not want him killed."

"Yes, my lord," the sergeant answered.

"As for these," Algar said, pointing to the bodies, "have some of the men gather them together and throw them into the race. The tides will take them out to sea by nightfall.''

''It will be done, my lord.''

''Viking,'' Algar said, ''tonight you will see how Christian men live. Tonight you will be my special guest at my wedding feast, and if you bark to my satisfaction, I will throw you a scrap of meat. Now attend to the task of putting the heads of your men on poles. . . .''

III

IN THE GREAT hall that was ablaze with torchlight for the wedding feast, Maida sat to the right of her husband. Over a smock of white linen, she wore a blue tunic of dark silk, embroidered with gold thread at the ends of the sleeves. Her long black hair was covered by a light blue head rail, the end of which crossed her bosom and reached below her knees. Her cheeks were flushed with excitement, and she laughed easily at the ribald jests made by various members of Algar's court.

The laughter was loud and merry. There was more food than she had ever seen, even in her father's castle at Christmas or Easter.

On each table there were pewter and wooden trays laden with sweetmeats of every kind, roasted suckling pigs, huge saddles of venison. Some trays were piled high with whole chickens, pheasants, and grouse, while others held huge salmon and trout that had been freshly caught and baked that very afternoon.

Mead and beer were brought to the tables in huge flagons, and there was even red wine from the land of the Franks for those who wanted it.

Algar ate a great deal of venison and two small chickens. He urged her to eat, but she was too excited to even be hungry.

From the little she could understand, much of the conversation was about Algar's capture and punishment of the Vikings. His vassals were loud in their praise of his victory, and she, too, was enormously proud of his accomplishment.

Several times Algar leaned close to her and purposely slowed his speech so that she could more easily understand him. He told her his kinsmen thought her beautiful and that they said that they would pray to God that she bore many beautiful children.

These words brought a bloom of fresh color to her cheeks, and smiling at him, she answered, "And if God grant my wish, my lord, the first will be a son."

Algar put his arm around her and drawing her to him, he said, "By the living God, I am sure it will be a son!"

One of the men offered a toast to the forthcoming child. Several more toasts followed that one. Some were for Algar and many were for Maida.

With his left hand, Algar rapped on the table several times. Then he stood up and shouted for silence. After a few moments, the great hall was quiet.

Algar said, "I have this day, made a slave of Geir the Viking. Let my slave be brought to me so that I may show him to everyone."

A door creaked open. A sudden breeze rushed into the hall making the torches burn more fiercely.

With a rope around his neck, Geir was led into the huge chamber. His hands and chest were stained a dull red from the bloody work he had done. He moved his eyes up toward the high ceiling, where the crossbeams were blackened with age; along the walls, where there were openings, and finally across the many tables to the huge door.

Geir realized that there was no way for him to escape; he would be cut down before he ever reached the door or any of the other openings in the wall.

"Viking," Algar shouted, "have you finished the task I gave you?"

Geir's eyes fastened on the woman seated next to Algar. She was the one he had seen in the opening above the courtyard; he was sure of it.

"He seems more interested in Maida than in anything else," Algar commented laughingly to his guests. "Here, give me the end of that rope. Viking, have you nothing to say, no words of praise for my wife or no wish that our union be fruitful?"

His eyes still on the woman called Maida, Geir remained silent. In his wretched state, he could still feel desire, especially for a woman as lovely as this one.

Maida tried to avoid the Viking's eyes but could not. Even in the wavering light of the torches, they were as blue as a summer sky. She could feel his eyes moving slowly over her breasts and then back to her own eyes.

She struggled to look away, but could not. His blood-stained hands repelled her. Her stomach twisted with nausea. The man at the end of the rope was hardly human. Yet she could not turn from him. Maida was shocked to find herself filled with a strange heat.

A second silence fell over the guests as they watched the Viking and Maida. Algar, too, was stunned by what he saw; then, flashing with anger at Geir's bold exhibition of lust for his still-virgin wife, he jerked violently at the rope.

Geir fell across the table, overturning a flagon of wine and spoiling a platter of sweetmeats. He looked up at the Saxon duke and said, "May the gods give you less than you gave to my men."

Easing his hold on the rope, Algar ordered Geir to stand. Then he said to Maida, "When I have trained him, you will be able to walk with him as you would any dog. See how he obeys . . . Viking, bark . . . bark for your meat!"

Geir flicked his blue eyes back to Maida. She seemed to be holding her breath.

15

"Bark!" Algar commanded. "Bark for my lovely bride."

"Yes," Maida suddenly said, with a ragged sigh, "please bark!"

Geir slowly shook his head.

"Dog," Algar shouted, suddenly leaping over the table to where Geir stood, "you'll bark for my new wife, or I'll have your tongue cut out." He grabbed the Viking by the throat and forced him to his knees. "Bark for my lady."

Geir fought to free himself. But with his hands still bound to the yoke across his shoulders, it was impossible. The best he could do was to prevent Algar from getting a good hold on his throat by twisting around as violently as possible.

Most of the guests urged their lord to throttle the Viking. But there were some who cried out, "Let him be . . . In God's name, let him be."

Intuitively Maida knew she was to blame for what was happening to the captive, but she powerless to stop it.

Algar was too enraged by Geir's lack of response to do Maida's bidding to heed anyone.

She tried to call out, but the sounds coming from her mouth were too weak to be heard above the tumult in the hall.

Algar and the Viking fell against the table. But suddenly in one of the openings at the other side of the hall, Geir caught sight of a flame-tipped arrow. He glanced at the nearer opening; there, too, he saw a flame-tipped arrow. The next instant, the whir of loosed arrows rose above the noise in the hall.

The women in the hall screamed; the men rushed for their weapons.

Algar let go of Geir and leaped for his sword.

More arrows came whirring down into the hall from the openings in the walls. Some were tipped with flames and others were not. Fire, smoke, and the cries of the wounded soon filled the room.

Again and again a battering ram smashed against the huge door until finally it broke away from its hinges and crashed to the floor of the hall. The instant it was down, the Vikings rushed into the hall. Shouting the name of Odin, they killed with sword, spear, and battle-ax.

Terrified, Maida cowered against the wall, and watched the slaughter, immobilized with horror. Then suddenly she began to scream and started to run.

Geir went after her and pinning her to the stones with his body, he rasped, "Do not run or you'll die."

Suddenly Geir heard his name being called.

"Here, Bjorn, here!" Geir shouted, recognizing his cousin's voice.

Moments later a helmeted Viking rushed out of the smoke.

"Cut me free," Geir told him, "and give me your sword. I have some killing to do."

"What about the woman?" Bjorn asked, looking at Maida.

"She's mine." Geir answered. "She's mine. See that no harm comes to her, cousin." And taking Bjorn's sword, he rushed to where the fighting was still going on.

Taken completely by surprise, Algar's men did not have the time to offer any hard resistance. Those who fought were quickly killed by the ferocity of the attackers. Most of the duke's men fled with him into the hills, where he hoped to re-form his units and mount a counterattack. But it soon became obvious to Algar that the men had had enough of the Vikings for one night and he would have to fight them another time. Full of hate for Geir, he silently swore to find and slay the Viking. There would be no other way for him to reclaim his honor other than to bring Geir's head back to his people and his wife back to the castle;

though she, too, would have to answer for her disloyalty.

Once the killing in the great hall was over, Geir returned to where he had left Maida. He was wet with sweat and stained with fresh blood. He stopped at a table to drink some mead and cut a piece of venison for himself.

"Algar escaped," he said, looking at Maida. "I would have respected him more if he had stayed and died like a man." Then, turning to his cousin, who was no older than himself, but not as tall and not as blond, he thanked him for returning. "If you had waited much longer, I might have lost my tongue," Geir laughed, tearing off a piece of meat with his teeth.

Bjorn shrugged and answered, "Perhaps I should have waited longer to see how you would have managed without a tongue?" Then, pointing to Maida, he said, "I will buy her from you."

Geir shook his head. "She's not for sale," he said, taking hold of her hand, pulling her to him.

"My share of the plunder?" Bjorn offered.

"Not for all of it," Geir answered. "This day she married Algar, but I'll be the man warmed by her tonight."

Maida tried to break away from him, "Devil," she cried, "murdering filthy devil! God forgive me," she wept, "I was foolish enough to pity you . . . But now— I'm sorry Algar didn't kill you.

With one swift movement, Geir slung the woman over his shoulder. He walked swiftly through the wreckage left by the fray.

Maida pounded on his back and pleaded with Christ, the son of God, to save her. Ashamed now of what she had felt for the Viking, she prayed to be forgiven and promised never to let herself lust after any man and to be a Christian wife to her husband, if God would return her to him.

Geir carried the woman down to where the dragon-prowed ships were beached and boarded one of them.

"It will be easier for you," he said, dropping her into the stern, "if you do not fight me."

"Kill me!" Maida cried, knowing he only wanted to despoil her, that he would take by brute force the virginity which she would have eagerly surrendered to Algar.

He laughed and roughly pushed her down.

She thrashed under him. He smelled of sweat. She raked his cheek with her fingernails.

"Bitch!" he shouted, slapping her across the face. "Saxon bitch!" He tore the top of her gown from her body and grabbed hold of her bare breasts.

"Oh my God!" she cried out, wincing with pain. His hands were all over her body.

He pulled the bottom of her gown over her hips.

His touch now was suddenly less violent than she had expected it would be. His fingers stroked her thighs and moved over the kinky hair of her womanhood. Her breath quickened. "Devil!" she gasped. "Devil, what are you doing to me?"

"No more or less than any man does to a woman," he answered gruffly.

Maida tried to push him away but couldn't. His hand was at her sex, touching her in a way that made her tremble.

"Holy mother of God," she whispered fervently, "protect me from—" Suddenly she felt his hard organ probing where his hand had been. "No . . . Dear God, no!"

She shouted. But her cries went unheeded. The Viking had already impaled her. She shrieked as he rammed through her maidenhead.

For several moments he pinioned her body with the weight of his own.

Tears flowed down Maida's cheeks. She could still feel

19

the searing pain where his organ had pierced her. Her virtue had been torn from her. She had been ravished by a barbarian on her wedding night.

Maida looked up at him. His face glistened with sweat. He was breathing hard and his eyes were no more than narrow slits. The pain lessened and she was beginning to feel the full thrust of him inside of her body. He started to move, ever so slowly. She began to move, though she tried not to. She closed her eyes. Suddenly she realized she was clinging to him.

"Yes," he said, "yes . . . it is something every man and woman learns to do quickly."

Maida couldn't tell if he was mocking her or not. She opened her eyes. Nothing in the face above hers indicated mockery.

His movement quickened. Never had she experienced the wonderful strange sensations that flowed from the depths of her. She moved her head from side to side and uttered a low, throaty sound. Her body became as taut as a drawn bow.

"I hate you," she wailed, "I will always hate you . . . Always . . . Always . . . Al—" Her speech faltered. The bow-like tautness suddenly snapped, leaving her trembling with pleasure. A moment later she heard Geir utter a low growl. Then, as he thrust hard against her, she felt the hot gush of his fluid.

Later, after Geir left her, Maida sat up. The castle and the houses of the village were in flames, and the Vikings were already bringing their plunder to the ships. Now and then she saw Geir or heard him order one of his men to do something.

Alone, on the stern sheet of the ship, Maida wept for herself, for Paige and Glenna, who no doubt had suffered the same fate as herself . . . perhaps even worse? She wept

20

also for Algar and for having been guilty of experiencing pleasure with the man who had raped her. . . .

The dawn came gray and heavy with the scent of burning wood. The Vikings returned to the ships, refloated them, and took their places at the oars.

Geir came back to Maida and said, "We sail for my uncle's stronghold."

"May God drown all of us," she answered, looking up at him.

He ignored her and climbing high on the stern, he shouted, "To Gottland, men. We sail for Gottland!" The oars skimmed the water and the ship began to move slowly toward the mouth of the cove, where the sea began.

IV

THERE WAS A chill in the early morning air that forced Maida to draw the heavy sheepskin robe more securely around her aching body. Soon the ship would be on the open sea, and everything she had known or had dreamed about would be gone forever.

She glanced back to the land. A pall of dark smoke hung over what had been, only the previous evening, Algar's village, her future home.

Maida shook her head with disbelief at what had befallen her. She dearly would have wanted to believe that it was all a bad dream, a nightmare visited upon her for having engaged the Viking's eye with her own in front of her husband.

"Dear Lord, make it a dream," Maida humbly implored, squeezing her eyes shut. In the few moments of self-imposed darkness, the sound of oars in their oarlocks and on the water became a series of loud squeaks and a continuous rhythmic splashing. She prayed more fervently but to no avail, as she could not deny the dried blood between her thighs, she could not deny, even with such prayers to Christ, the reality of where she was. Maida opened her eyes and glared up at the man who had raped her.

He was standing just a short distance from her. His right hand was on a huge oaken staff that was connected to another object. By moving the staff, she realized he could change the direction of the ship.

In the pale gray light of the morning, Maida was able to study Geir. He was broad, and from the force he had used to subdue her, she knew he was very, very strong.

The memory of his hands on her body, of his organ sheathed in her body, inexplicably quickened the beating of her heart. She frowned. His initial assault had rent her apart, or so it had seemed. But afterward she had experienced more pleasure, more delight than she had ever believed she would, and it had come to her when she was being despoiled by one of the Devil's very own, a Viking.

Maida flushed guiltily and she looked away from Geir. The pleasure she had felt had been no more than the Devil's temptation, of that she was sure. And when next she would go to confession, she would purge herself of it. She would ask the priest to give her a harsh penance, something that would never let her forget that she felt delight, when she should have been filled with revulsion; that she had experienced pleasure, when pain would have pleased God more and that even now, she could not free her mind from the ecstasy of Geir's wild, overpowering embrace.

To stifle a cry of shameful rage, Maida bit her lip. With the back of her hand, she wiped the tears that streamed out of her eyes.

Suddenly Geir shouted something, and in unison the men lifted their oars out of the water.

Maida swung toward her captor. In an instant, she hurled herself at him, hoping to tumble him into the water. But at the same moment she moved, he looked at her.

With a burst of laughter, Geir nimbly leaped aside.

Maida sprawled across the railing of the ship, and she found herself looking down at the water.

The other Vikings were now also laughing.

Geir lifted her up and said, "I told them what you tried to do. They think it was very foolish of you to try to push me off the ship."

"And I suppose you could not be thrown off the ship?" She questioned, glaring at him.

"By a half dozen of my men, yes. But by you, no." He shook his head and began to laugh again.

"Jesters are to be laughed at," Maida screamed, flinging herself at him. No one had ever laughed at her; she would not permit anyone to treat her that way. With her nails, she went for his eyes.

Laughing even harder than before, Geir fended off her flailing hands.

The men at the oars shouted and continued to laugh.

"I meant to kill you," she shrieked, "I want to kill you."

Geir grabbed hold of her, clamping his large hands around her waist. Then, with one swift movement, he swept her off her feet and sent her hurtling down toward the stern sheet.

She uttered a wordless scream of terror. Until she crashed painfully down on the ship, Maida was certain that she was being thrown overboard.

She gasped for breath. She tried to rub the pain out of her arms and shoulders, where she hurt the most. And though tears came to her eyes, she would not give Geir and the other devils with him the satisfaction of seeing her weep.

Geir spoke to his men and they answered him. "I told them," he said, looking at her, "that it took courage for you not to shed tears, and they agreed with me."

"It will take more, much more than that to make me cry," she said proudly.

24

"But it also takes much less," he commented with a grin, "to make you moan and thrash around with love."

Her color heightened. She was ashamed he could chide her for that. "Only a heathen devil would mistake disgust for love," Maida responded hotly.

A thickset, grizzled bearded man at the oars called out to Geir and he spoke to him, taking a long time before he finished. Then he said to her, "Since my men do not understand your language, Sven asked me to tell them what we were talking about."

"And you did?" she asked, coloring again.

"I did," he told her, with a vigorous nod. "They have a right to know, since I owe them my life."

"Oh!" she exclaimed several times before she realized every one of the Vikings was again laughing at her.

The sun was up. The gulls wheeled and screamed at one another as they flew in a gray sky.

Geir signaled to the other ships to stop. There were only two of them from what Maida could see. Not more than ninety men had defeated a force five times their size and had put the whole town to the torch.

Though she could not see them, Maida could hear the sounds of the women captives in the other ships. Some wept; others moaned. Like herself, no doubt, they had been ravaged and then had been put aboard the ships to be taken to Gottland, wherever that might be, and used to satisfy the lust of their captors or sold to other heathens for whatever devilish use they would put them to. She crossed herself and silently prayed to the Blessed Virgin to succor her and all of the other women who had fallen into the hands of the Vikings.

The ships lay within hailing distance of one another, but none started for the mouth of the cove. There was a great deal of conversation between Geir, Bjorn, the man he had called cousin, and a third Viking whose name, from what she could understand, was Thorkel.

The three men shouted to each other from the sterns of their ships and made great sweeping gestures with their arms.

Maida listened to what Geir was saying. Some of the words sounded almost familiar, but Geir was speaking so fast that she was unable to identify any of them. But the language of the Vikings was harsher than her own and stranger to her than the Saxon dialect spoken by Algar and his men.

More from the disturbed expression on Geir's face than from any comprehension of what he was talking about did she come to realize that he was troubled by something and that knowledge pleased her greatly. She would have willingly forsworn a year of pleasure to see him tormented by the flames of hell for only a few minutes.

The conversation between the three Vikings ceased. Then Geir, with his brow deeply furrowed and his blue eyes dark with anger, turned to Maida. He looked at her for a long time without speaking.

The hard ice-blue stare of his eyes made her uncomfortable. She desperately wanted to look away. Though he made her feel completely naked, she would not give him the satisfaction of disengaging her eyes from his.

"Bjorn claims you," Geir told her. "He says that he gave me my life, and now he demands that I give you to him."

Maida sucked in her breath and slowly exhaled. She did not know what to say.

"I owe Bjorn my life," Geir said, almost as if he were weighing that debt against his claim on her.

"And will you give me to him?"

Geir shook his head.

Maida sighed with relief. The prospect of being used by

yet another man the way Geir had used her was unbearable.

"Now he demands that we sail to his father's stronghold, where the matter will be settled."

"But you just told me you would not give me to him," she challenged. "Will you go back on your word once we are in his father's stronghold?"

"I will not give you up," Geir responded harshly. He suddenly moved his eyes from her to where Bjorn was on the stern of his ship and he shouted, "We will not sail until the men are rested and their wounds tended."

Bjorn shouted something back.

"He says," Geir explained, "that he will sail without me."

"Will you let him?"

"No," he told her. "I am chieftain of this party. He will have to kill me in order to take command. He knows that and so do all of the men."

"What does Thorkel say about the matter?" she asked.

Geir acknowledged her use of the other captain's name with a nod of approval. Then he called out to Thorkel. After the man answered, he told Maida, "He says he will not go against me or aide Bjorn." Then Geir shouted to his cousin, "In this fight it will be friend against friend, and how will you answer to your father for that and for disobeying my orders?"

Bjorn rubbed his jaw.

"When he does that," Geir said to Maida, "he is not sure of his thoughts." And again he called out to Bjorn, saying, "Come, cousin, our men have served us well; let us not turn them against one another like wolves turn against their own. Though all our warriors hope to enter Valhalla, let us not be the means by which they open its doors. It would be a better death for those who would die if they died while fighting Saxons, Franks, or even Moors.

27

And our fight would give great joy to Algar, who is probably on the shore watching us."

Hearing Geir speak Algar's name made her turn and look back toward the town. There were only wisps of smoke now coming from the charred ruins of some of the houses and the castle. With tears once more blurring her vision, she turned away.

Bjorn considered Geir's words for several moments before he spoke. "I do not want the blood of my men on my hands," he said. "I will wait until we reach the stronghold to settle our differences."

"Well spoken!" Geir responded.

"Well spoken!" Thorkel agreed.

Only when Maida had once more turned away from the sad remains of the town, did she suddenly become aware of the terrible tension that held all of the Vikings in its grip. The men in the ship had slipped their shields from the sides of the vessel, placed them on their left arm, and with their right hand took hold of their spears. Though some of them were splotched with dried blood from the previous night's battle, they were ready at Geir's command to once again throw themselves into the fray; they were grim looking berserks, and she had no doubt that the same kind of tension prevailed on Bjorn's ship.

As it became clear that Bjorn was not willing to risk a bloody encounter with Geir's men, the shields were replaced in their respective slots along the sides of the vessel, and each man set his spear down at the side of his rowing bench.

With the threat of battle passed, the men called easily from ship to ship, and there was much laughter between them.

Maida was taken completely surprised by the swiftness of change in the Vikings. Within minutes they had gone from the willingness to shed one another's blood to an easy exchange of jests that caused laughter among the men of all three long ships.

The troubled look on Geir's face was gone, and he stepped lightly down from his place in the stern to go among his men and see to their wounds.

From the way they slapped him on the back, Maida did not have to understand their language to know that his men held him in high regard.

All of them made light of their wounds, though it was obvious from the attention he gave some that their wounds were severe. Several times he stood above one or another of the men and sadly shook his head. Then, quite without warning, he called to her.

Maida did not move.

"Several of my men are badly hurt," he said. "They need more attention than I can give them, if they are to survive."

She did not answer, or make any attempt to move. She was the daughter of a duke and not just some woman whom he happened on.

Geir was standing toward the bow of the ship. The man on his right side was slumped over his oar. "If he dies," he told her, "I will not only put you in his place at the oar. But I will sell you—"

Full of anger, she started up and shouted. "You raped me and then carried me off on the night of my wedding. Now you ask me to help you?"

"I ask you for nothing. I *tell* you to help him," Geir answered, placing his hand on the man's shoulder. "His wound needs tending."

"I will help none of you," she cried.

Geir barked an order to two of his men.

In a trice, Maida found herself being dragged to where Geir was standing. He pointed to the injured man.

She moved her eyes toward a member of the crew. His

left side was rent by a long gash and his chain mail shirt was sticky with blood. The sight of the wound drove the color from her face.

Geir said, "If you can stop the bleeding, he might live. He is young and strong enough to sustain such a wound. I myself did when I was his age—younger perhaps by a year or two."

Maida's lips trembled. "You should have died, Geir."

He shrugged and pointed to the young Viking and told her, "You can see me into Valhalla some other time. Now it is up to you to keep him alive. His name is Elnar, and I promised his old mother I would bring him back."

"You should have thought of your promise before you let him take part in the fighting."

"Sooner or later he would have fought," Geir answered. "It is best to begin sooner. Will you tend him?"

Without answering, Maida bent down alongside of the young man. She did what she could to stanch the flow of blood, but she told Geir that it would be a miracle if the boy lived. Then, at Geir's side, she looked at the wounds of the other men. Some she was able to bandage with the rags that were handed to her. Others remained open and would eventually heal in long, terrible scars.

When she finished, she said to Geir that he would probably lose five of his men.

He nodded and spoke to his crew. When he was finished, he explained that he told them what she had said.

"But why make them miserable?" she asked, sitting down in the stern sheet again.

He shook his head.

"They are going to die!" Maida exclaimed.

"Their wounds are honorable," he answered. "They will enter Valhalla and forever afterward live in the great hall enjoying the life of a warrior."

Maida did not even bother to shake her head in denial of

30

what Geir had just told her. Vikings were heathen, and when they died they went straight to hell without hope of redemption, even when Christ would come again and harrow hell.

"My men are grateful for what you did for them," Geir said.

"I do not accept their gratitude," she told him haughtily. "I did it because you threatened me with—"

"But you did do it," he said, interrupting her.

With a sigh, she nodded. Then she asked, "Do you always get your way?"

He shook his head and answered. "Only when the gods smile on me. Otherwise, like most men, I must fight for whatever I want."

Maida did not understand him or his words. In her father's castle she never had to ask for anything. Everything was there for the taking, and had Geir not come to steal her away, she would have expected her life with Algar to be much the same as it had been in her father's castle. She would have had everything she had ever wanted. Now she was a slave—and worse. The loss of that prospective contentment filled her with an overwhelming sadness. She buried her face in her arms and began to weep softly.

V

THE SLOW RHYTHMIC heave of the ship riding on the waters of the cove had a lulling effect on Maida. The tears stopped flowing from her eyes, and she felt the weariness in her body slip its long mysterious tendrils around her arms and legs. Never had she felt so tired, never had she gone so long without sleeping.

She let the heaviness in her eyelids have its way, and with a deep sigh of relief closed them. Now all she could hear was the creaking of the wood and the mournful cries of the gulls that at times almost sounded human.

Within moments she was in a deep, dark sleep and sometime after that she was back in her father's castle. He was sitting at the huge table in the great hall. Though she could not see his face, she knew it was her father by the timber of his voice. It was full and rich for a man of his years. There was a good fire going in the hearth behind him. His words floated across the table.

"I have arranged for you to marry Algar, an ealdorman of some wealth who lives on the coast of the north country," he said.

"I would rather abide with you," Maida answered.

"The years weigh me down," her father said. "Algar will be a fine husband. He stands high in King Alfred's esteem."

"And when will I marry him?" she asked.

"I will send you to him in the fall of the year," her

father told her. "You will take your serving women Paige and Glenna with you."

"And will you come, too?"

"I am too old," he answered sadly. "I must spend the rest of my days preparing to meet God. But my blessings and my love will go with you."

Maida shuddered in her sleep. She loved her father, and even in the dream it saddened her to realize she would go forth to her marriage with only her serving women for company. But in his younger days, her father, Edward Penrose, the duke of Wickhamshire, had sinned much, having killed many men in his rages and having taken many women to satisfy his lust. And now, with the aid of Father Quinell, he was endeavoring to undo as much as he possibly could before giving up his ghost.

"You must be obedient in all things toward Algar," her father told her. "And do nothing that will bring dishonor to his name or to your own."

"Yes, father," she answered.

"And bring forth sons," he told her. "The first will bear my name."

"Yes, father."

The old duke sipped beer from a copper tankard and wiped the suds from his beard with the back of his hand. "Have you anything to say? he asked.

"Have you seen this man who will be my husband?"

"Last year, when I went to London town."

"What manner of man is he?"

"A good enough man for you," the duke answered. "I would not have struck an agreement with him if I did not think he would be good for you. But it will take you sometime to understand his manner of speaking. Some words are similar to ours, but many are not. I pray you listen carefully and learn quickly."

33

"I will do my best, father."

"Aye." He laughed suddenly. "I am sure you will, and when you are abed with him do not be afraid to give him good sport, as your dear mother, may God grant her eternal bliss, did for me."

Maida laughed.

"Do not take my words lightly, daughter," he said, waving his long bony forefinger at her. "It is the way for a wise woman to keep her husband happy and contented."

"And what if he should not give me good sport?" she asked.

"The answer will come to you without my having to tell you in advance," he responded. "But I warrant you, from the looks of him, Algar will not disappoint you. And now go tell your serving women that come autumn you will be mistress of your own castle."

The dream was so pleasant that Maida smiled in her sleep and was just about to take leave of her father when suddenly sleep was rudely torn from her by a sudden outburst of noise, a hubbub of hard guttural shouts in a strange language.

Maida opened her eyes and lifted her head. The gray sky was dark with twilight. For a few moments, she did not know where she was. She bolted up! Immediately she felt a strong hand on her shoulder, forcing her down.

"Sit!" Geir commanded.

Startled, she turned and looked up at him.

"Algar and his men," he said, pointing to the dark forms on the beach to their right. "I did not think he would venture down from the hills so soon."

Suddenly a fire-tipped arrow came streaking toward them with a hissing sound. It fell several paces short of the ship. Within moments more flaming arrows came their way.

34

Maida noticed they left a thin line of dark smoke behind them.

"A waste of good arrows," Geir commented with a shake of his head. The disdain for such a foolish gesture was clearly evident in the sound of his voice. "Algar should know we are beyond his reach."

In defense of the man to whom she was wed, Maida said, "His bowmen are among the very best in the land."

Suddenly Bjorn shouted, "I told you we should have sailed."

Geir translated his cousin's words for Maida and added, "His anger will cause more trouble than Algar's arrows." Then to Bjorn he said, "By the next dawn we will be on our way."

Bjorn did not answer.

The number of flame-tipped arrows lessened, and after a short while ceased altogether.

Geir came down from the stern deck and sat next to Maida. "You were smiling in your sleep," he said.

"I was visited by good dream," she answered.

"Good dreams are scarce," he commented. "Most dreams leave a bad feeling here and here." He touched his chest over his heart and the side of his head.

"I did not know that heathen dream as Christians do," she told him.

Geir guffawed and quickly explained to his men what she had said. They, too, laughed heartily.

Flushed with rage that she was the cause of their merriment, Maida looked haughtily at the Viking next to her. "Christians dream because God wants to please or frighten them, or—"

To silence her, Geir held up his hands. "You will soon learn that all you do, our women do, and all that your men do, our men do. The differences between us is not what we

35

are, or what we do but rather in what we believe guides us to our end and what we hope to find after our breath leaves our body.''

She did not know what to answer. His words were well spoken, and though they were said by a heathen, they seemed to be full of meanings which she could not quite understand. Then she recalled how deftly he had worked Bjorn around to agreeing with him. It was entirely possible that Geir's words were given to him by the Devil, or one of his ministers.

Her father's priest, Father Quinell, a thin, cadaverous-looking man with burning light in his eyes, just this past Easter had preached a long sermon on how the Devil uses words to trap the unwary; and how though he may speak the truth, it would be for the purpose of ensnaring another soul to carry down to hell with him.

Maida glanced quickly at Geir. From all he had done, there was no reason for her to doubt what Father Quinell had said. But it was difficult for her to understand how God could have made such a handsome man and allow His work to fall into Lucifer's hands?

"It is time to look at the wounded again," Geir said.

She was about to protest, but he took hold of her hand and pulled her along with him.

Many of the wounded seemed to be better, and Maida bathed their cuts with saltwater. But the young man with the slashed side could not even lift his head, and the four others who had been mortally wounded were very close to death.

Geir patted them on the back and spoke softly to them. "They are all brave men," Geir told Maida when they returned to the stern thwart. "I gave my word that I would speak well of them when we return to the stronghold so their families would be proud of them. Then I said good-bye and told them I would again meet them in Valhalla.''

"But you already told them—"

"That they were going to die? Yes. But this time I said good-bye. They will not be here when morning comes."

"I do not understand," she told him in a low voice. Geir pointed to the water.

"But that is against God!" Maida exclaimed with horror at the idea of man taking his own life.

"Only against your God," Geir answered. "They will go to meet their fate as a man must if he is to be considered a man by other men."

Maida trembled.

"And each of them know they would be no good at the oar. It is a just way for them to die and for us to live."

"Even for the boy whose mother you promised to return him to?" she questioned in a tight whisper.

Geir shrugged and with a deep sigh, he said, "It was a bad promise, no doubt put there by Loki to make me look foolish."

Maida did not know who Loki was and did not ask.

"If he lives through the coming of morning," Geir told her, "then he will live. The hours just before dawn are the worst. Then all the doors to Valhalla are open, and he will be sorely tempted to enter one of them. It was that way with me when I was wounded as badly."

Maida did not remember seeing or even feeling Geir's scar when he slipped between her naked thighs. She could not recall anything about him except his weight and the heat of his organ as it moved deep inside of her.

Geir called out to his men, and one of them went to the bow of the ship. "I told him that it is time to eat. We have some salt pork and herring on board and some very hard bread."

The mention of food was enough to make Maida's stomach contract with hunger. She had eaten nothing all day, and though she would not ordinarily eat such fare,

37

she knew if she refused it, she would not be given anything else.

In a short while she was tearing away at a piece of salt pork as viciously as any of the Vikings. She drank some ale from a wooden cup and then, as the night settled down on them, she drew her sheepskin robe around her and leaned against the side of the ship.

Geir moved closer to her and slipped his arm around her shoulders.

She tried to push him away, but she lacked the strength to move him. His hand slipped inside of her gown and his fingers spread over her breast.

"Sleep," he said gently. "Sleep and have good Christian dreams."

"Not with a heathen holding my breast," Maida responded hotly.

He chuckled. "With me, it is just the opposite. With your breast in my hand, I will have good dreams—very good ones indeed."

VI

MAIDA'S SLEEP WAS alternately restive and deep. Her dreams were confused and full of the violence she had recently witnessed in Algar's great hall.

Often when she was close to waking, she stirred uneasily. Almost awake, she heard the splash of something falling into the water, which was immediately followed by the sounds of low voices.

One of the voices was closer to her than all the others and it always said, "Sleep easy, sleep easy, my Saxon woman. Morning has not yet come." There was such strength in that voice that she did not make any effort to become fully awake, and she placed her own hand over the hand that held her breast.

Sometime during the night a thin rain began to fall. She could feel it on her face and turned to avoid it.

"Move closer to me," Geir said, "and I will bring the robe up over your head."

Maida opened her eyes. His face was very close to hers. His hand was on her breast; his palm rested on her nipple. Suddenly she was filled with a strange warmth. Her breath quickened. Her nipples became turgid and hot. She tried to speak, but the words would not form on her tongue. She longed to have his strong, muscular arms around her, to have his hardness in her. Ashamed of herself, she silently prayed to God to give her the strength needed to resist the temptation of the flesh that now was set before her by one of the Devil's own.

39

"I feel as you do," he whispered, caressing the nipple of her breast with the tips of his fingers.

Afraid she would yield to him, Maida tried to pull away. "I feel nothing," she told him. "Nothing but hate for you."

Holding the erect nipple of her breast between two fingers, he chided her for lying.

"You would take me here?" she questioned, fearful that she would be used in front of the other men.

Geir shook his head. "I will wait until you come to me of your own accord."

"Then you will indeed have a long wait!" she exclaimed angrily. The impudence of the man was more than she would have imagined a barbarian to possess. He was talking to her as if he were some great lord and she, a woman of lesser degree. "You will not have me again," she told him in a low, harsh voice, "unless you take me by force and against my will."

"If it will have to be that way," Geir answered with a growl, "then it will be. And as for your will," he told her, "it must give way to what you yourself want."

Maida did not answer. She would not demean herself by discussing the matter any further with him. She closed her eyes and listened to the creaking of the wood. After a while, she began to drift into a light slumber.

The instant Geir removed his hand from Maida's breast, she awoke with a start. A mizzling rain was still falling. Though it was still dark, the sky to the east was already beginning to lighten with the coming of dawn.

The shores of the cove were obscured by the rain and the members of the crew were no more than dark forms, though the two closest to her were less than a pace away.

Geir was standing by her.

The darkness dissolved in the spreading light. But a heavy mist clung to the shores and the waters of the cove.

40

Maida looked toward the bow of the ship. Four places were empty. She glanced up at Geir, but he was intent on scanning the waters around the ships. Of her own accord, she went to where the young man was. He was still alive. She called out to Geir and told him.

"Silence!" he ordered.

The oarsman next to her put his finger over his lips and whispered something she did not understand. Stung by Geir's response, she hastened to where he stood and she said, "He lived through the night. You said if he did that, he would live."

Geir turned to her. His face was dark with rage. "If you do not keep still," he growled, "none of us will live." And then he barked something at the two crewmen closest to him.

In an instant, Maida felt herself being dragged down to the ship's deck. She realized Algar must be close by. And shouting his name, she yelled, "I am here, Algar. Here . . . Here. . . Here—" A callused hand was clamped over her mouth. She bit it, drew blood—but it would not yield.

"Maida?" Algar called out. "Maida, where are you?"

She struggled to free herself but could not. She looked up at Geir. He was pointing to the mist behind the ship.

Bjorn and Thorkel were also on the high sterns of their vessels. They, too, were staring hard into the mist.

Algar shouted Maida's name again.

Geir turned to his crew and signaled them to begin rowing. Then to Maida he said, "Make any sound and I will kill you myself." He motioned the men away from her.

The ship slid through the water. The other vessels followed.

"They are moving," Algar called out. "I can hear them. Listen! . . . there is the creaking of their oars." He stood up in the bow of the small boat and tried to catch a

41

glimpse of his elusive enemy. "I swear by the blood of Christ," he stormed, "that I will follow you, Geir, and when I find you, I will kill you."

Geir held the huge staff in his right hand; with his left, he signaled to the other captains.

The three ships kept together, though Geir's was always slightly in front of the other two.

The sound of the sea pounding on the rocks along the shore became louder and louder. They were running for the mouth of the cove. Maida knew once they reached the open sea Algar would not be able to follow. The tempo of the rowing became swifter. The men took great gulps of air as they raised, lowered, and pushed the oars against the water. It was light enough for Maida to see that every one of them glistened with sweat.

Despite the fact she did not doubt Geir's threat, Maida could not just stand by and watch her only hope for escape become lost in the mist. She leaped up to where Geir stood, and wrapping her arms around the long dragon tail, prayed the mists would part in time for Algar to see her and he would be able to rescue her. She wept but the mist held fast to the waters.

When she finally felt the ship plunge into the swell of the sea, Maida looked up at Geir. It was difficult for her to believe that God in His infinite wisdom had given her to a Viking, who would use her as he willed. She could not reconcile what Father Quinell had told her about God's mercy and how He answered those who are truly in need of His help.

Geir headed straight out to sea. Within a short time, the coast was obscured by the rain. The men did not row as hard, and the three ships moved to each other.

"We will sail across the open water and then turn north along the coast," Geir called out.

Bjorn shouted, "I will not continue unless we sacrifice to the sea people."

Geir ordered his men to ship their oars. The crews on the other vessels did the same. The ships drifted very close to each other.

Bjorn said, "The sea people will take more of our crews before we reach our own shores, if we do not give them blood now."

Geir rubbed his chin. In the past he had often sailed without sacrificing to the sea people, and nothing terrible had happened to him. He had weathered fierce storms and had always managed to sail through them.

"We will have better weather if we give them their due," Bjorn predicted.

"What do you say, Thorkel?" Geir questioned.

"It cannot hurt us," the captain answered.

Geir could not deny that, and he asked what they thought might be an appropriate sacrifice. Neither one of them wanted to give up any of the livestock they had taken aboard.

"One of the women," Bjorn suggested.

Geir quickly waved that proposal aside. He knew exactly where his cousin's thoughts were tending, and he would stop them from going any further, if he could. "We do not sacrifice our own kind the way the Wendols do," he responded.

"They are not of our kind," Bjorn shot back. "They are Saxons. Their chief Algar did not hesitate to put the heads of our men on poles to satisfy their God, and we should not hesitate to give the blood of one to the sea people. One is as just as the other."

Crews loudly agreed to what Bjorn said.

Thorkel commented, "We can do not less for the sea people than they did for theirs."

"Then you would spill the blood of six of them," Geir questioned, "to equal the same number that Algar had killed? Six good thralls."

"One will do," Bjorn answered.

"One?" Geir responded. He could no longer stop his cousin from rushing headlong into a snare of his own making.

"Everyone has heard me say only one," Bjorn said with satisfaction. "The sea people are never greedy."

"We shall make the sacrifice," Geir said, "but as your chieftain, I claim the right to make the choice of who it will be."

"It must be her," Bjorn shouted, pointing to Maida, who understood nothing of the exchange between the three captains, though she intuitively sensed it was very serious and was instantly filled with dread by what was happening.

"Put down your hand," Geir said quietly. "There is no reason for it to be her. As you yourself just said, the sea people are not greedy; they would just as lief take the blood of goat to the blood of cow. We all know that, too."

The men agreed with him.

"Besides, Bjorn," Geir told his cousin, "it cannot be her because if we sacrifice the woman, your father will not be able to settle the prior difference between us. She must be there since she is the cause. No, I give you Einar or rather I give him to the sea people. He is of no use at his oar and is more than likely to die before we reach Lid's stronghold."

"He is kinsman to my mother's brother," Bjorn said in a voice tight with anger. "His death will cause hard feelings between my father and his mother and brothers."

"He is of no use to me," Geir responded and leaping down from the high stern to the deck he went to where Einar sat slumped over his oar. He reached down, and grabbing the young man by his hair, he lifted his head up. "See," he shouted to Bjorn, "he will soon be food for the fishes anyway."

Horrified, Maida grasped the nature of the situation. Her hands trembled; she could scarcely keep her knees from buckling. She forced herself to move where Geir stood and in a tremulous voice, she said, "He will live if—"

Geir pushed her aside and told her to keep her mouth shut. Then to Bjorn he said, "I will slit his throat and let his blood run down my bow."

"No," Bjorn shouted. "I will kill a goat and give the sea people its blood from my bow."

Geir let Einar's head fall across the oar. Then he walked slowly back to the stern of the ship. "Make your sacrifice so we may continue our journey home."

Maida joined Geir and from the stern of his vessel she watched as Bjorn slit the throat of a goat and let its blood run down the prow of his ship; then he let the body fall into the sea.

Geir ordered his men to begin rowing again. Once more the ships plowed into the dull gray waters of the sea.

The rain continued throughout the day. There seemed to be very little space between the sea and the clouds. At times the top of the mast was lost in the bottom of the clouds.

Maida went to look at the wounded. Though they would all be scarred, the wounds would heal. When she came to Einar, she took a great deal of time to clean his wound and try to make him as comfortable as possible. But the best she could do was to set him against the side of the ship. He looked no more than seventeen or perhaps at the most twenty. His face was very white and the freckles on it very brown.

She glanced at Geir; it was hard for her to realize that

once he was as young as Einar, or as close to death.

When she returned to the stern, Geir ordered the food to be broken out. She ate herring and salt pork and drank the ale given to her. Then she wrapped the heavy sheepskin robe around herself. The wind had freshened and it had a bite in it.

Geir called one of the men and gave the heavy shaft to him. He settled down next to Maida and asked if Einar had bled any more.

His solicitude surprised her and she said, "You were so willing to see his blood flow down your bow, I did not think you cared whether he lived or died."

His eyes became slits.

"But I imagine it easy for someone like you to offer another's blood," she commented with a shrug.

"It would have been much easier," he growled, "to let Bjorn sacrifice you to the sea people."

Though she had known instinctively her life had been at stake, she had not wanted to believe it. But now that Gier told her, she blanched with fear and could hardly keep her hands from shaking.

"To be afraid now is foolishness," Geir told her disdainfully.

"I was afraid then," she murmured. "I knew what he wanted when he pointed at me."

Geir looked toward Bjorn's ship. "You have lighted a fire in him that has never burned there before in the same way."

"And for that he would have me dead?" she asked.

"Because I have you," Geir answered, looking straight at her.

She flushed.

Seeing her color, Geir slapped his thighs and with a laugh, he said, "See, you know I have you."

"I know nothing of the kind," she answered, turning an

46

even deeper shade of red. "You have me because you stole me from my rightful husband. But I am not yours and never will be!"

"Never," he responded, "is a long, long time. And right now I have to see to my ship." He returned to his place at the shaft.

VII

IT RAINED THROUGHOUT the day. The sea and the sky were slate-gray, though in the distance, first in the south and then in the west, sunshine poured through huge holes in the clouds. Once Maida was even certain she could see the high hills that were behind Algar's village and would have asked Geir if they were, but she would not give him the satisfaction of talking to him.

The men at the oars varied the tempo of their rowing. Hour after hour they labored at their task. They spoke, laughed, and sometimes sang.

For the most part, they seemed to be oblivious to Maida's presence, except when she went amongst them to tend their wounds. Then they spoke to her in their atrocious langauge that sounded to her ears more like the low growl dogs make just before they bite. But she realized they were tendering their thanks to her, especially those men who were seated close to Einar.

Maida soon discovered that Geir did not always stand at the stern of the vessel, holding the shaft to guide it through the water. He moved about the ship a good deal and he often spent hours in the bow, where he stood alone, usually with one hand braced against the awful neck of the sea dragon, whose carved head decorated the very top of the ship's prow.

From where Maida sat in the stern sheets, Geir seemed to be a remote person and somewhat forbidding with his dark blue cloak wrapped close to his body. Now and then she would see him look toward her, but it was never more than a glance; as if he were trying to make up his mind about her, though she could not even begin to guess what thoughts ran through his mind. After all, he was a heathen and according to Father Quinell, a heathen could think only those thoughts that were put in his head by the Devil or one of his helpers.

The afternoon passed. Twilight slid out of the east and closed over the ocean, but the sky in the west was filled with a brilliant yellow that turned to orange, became blood-red and finally changed into a deep, lingering purple. Then night came.

The rowing slackened. Food and drink were given out. The wind had a bite to it, and Maida wrapped herself in the heavy sheepskin robe. She soon understood that the men rowed and slept in shifts, though she did not know how they knew when it was time for one group to wake and row and the other to sleep.

Geir did not come to her as he had done the previous night. Instead he replaced the man who had been at the shaft for most of the day. But much later in the night, she felt him next to her and for the warmth of his body, she moved closer to him, while he eased his hand into the top of her torn gown and held her breast, as he had done the previous night.

When she awoke, Geir was already standing at the shaft. The sky was clear and the sun was just beginning to show itself in the east. Several gulls flew low over the mast head and one white one with gray-tipped wings rested on the head of the dragon.

Maida ate and drank with the rest of the crew; then she went to look after the wounded. Einar was very much better. He looked up at her with big brown eyes and whispered something.

She nodded and told him he was going to get well,

though she knew he no more understood her than she did him.

"What Einar could use," she told Geir, when she returned to the stern, "is some hot broth."

"All we have aboard," Geir answered, "is what we have been eating."

"That can hardly be called food."

"I have eaten worse," he said with a shrug. "But maybe when we reach the Frankish coast we will pause for a day or two and bring some fresh meat aboard."

"And how long will it be before we reach the coast?" she asked.

"By nightfall. If the wind veers round and blows from the west, we will raise sail and be there in the afternoon."

Maida clambered up to where Geir stood.

He looked at her warily.

She shook her head and told him she would not try to push him overboard.

"That is good," he answered, "because then I would not have to throw you down to the deck again."

She rubbed her bruises and said, "I still hurt, and the black and blue will be there for a long time."

"It was a hard lesson," he said with laughter in his eyes.

Unable for the moment to match his wit with words, she made an ugly face.

He returned the gesture.

She pulled back the skin around her eyes, making them slanty, and bared her teeth.

Geir said something to the men, and they roared with laughter; some of them laughed so hard that they fell off the rowing bench, while others developed a fit of coughing.

"What did you tell them?" Maida asked.

"That when you make a face like that," he answered,

"you burn with passion for me, and when I am finally inside of you, you make low throaty sounds like a contented cat."

Maida looked at the laughing men, and flushed with anger, she said, "If I could speak your language, I would tell them that your organ is no bigger than the nail of my thumb and could not possibly satisfy any woman." And holding her thumb of her right hand with the fingers of the other, she showed it to the men and then pointed to Geir's groin.

The crew laughed and stamped their feet. Some of them shouted, and Geir told Maida that many of them would be more than willing to see if the size of their organs would satisfy her.

One of the older men called out to Geir, who answered him.

"And what was that all about?" Maida questioned.

"He said you were a beautiful woman but when you are angry you are even more beautiful. He also asked if you are worthy of having a man between your thighs."

Maida was so incensed that she had lost the means to speak.

"I thanked him on your behalf for the compliment," Geir told her. "Also I said you were indeed worthy of having a man between your thighs. And he answered that he did not doubt it."

That she was the subject for such a coarse jest was more than Maida could bear. She could do nothing in her own defense against their lewdness; she was helpless. She turned her back to them. The sea was vast and empty. There was nothing except the wake of the ship, a few lonely gulls, and the continuous movement of the waves flashing in the bright sunlight.

"Do not think harshly about them, Maida," Geir said softly using her name for the first time. "They are good

51

men and all would gladly die in your defense in payment for the small kindness you have given them. It is our way to jest about those we consider our friends."

"I am your captive!" she exclaimed, facing him.

Geir did not start; he remained steady at his task of holding the ship on its course. His eyes locked with hers. For a fleeting moment, he recalled how he had first seen her: when she had leaned bare-breasted out of the castle tower and he had chanced to look up. Then as now he wanted her!

His sharp blue eyes were too much for her; they stripped her naked and made her feel tight in the depths of her being, made her feel warm and quickened the beating of her heart.

Maida cast her eyes downward and in a low voice, she said, "I am not used to being laughed at. It is not our way."

"And it is not our way to turn our backs on friend or foe alike," he said, gesturing with his head toward the crew.

She glanced at them. All of them were looking at her with such a sad expression on their weatherbeaten faces that she could not help but understand she had insulted them by her actions.

"Say something more to me," Geir told her, "and I will tell them that you apologize for being rude."

"And they will forgive me?"

"If I tell them to," Geir said and then he spoke to his men. Immediately they began to nod and smiles broke the hard line of their closed lips.

Several of the men lifted their hands toward her in a gesture of friendship, and Geir urged her to answer them the same way. When she finally did, they were so pleased that several of them offered her the opportunity to sit next to them and help them at the oar.

Geir waved their offers aside and told his men that

Maida was highborn, the daughter of a chief in her country, and could not do such hard work but she would continue to look after the wounded.

His men voiced their satisfaction of the arrangement. When Geir was finished speaking with the crew, he translated for Maida all he had said to them and what they in turn had said to him. He purposely used several words many times to see if she would understand them.

She did, and by that afternoon she had learned the Viking words for man, men, ship, and crew.

By late afternoon the wind came around, and Geir ordered the sail set. The men shipped their oars and Geir gave charge of the shaft over to another man. Then he took her by the hand and led her to the bow. The huge square sail billowed out toward them, and she saw that it was decorated with a fire-breathing dragon.

The sails of the other two ships were decorated in the same way. Bjorn's vessel was on their right and Thorkel's on the left.

Though it was difficult for Maida to admit, the ships looked beautiful as they sliced through the water. They almost seemed not to be in it, but rather, like huge birds, just skimming its surface. She said as much to Geir.

He nodded and in a sad voice he told her that when Algar had taken him prisoner, he had lost Bluetooth, "A long time will pass." he said sorrowfully, "before I find as good a companion."

At first Maida thought that he was speaking about one of the Vikings who had been killed, but when she realized he was lamenting the loss of his weapon, she could not help but laugh at her stupidity and his foolishness.

His face darkened with anger.

Hastily Maida explained her confusion and assured him that one sword was as good as another.

Geir shook his head. "Like men, or for that matter like

women," he told her with serious frown, "one sword is very different from another. One will break apart just when you need it the most; another will take rust even in the hot dry months; and a third will dent and dull when kissed by another blade. Bluetooth had none of these faults. I won him in fair combat with a Frank."

Maida thought it best to hold her tongue in check. If she were less frightened of him, she would have said that heathens might revere a sword or some other object, but Christians were not permitted, by God's own injunction, to have such feelings for anything or anyone but God Himself. But Geir, or any of his men, would not have understood such teachings.

"It is a bad thing for a man to lose his sword," Geir commented in a low voice. "I have often heard the old men say that when it happens to a man, he can be sure the gods are angry at him."

"Is that what you are afraid of?"

"I am not afraid," he told her. "My destiny will be what it will be. If the gods are angry at me, I must first discover why—and then how I might be able to change their anger into something less dangerous."

Maida saw the contradiction in what he said but dared not point it out to him. He was as afraid of his gods as she was of her one God. Mortals were full of weaknesses. It made no difference if they were heathen gods or the one true Christian God; they seemed to know all of them.

She nodded sympathetically and assured him he would eventually find another sword to replace the one he lost.

Geir climbed high on to dragon neck of the ship and after a while he shouted to her, "Land . . . land . . . the Frankish coast." He quickly told his men, and when he came back to where Maida was standing, he said that by nightfall she would have fresh food for herself as well as for Einar.

The three ships made straight for the coast. At first it looked like no more than a low-lying cloud. But as they sped toward it, the cloud became more defined. The hills came into view, and as they drew even closer, the shore emerged. Finally they could hear the thunderous roar of the waves as they broke white along the rocky beach.

The ship's sail was hauled down and stowed away in its special place beneath the deck. The men returned to the oars and Geir went back to the shaft.

The ships moved along the coast for some time. Then Geir pointed the prow of the ship into the mouth of a small river.

Maida guessed he had previously sailed these waters and knew the coast as well as any man could. They crossed over a shallow bar and went slowly around the first bend in the river.

Geir guided the ship into the right bank of the river. They eased up on the land. Within moments, the Vikings spilled over its sides taking with them huge logs which they placed under it. And then they put their shoulders against its sides and rolled it high out of the water.

The other ships were treated in the same fashion, and as soon as all of them were securely beached, Geir went over the side and waited for his other two captains to join him.

"We will make camp here for a day or two," Geir told them, "and have our men gather what fresh meat and water they can."

Bjorn and Thorkel agreed and they returned to their crews to set them about the work that had to be done.

VIII

GEIR HAD NO time for Maida and he left her alone in the stern of the ship. She was amazed how quickly the Vikings organized the camp. Now and then Geir or one of his other captains shouted an order, but for the most part each man knew his task. Everything was accomplished with extraordinary swiftness.

A fully armed group of men immediately detached themselves from the main body and they spread themselves out in a semicircle to guard the campsite. Another armed group went to hunt and forage for food. The remainder of the crews began to unload the ships.

In hardly any time at all, the tents were set up, fire pits dug and cooking fires started. Then the livestock that had been stolen from Algar's lands was removed from the ships and securely tied down in the center of the camp. There were not too many animals: three cows, four horses, a dozen pigs, five goats, and one ass.

After the camp was completely set up, the other captives were led off the ship. Maida gasped when she saw them. They were a pitiful lot.

A half dozen men were bound to one another with lengths of rope twisted around their necks, and each had his hands tied behind his back. The women and young girls were just bound around their waists. Those who were old enough to have their monthly blood flow had been raped. All the women had part of their clothing torn away.

The sight of them wrenched a cry of despair from

Maida's throat. She could not believe that such wretchedness would be tolerated by Christ. Her father had slaves, but he treated them with Christian kindness . . . Then suddenly through her tear-blurred vision, she saw Glenna and cried out to her.

Glenna paused and looked at her mistress.

"Wait," Maida shouted. "Wait . . . I will come to you."

But the guard was impatient, and pushed Glenna along with the others.

Maida shouted to her again. Then she ran toward the center of the ship and started to go over the side when she came face to face with Geir.

"Glenna, my serving woman," she cried, "is with the other women. I must go to her!"

Geir blocked her way and quietly said, "She no longer belongs to you."

Wide-eyed, Maida looked at him. Then very slowly she moved back into the ship. She nodded and in a low, sad voice, she said, "I forgot . . . I am as much as a slave as she is." '

Geir did not answer.

"Am I not your slave?" Maida cried, looking up at him.

Geir gestured behind him and said, "I have brought two men to help carry Einar to a shelter. Will you go with him and tend his wound?"

"But Glenna—"

"Einar is my interest now," he told her sharply.

"I will go," she replied, her body trembling with grief.

Geir spoke to the men. They went quickly aboard the ship, lifted Einar, who groaned in agony but did not cry out, and carried the wounded boy between them to a roughly made shelter of sailcloth and pine boughs.

Maida knelt beside Einar and for the first time lifted his

clothing away from the wound. It was still very raw and ugly, but it was beginning to heal. She asked Geir for boiling water and he had a large pot brought to her. She washed the wound again, and tearing a piece of cloth off the bottom part of her ragged gown, she made a dressing for it.

"He will have hot food soon," Geir said, as he helped Maida to her feet.

"I think you will uphold your promise to his mother," she said.

"That is the kind of promise I will never again make."

"Will I be able to speak to Glenna?" Maida asked suddenly stopping.

"I cannot say," he told her. "I will ask the man who owns her and then perhaps—"

"But you are their chieftain," she exclaimed, "and can order the man to let me speak to her!"

"My authority does not extend to any man's property," he told her. "Each man owns what he has taken."

"But you do not understand!"

"It is you who do not understand," he answered. "Our ways are different from those of your people. I must follow the ways of my people."

"The ways of heathens," she said disdainfully. "Heathens who plunder and rape."

"We do what we must do in order to live," he told her.

She pointed to the captive women, who were now huddled around a fire at the other side of the camp. She scornfully said, "And what you see there enables you to live; those miserable women were once wives, daughters, and sweethearts. Now they are no more than thralls of your men."

"They will be sold, and each of their owners will have more silver than he had before."

"Will I, too, be sold?" she questioned.

"No," he answered. "I would not sell you."

For several moments they stood and looked at each other; Maida with an angry glare in her black eyes and Geir with an unfamiliar and uncertain softness in his.

Then he said, "Our shelter is that tent over there."

The hard anger in her eyes became more intense and she told him, "I will not open my thighs for you."

He shrugged and walked away, leaving her standing alone.

Maida called after him, but he would not stop or even turn to acknowledge he heard her. In a rage, she stamped her foot and shouted "You and the Devil are one!" But when she realized many of the men were looking at her and laughing, she hastily withdrew into the shelter of the tent.

Several of the Vikings caught fish and were busily cooking them over the open fires. The smell of food brought Maida out of the tent. Her mouth watered but she did not know how to ask for food.

Not far from where she stood were several members of Geir's crew. They were sitting around a cooking pit eating some eels that had been cooked. She approached them.

Several of them spoke to her.

She smiled.

One of them picked up a piece of eel and handed it to her.

She accepted it from him and immediately took a generous bite out of it. She had never been fond of eels, but this one was delicious; so good in fact that she pointed to another piece which the men generously gave her. She asked for a third piece. But this time the men muttered to each other; they seemed to be displeased.

"But it is not for me," she told them. "It is for Einar."

They understood the name and one of the men repeated it.

Maida pointed to the shelter where the young man lay and said, "Einar."

One of them gave her two pieces of eel and gestured toward his injured friend.

Maida could not even begin to guess what he said to her. But she nodded and smiled. Backing away, she moved toward the shelter. When she was several paces away from the fire pit, she turned and hurried to feed the wounded Viking.

Before twilight wove its way through the branches of the trees, the men returned from their hunting and foraging. They came back with three sheep, a good-sized boar, and two captives. Both were men.

Geir brought meat to Maida. She spitted part of it and cooked it over the fire; with the remainder she made a rich broth for Einar. The meat tasted even better than eels. When she finished feeding Einar, she went back to the fire and cut herself another piece.

There were at least a dozen fires in the campsite, and the light from their flames cast a reddish glow over everyone and everything. It almost seemed to Maida that she had been cast into hell and that the dark forms seated around the fires were demons. To reassure herself, she looked up and saw the star-filled night sky.

"Einar will owe you his life," Geir said, after remaining silent for a long time. "He has probably told you that already."

"I would not know," Maida answered. She was still angry with Geir for having walked away from her. "But I do know, from what you yourself told me, that it is rude to turn your back on friend or foe."

"Had I not been rude," he said, "I would have struck you. I do not think you would prefer that to having your pride wounded— or would you?"

"I have not been struck since I was a child," she told him, "and even then hardly ever."

He laughed and said, "I had to fight in order not to be struck. When I was strong enough to strike those who struck me, I was no longer struck." He left the fire and a short time later, he returned and handed her a cup of ale.

She sipped it slowly.

"Einar's mother brewed it," Geir told Maida. "It was her gift for the success of the voyage."

With a gesture that encompassed the entire campsite, she said, "It has obviously brought you good luck. You will return with much booty and many prisoners."

Geir rubbed his chin. Then, more thoughtfully than she would have suspected, he said, "The best of what we have seldom returns with us. A dozen men have entered Valhalla so that the rest of us might live and bring back what you see. Sometimes, we lose more men for a great deal less."

She drank the rest of the ale; its taste was fuller than the ale she had drunk on board the ship. And she asked if she might have another cup.

Geir obliged her. But he said, when he gave her the second cup, "This has been made with special herbs and spices. Too much of it quickly puts fog in the head of the drinker."

"This would have been the third night of my marriage to Algar," she said in a melancholy voice.

"I will kill him the next time I see him," Geir growled. "For each Viking head I stuck up on a pole, I swore that I would kill him."

Maida shuddered. She had quite forgotten the harsh judgment meted out by Algar to the other Vikings. No, she had not really forgotten about it, but rather she had accepted it as being just.

61

"They were good men all of them," Geir said. "They died with Odin on their lips."

She made a motion with her hand to indicate that she did not want to continue the conversation. The ale had indeed put fog in her head. She looked around the encampment. The fires were burning low. Many dark forms were stretched out close to them. Now and then the stillness was disturbed by the hoot of an owl or the moan of one of the women, who was being forced to submit to the will of her captor. She hoped it was not Glenna.

Without saying anything more to Geir, Maida crawled into the tent and stretched out on the bed of pine boughs covered over with a piece of sailcloth. After a while she sensed Geir's presence.

He pulled a sheepskin robe over the two of them.

His hand found her breast, but this time he touched her two nipples with the tips of his fingers in such a way that they grew hard and tipped with a delightful warmth that spread deep into her.

The fog was most certainly in her head because she moved closer to him and ran her hand over his chest. She breathed deeply, inhaling the salty scent of him.

Geir nuzzled her ear and said, "I told you not to drink so much."

His hand slid between her thighs, and when he touched her sex, she splayed them for him.

He whispered her name, and baring her breasts, he kissed one and then the other.

She moaned with delight and held the back of his head tightly to keep his lips on her breast.

Slowly Geir's caresses brought moisture from her sex and he eased himself between her bare thighs.

She reached down, took hold of his organ and fondled it; then with a laugh of delight, guided it into her body. She trembled with pleasure and almost instantly threw herself against him. Despite the fog in her brain, Maida could feel his every movement.

"Geir," she told him, in a low throaty voice, "Geir . . . I have had this burned into my brain ever since you took me."

"It has been with me, too," he told her, breathing hard.

"Geir, please buy Glenna for me," she cried. "I will lie with you whenever you wish. But bring Glenna to me."

He stopped moving. "Is that why you are with me now?" he asked, looking down at her.

She shook her head. "But I was told that a man in his passion seldom could refuse a woman anything," she said.

He started away from her. He did not want to be used.

Maida clutched him and whispered, "For the love of God, I, too, am in my passion, Geir. I do not have so much fog in my head not to know what I am doing or why." To prove her words, she played her fingers over the sac of his manhood.

He moved deep into her again.

She sighed with delight and asked him to plunge hard into her. "Yes," she told him, "like that . . . like that . . ." Her body became as taut as a well-pulled bow string. Then suddenly it was let go; his fluid gushed into her. The arrow seemed to strike deep into her, making her writhe in an exquisite agony, a kind of death that was more, so very much more than life itself. She cried aloud and clung tightly to her Viking lover!

When he could speak without having to gulp for air, Geir said, "I will first see if Glenna's owner will let you speak to her. And when we reach the stronghold, I will try to buy her but unless her owner is willing, nothing can be done."

Maida kissed his face. The ale had given her more

courage than she would have ordinarily possessed. She had let him use her so that she in turn could use him, though she could not deny the experience gave her great pleasure—much more than when he had taken her against her will. But by letting him conquer her, she had conquered him. That her body was a weapon equal to and in some ways probably more potent than his sword was a discovery that amused her greatly. In time she was sure she would learn to use it much more skillfully. She smiled and drifted off into a deep and contented sleep.

IX

MAIDA AWOKE TO the clamorous honking of flocks of wild geese and the gleeful shouting of the Vikings as they killed many of the birds with their arrows.

Geir was nowhere in sight. Because all of the men, with the exception of the guards, were occupied with the geese, Maida hastened to the coffle of women captives.

They were gathered around a fire pit at the far end of the camp. They had not yet been given food and drink. Many of the women were wide-eyed with the blank stares of unfortunates whose wits have left them; others were moaning to themselves. But there were many as sound as she herself was.

Maida went straight to Glenna and embraced her warmly. "Did you see Paige?" she questioned, hoping that her other serving woman might also be among the captives.

"She was killed," Glenna answered. "One of the Vikings went for her. She fought him off, and in a rage, he smashed her head open with his battle-ax."

Maida's hand flew to her mouth. But the cry of horror could not be stifled, nor could the sudden welling up of tears be stopped. She shook her head and bit her lips.

"I saw you being taken the night of the raid," Glenna said.

Maida pushed away the sorrow in her heart and told her serving woman that Geir would try to buy her when they reached the Viking stronghold. "Tell me the name of your captor," Maida asked, "so that I will be able to tell Geir."

"His name is Jon," Glenna said. Then she asked, "But

why would Geir want to buy me when he already has you?''

"He will do it for me," Maida said proudly.

"In exchange for what you do for him?"

Maida nodded, flushed, and then seeing the knowing smile on Glenna's face, she, too, smiled. "I would do anything to have you with me and to gain our freedom." She looked downstream to where the Vikings were still shooting the geese. "Though Geir has made me feel passion, it is not more than a lust which he conjures into my body. There is no love in what I give, no love at all."

"And for him is there any love?"

"I care no more than that about his feelings," she said, snapping her fingers. "He did not think of my feelings when he ravaged me."

"Not more than a few days past you were just a girl," Glenna commented. "Now you are a woman full of vengeance."

"Only because I have been quickly taught to hate."

"Be careful, Maida, that the snare you set for Geir does not entrap you as well."

"My heart will be dead until I am returned to my rightful husband," she answered. Then she embraced Glenna and said, "We will soon be together again, I promise you. Remember when I come with Geir you must pretend it is our first meeting."

"I will remember."

Maida let go of Glenna, turned, and found herself looking at Bjorn.

Several dead geese hung from his belt. She started to walk around him, but he stepped in front of her. She tried again to go around him, but he blocked her way. He spoke to her, but she did not understand anything he said except Geir's name.

Bjorn made a grab for her. She screamed. Then some of the women captives also began to scream.

Several of the Vikings dropped their catch of geese and ran back into the camp with their swords drawn.

Bjorn pointed to Maida and shouted to the men, "She was trying to set the women free."

They were very angry. A few of them demanded that something be done with her. And one man said that Geir should be summoned and be told what his woman had tried to do.

Bjorn ordered, "Seize her and bring her to my ship. I will hold her there until Geir returns."

The Vikings did not move.

Bjorn called upon the men of his crew to execute the order.

Maida was terrified. Her heart beat wildly. She looked around her. Many of the men were from Geir's ship.

Suddenly the gray-bearded man whose oar was across from Einar's moved toward her and at the same time, he spoke to Bjorn, telling him, "We have only your word for what she did. None of us here can speak her language. Besides, she belongs to Geir and to our ship; we cannot give her to you." Even as he spoke, several more of the ship's crew came toward Maida, and they formed a protective circle around her.

Bjorn's face became dark with anger.

Other crewmen joined those already guarding Maida, and the old Viking said, "We do not want to spill the blood of any man, but blood will be spilled if anyone is foolish enough to try to take her from us. Now if you will let us pass, we will return to our place on the other side of the encampment."

"She has bewitched all of you!" Bjorn raged. "From this time on, there is hard feeling between us."

"I am too old, Bjorn, to worry about your feelings,"

Skled shouted back, causing the men with him and all of those who were watching the incident to laugh heartily. "But I thank you for caring about mine."

When they reached the vicinity of Geir's shelter, the Vikings broke the circle they had formed around Maida and Skled used the point of his sword to draw a line in the earth. He gestured to the prow of the ship and then to a tall maple tree to indicate that she must not go beyond the invisible line that extended between those two objects.

She nodded and spoke his name; then pointing to herself, she told him her name.

Skled repeated it and gesturing to several men that had come to her defense, he identified each of them by name.

Maida walked from man to man and with a nod spoke his name; then she pointed to where Einar lay and said his name.

They understood that she wanted to go and tend him and with smiles on their faces, they left.

Maida went directly to Einar, and as she washed the wound, she realized the men who had formed a circle around her had been ready to die for her. That kind of fierce loyalty was something she had heard existed only between soldiers and almost never between men who were not called upon to face death together.

She took a deep breath and said to Einar, "I have done no more than my Christian duty for you and your friends have made much of it, much more than I would have thought them capable of, considering that all of you are the Devil's own."

Einar smiled at her and spoke a few words to which she nodded.

When Geir returned, his eyes were ice-blue and hard with anger. He had been met by one of his men and had been told what had happened between Maida and Bjorn and then between Bjorn and Skled. He did not speak to her and sat down by the fire to think about the situation.

Maida endured his silence for a long time before she said that Einar was much stronger, and if Geir would bring her meat, she would make more broth for him.

"And you did nothing more than tend Einar this morning?" he asked.

"No more than I thought fitting," she answered guardedly, realizing that he already knew what had taken place.

He repeated the word "fitting," and removing his knife from its sheath, he flung it with a sudden flick of his wrist. The point stuck in the earth next to where she sat.

So swift was his movement, that her mouth dropped open in wordless terror. She had seen the flash of the blade and the very next instant it was quivering in the ground, making a strange low humming sound.

He reached across the fire pit and, retrieving the knife, he said in a low, flat voice, "I will not let what you thought fitting to do cost the lives of either Bjorn or Skled."

"I went only to learn the name of the man—"

"Bjorn accused you of bewitching me, of working trollcraft on me."

"I am a Christian."

"The worse for you," he answered. "Your priests have been known to bewitch us with their strange mutterings and singing."

"I went to speak with my serving woman."

"She is no more your *anything!*" Geir shot back at her. "She is a thrall and you are a thrall. The only difference between you is that you are my thrall and she belongs to Jon."

"You were not so eager to shout at me last night," she said.

"Last night was last night,' he answered harshly. "Now you have caused more trouble than I am willing to bear; I should give you to Bjorn and have done with it."

Maida shook her head. She began to tremble.

Suddenly he reached across the fire pit, and dragging her across it, pulled her after him.

She screamed at him and swore she would not go beyond the line shown to her by Skled.

But Geir was deaf to her cries.

He pulled so fast that Maida stumbled over her own feet and had to scramble to regain them, or he would have dragged her along the ground.

Geir shouted to the men and they followed him. He shouted to Bjorn and to Thorkel. When all the Vikings were gathered around them, he said, "Bjorn, tell me now what my woman is accused of."

"I came upon her when she was trying to set the other women free."

Geir translated for Maida what Bjorn said and he asked for her answer.

"As God is my judge," she told him, "I came only to speak with Glenna and ask her the name of the man who owns her."

Geir told his followers what his woman claimed.

"And who is the woman she came to see?" Bjorn challenged.

"Bring the woman here," Geir ordered. When they were brought into the center of the Vikings, he told Maida to point out her serving woman.

"I am she," Glenna declared, stepping as far in front of the others as the rope that bound her would permit. "I am her serving woman."

She was younger than Geir had expected and much better-looking. He explained what the relationship between the two women had been. And then he said to Jon,

"I would have come this afternoon to ask your permission for my woman to speak with yours."

Jon nodded. He was a tall barrel-chested man, with a black beard and black eyes. He was a strong fighter and not given to bad humor. He looked thoughtfully at the two women and then at Geir before he said, "I accept what you say; I have seen other women do the same thing."

"Thank you," Geir responded. "I have also seen men do it."

"Yes," Jon answered. "To be taken captive is not a good fate for man or woman."

Geir looked at Bjorn and asked what else his woman was accused of.

"Trollcraft," Skled called out.

"Is that true, Bjorn?"

And Bjorn answered, "I know what I know."

Geir accepted his cousin's answer with a nod and said, "Would you still accuse her of trollcraft if I offered her to you?"

Bjorn began to stammer.

Geir quickly explained to Maida the gist of what was happening.

"But you would not give me to him," she cried. "You said you would not do it willingly."

He glared at her and said, "I was not the one who became involved with Bjorn; it was you who took it upon yourself to do what I said I would do."

To keep from being laughed at, Bjorn was forced to admit he might be wrong, that her trollcraft was no more than her Christian ways.

Geir accepted the explanation but to push his cousin even more, he again offered Maida to him. "She might bring you more peace," he said, "than she has brought to me." These words did make the men laugh, but their laughter was directed against him rather than his cousin.

"But since I began it by taking her maidenhead," he continued, "I will suffer with her until I tire of her and then for my trouble perhaps I will receive a few pieces more of silver or one or two gold coins."

"There is still the matter to be settled by my father when we reach the stronghold," Bjorn reminded him.

"I have not forgotten, cousin," Geir answered. He grabbed hold of Maida's right hand and once again cruelly dragged her back to where they had started from. She bit her lip to keep from crying out in pain as he twisted her arm behind her back.

"Next time you do something to set one man against another, I will have you stripped in front of all of them and each man will have the opportunity to take his pleasure with you."

"Even *you* would not—"

"I would," he told her sharply. "If I could keep my berserks from fighting one another, I would let them use you until you were gutted out."

She shook with fear. From the tone of Geir's voice, Maida knew he would not hesitate to carry out his threat.

"What kind of man are you?" she questioned with a quavering voice.

"Not any kind you have known," he answered with disdain.

"A Christian would show some mercy."

"A Viking does not know what mercy means," he said. "He has learned to live without it."

Maida did not answer; she knew too well that it was true.

X

FOR THREE DAYS and three nights the Vikings remained encamped on the bank of the small river. During the brief interval, Geir ordered that the ships be scraped and planking relashed.

Throughout the day, the men were at one task or another. Geir was busy from sunup to sundown. When he returned to the fire pit at twilight, he was very tired.

Though Geir slept with Maida in the same tent, he made no attempt to possess her, and when he spoke to her, it was only about essentials. He did not engage in any polite conversation. He ate what food she prepared and then sat staring at the fire until it burned low; then he crawled into the tent next to her. But he did not even put his hand on her breast.

His remoteness isolated Maida. And though she told herself it did not bother her, it did. She was not used to being treated as if she did not exist.

Several times she commented that Einar was making good progress and that he was now teaching her many Norse words.

Geir replied that once the young man had lived through the second night, he never had any doubts about his survival.

Then Maida spoke to Geir in his own language, using the words she had learned. But he paid no attention to her and she became so angry that she said, ''From now on, I will be silent, too.''

Geir did not answer.

On the third day, the two Franks that had been taken captive and two of Algar's men were brought to the side of Geir's ship and four of them were tied down to the front of the bow.

Maida stood and watched what was happening. She now had learned enough of the language from Einar to ask the two Vikings who brought the men to the ship what the captives would be used for.

"At the oars," he answered. "We are four men too few."

She thanked him and nodding to Maida he went away. One of the men taken from Algar's village seemed vaguely familiar to Maida. He was a fair-haired man with freckles on his face and arms. His hair and beard were a brownish-red. He was a well-built man with muscular arms and a bull-like neck.

For a moment, Algar's great hall came back to her the way it had been just before the first flaming arrow struck the table. Then she remembered that the man she was looking at now had been seated at the table to the left of Algar.

"Lady," the man said, "my name is Harold; I was one of Algar's vassals and served him well until I was captured." He spoke slowly so that the difference in their manner of speaking would not interfere with her understanding.

"I recognized you," she responded. "But not the other man."

"He was a carpenter who lived in the village."

"And the other men who were taken with you?" she questioned. "What were they?"

"Two were soldiers and the others of no degree at all," he answered. Then he asked if she knew why they were brought there.

"To man the oars," she told him. "Until we reach their stronghold."

He took several deep breaths before he said, "If you cut the two of us free, we will take you back to Algar."

Maida raised her eyebrows.

"You have complete freedom," he said. "Bring me a knife and I will do the cutting."

"You will not get beyond the line of guards." she warned. "They will cut you down before you could begin to run."

He shook his head. "We would not go that way," he said. "We would go up the river at night. By morning, we would be far enough upstream for them to think twice about going after us."

"And then what?" she asked, wondering if it was that easy to escape.

"We will buy our way home."

"With what?"

"Your rings and brooch, my lady; they will fetch a good price. Thank God that they were not taken from you."

"And the other man," she asked. "Will we take him, too?"

He thought for a few moments and then he answered, "Our escape is more important than his. But he might render us some service along the way. I leave the decision up to you."

She nodded and told him she would think about it.

"It must be done while we are here," Harold urged. "Once we put to sea again, there will be no other opportunity to escape."

"I said I would think about it," Maida answered and turning from the four bound men, she went back to Einar.

Throughout the afternoon she found it very hard to think about anything other than the plan for escape put to her by

Harold. She was slow-witted when it came to the words that Einar was trying to teach her. At least a dozen times she wanted to run down to where Harold was and speak with him about the escape. But she did not, for fear that she would be seen.

She asked Einar if anyone ever escaped from the Vikings.

"Few," he answered. "But it is not easy, especially once we reach the stronghold."

From him, she learned that there Bjorn's father, Lid, was the chieftain. And that the stronghold was always guarded by men and fierce dogs.

At sunset, when she was preparing food for Geir, she saw him at the ship. He was speaking to one of the men, though from where she was, she could not tell which one it was.

Geir came to the fire pit and sat down. He said nothing. But to Maida the expression on his face was less severe, than it had been on previous evenings. She made no attempt to start a conversation. But from time to time she glanced at him.

Then he said, "I have four more men for the oars."

"You should have five," she answered. "Einar is not well enough to work at an oar."

"Four will do," Geir told her. "Einar would not want another to do his work."

"If his wound should open," she warned, "you cannot blame me or anyone else; you will not be able to say that it was the work of trolls or the sea people. Einar should not be put at the oar."

"Two of the men are from Algar's village," he said, completely ignoring her words.

She did not answer, but her heart missed a beat and then it began to race. Suddenly she distrusted Harold and saw a trap in his proposal for an easy escape. It was clear the men were not brought here just to man the oars. She was sure Geir had another purpose for Algar's men. He was trying to test her. Perhaps he was even trying to have her killed without having to raise his own hand to do it.

"Is anything wrong?" he asked, looking hard at her.

"Should anything be wrong?" she responded.

Geir shrugged and returned to gnawing on a bone.

That night he did not sit by the fire very long. He came into the tent and settled down next to Maida long before all the faggots in the fire were reduced to glowing embers.

She pretended to be asleep.

Geir slipped his hand over her breast and in a low husky voice, he said that he wanted her.

She did not move, still feigning sleep. But already his fingers had awakened her nipples. They were hard with excitement and seared with heat. She tried to control her breathing, but her body would not respond, and her breasts rapidly rose and fell to the quickened pace of her heart.

"I know you are not asleep," Geir said.

She opened her eyes and told him that since she was his thrall, he could do what he wanted with her.

"That is not the way I want it to be," he said.

"You took me by storm once," she responded. "I am sure you can do it again."

"Why do you want to anger me?" he asked.

Maida did not answer immediately. She had not expected him to ask that kind of a question. But after a few moments, she said, "Your anger or mine is all we have between us, all that we can truly give each other."

He denied it.

"We are enemies to one another," she told him.

His lips found hers. And with his hand, he caressed the mound of her sex.

"Lust," she whispered, breathing shallowly. "Only lust—" Again his lips found hers.

Geir splayed the moist lips of her womanhood.

"I cannot deny you," she told him. "You work your demon magic, and I am no longer in possession of my soul or my body. Do what you want with me, Geir; I cannot stop you."

He moved between her open thighs.

She uttered a deep sigh of contentment when he entered her, and she told him that she would burn ten thousand years in hell for taking pleasure from what he did to her.

He laughed and said, "It is no more than any man does to a woman."

Despite her resolve, Maida could not remain passive. Her hands moved over his bare shoulders, his chest and finally to his manhood. She strained against him, wanting to feel his organ as deep in her body as nature would permit it to go. She moaned with delight and thrashed her head from side to side. "It is better, oh so much better," she gasped. Her arms encircled his neck and she guided his lips to her nipples. "Ah, yes . . . yes . . . yes. . . . harder . . . score them with your teeth!"

Geir quickened his movements. He delighted in the grace of her body and quickness of her response. He was almost ready to believe that he could indeed conjure her passion.

Maida writhed with ecstasy. A tremendous knot began to gather itself together deep inside of her. It was frighteningly intense. The faster Geir moved, the tighter the knot became. She gasped for breath; her throat was dry; colors danced on the inside of her closed eyelids.

"Geir," she moaned. "Oh, Geir!" And then the knot suddenly gave way, flinging her body against his, making her shudder with ecstasy as tremor after tremor of ineffable pleasure passed through her body.

She heard a manly growl of delight and felt his hot fluid come into her. Then, after a few moments, she became aware of his weight on her. "Would you have had me killed?" she asked.

"No," he answered. "I would have killed Bjorn first."

"I mean if I escaped?"

"I would have captured you," he told her, tonguing her nipples.

"Even if I went upstream?-' she asked.

"Upstream or down," he said, "I would have come after you." And he went back to teasing her nipples.

"Stop that for a bit."

"But why? I am enjoying doing it and you enjoy having it done," he said.

She tried to think, but with Geir at her breast, it was difficult. Suddenly Maida realized that Geir had planned nothing with Harold, that by believing he had, she had entrapped herself. For a moment, she struggled against Geir. But his passion had come to full flame again and she could not quench it. Indeed, she was so chagrined with herself for succumbing to her own doubts that she closed her eyes and once more let his heat bring fire into her body.

Long before dawn came, the whole encampment was astir. The tents were taken down, all the supplies were loaded onto the ships, the livestock was boarded, and then the ships were rolled over logs into the river. By first light the captives were placed on the ships.

When Maida came on board with Geir, Harold looked up from where he was shackled to his oar and spat.

"And what was that for?" Geir asked him.

"For your whore."

Geir's hand flashed through the air and smashed against

the side of Harold's face. "I hear that from you again, Saxon," he said in a flat voice, "I will make the blood eagle fly across your chest and then hang you from the prow of this ship."

"Algar will reckon with you," Harold answered balefully.

Geir told his crew what the slave had just said, and they laughed heartily.

Geir went to the stern of the vessel to guide it downstream to the sea. The ship led the other two, and when he brought her around the bend in the river, his eyes scanned the banks on either side.

The vessel moved swiftly. Then suddenly Geir called for the other man to guide the ship.

He ran forward and shouted for several of his men to follow.

"Einar," Maida called, "what is happening?"

"A heavy line is stretched across the river mouth," the young man shouted.

The men at the oars began to backwater, but the movement of the ship could not be stopped.

Geir and several of the men hung off the bow with one hand and with the other held their swords.

Maida looked at the other two ships. Bjorn's vessel was slowing down and Thorkel's had stopped.

"I see the rope," Geir shouted. "There it is!"

An instant later, the air was filled with shouting and the whir of arrows. They struck the shields along both sides of the ship with a pinging sound.

Geir and the men with him slashed at the rope.

More arrows came whistling through the sky from the shore. Several of them were tipped with fire.

"I will have to go down into the water to cut it," Geir shouted and the next moment he was in the water.

Several horsemen charged into the river and raced across the sandbar to stop their lines from being cut.

The two Franks on board shouted to those onshore.

Waist-deep in the water, Geir grabbed hold of the rope and began to hack away at the thick line.

The riders bore down at him.

Several of the crew leaped up and took hold of their spears. An arrow caught one of them in the throat. He screamed the name of his god Odin, and he pitched forward with blood spurting from his neck.

The ship was beginning to swing sideways.

"The line is parted," Geir shouted. "Bring the *Sea Bird* through."

The men at the oars bent their backs to the task of putting the vessel on its course. More arrows came at them. The men who ran to the bow raced back to their oars.

The ship was responding; it was moving slowly toward the mouth of the river.

But Maida saw nothing of Geir; she did not even hear his voice. And Harold shouted at her, "Your man is dead, and you will be thrall to all of these heathen."

The vessel passed over the bar and rose to meet the sea.

Maida shouted for Geir.

"He is here," Einar told her.

"Where? Where is he?"

"Holding fast to my oar," he told her.

She ran to Einar and looked over the side.

Geir had wrapped his feet and his hands around the huge oar. An arrow was lodged in his right shoulder.

Slowly Geir climbed up the oar and into the ship. As soon as he was aboard, he slipped his knife from its sheath and called to Harold. When the man faced him, he threw the knife. It entered the man's chest with a thud.

"Take my knife out of him and throw his body over the side," Geir said. Then he turned to Maida and told her she would have to cut the arrowhead out of his shoulder.

She nodded, and filled with pride, helped him to the stern of the ship. That he had killed a man because of her had a strange and exciting effect on Maida; it made her feel heady, the way too much ale always had. But it also gave her a sense of strength and power that she had never felt before!

XI

"YOU LOOK GREEN," Geir told Maida, as she worked to free the arrow from his right shoulder.

She shook her head and bit her lips. Beads of sweat stood out on her forehead. Geir's warm, sticky blood covered her hands. The knife was slippery. She was unable to get the point of the blade under the tip of the arrow without enlarging the wound.

"Better give it to me," Geir told her.

She handed the bloody knife to him and hurried to the side of the ship, where she vomited up what she had eaten for breakfast. By the time she was able to lift her head and turn it toward Geir, he had removed the arrow.

He held it between the thumb and forefinger of his left hand and commented to his men that if it had been barbed, he would have had much more trouble removing it. Then he called to her and asked her to help him stanch the bleeding.

Maida washed the wound with saltwater. Then under Geir's direction she filled the opening with bits of wool soaked in seawater. The blood soon stopped.

Geir stood up and took his place at the shaft, which he explained to her was called a helm. "The helm," he said, "is part of the steering oar." He spoke first in her language and then in Norse.

She repeated what he said in Norse.

Skled told Geir, "She will soon speak our tongue as well as any of us."

83

Geir began to translate, but Maida responded that she understood the sense of what Skled said. She thanked him for the compliment.

The sun was well up in the morning sky and the sea was very calm. The ships moved in a line, with Geir's in the lead. They stayed within sight of the coast, oftentimes close enough for Maida to see a house made of stone and roofed over with thatch. Now and then she even saw cows or horses. It was impossible for her to tell what they were because they were too far away. But she was sure that if she asked Geir whether they were horses or cows, he would be able to tell her.

The morning drifted into the afternoon. The men rowed at an easy pace. The sun was off the right side of the ship.

Geir was relieved by the other helmsman, whose name was Hougen.

Maida expected Geir to join her, but he went to the prow of the ship and stayed there a long time, with his left arm wrapped around the dragon's neck. She considered going to him but decided that if he wanted her with him, he would have called for her. Besides, she was afraid he would misinterpret such an act; he might very well think he had captured her heart, when in truth, he held nothing more than her body.

The exhilaration Maida had felt when Geir had killed for her was gone. In its stead was a sense of shame. Whatever else he was, Harold was a Christian, and she had rejoiced at his death. Her guilt was even greater than that of Geir's. God could not expect him to show Christian virtue, Christian kindness.

Geir killed without so much as a flicker of feeling.

He did it as naturally as he breathed. But she might have stopped him; she might have pleaded for the man's life rather than reveling in his death.

She closed her eyes and prayed to Christ for forgiveness; she prayed that whatever feelings of lust had been awakened by the shedding of blood, be stilled forever; that God reach out his hand to her and stop her from slipping any further into the grasp of the Devil. "Protect me, God," she murmured. "Protect me!" Then she opened her eyes and saw Geir coming toward her.

"Were you praying?" he asked, sitting down next to her.

"What would you know about that?" she answered.

"I have seen Christians and other people pray," he told her. "They always have that same look on their face, as if they were in pain."

She did not know what to say other than to admit she was praying.

"What were you praying for?" Geir asked.

"For my salvation," Maida answered and seeing that he did not understand, she added. "And that I might soon have Glenna again."

"I know nothing about salvation," he said, "and as for Glenna—" He was going to tell her that he was not going to become entangled with that foolishness again, but he could not.

"If Paige was here," Maida said, "I would ask for her, too. But she was killed in the raid."

"You had two serving women?" he asked.

"I am the daughter of a duke," she said proudly. "I would have had even more if I had not been taken from Algar."

"If you could have had so many more, why were Glenna and Paige so important to you?"

She told him how her mother had died from the coughing sickness shortly after she had been born. She explained that both women had been slaves and that Paige had shared her father's bed. "Paige was a mother to me, and Glenna was my older sister."

85

With a thoughtful expression on his face, Geir remained quiet for a long time. Then he said in a low voice, "My mother died after bearing me. My father was killed during a raid on the stronghold. I was raised by my uncle Lid, Bjorn's father."

"And you went to sea when you were ten years old," she said.

He nodded and was pleased she had remembered. "We do not call it going to sea," he explained. "We say that we went a vi-king."

"But that is what you are called."

"That is what we do," he said.

"Then Bjorn and you have been friends all of your life?" she questioned.

Geir nodded. "He has been angry with me since we left the stronghold. The men told Lid they would not sail if Bjorn was their leader; they asked that I be made their chief and Bjorn captain one ship. If it was not for his stubbornness, I would not have been captured by Algar and so many of my men would not have had their heads stuck up on poles. Bjorn refused to join the fight when I sent word to him to come to aid me and my men. He stood offshore, out of sight and watched. Thorkel's ship was too far offshore to be of any help."

"Perhaps he wanted you killed?" Maida suggested in a low voice.

"No, I do not think so," Geir responded. "I think he wanted to teach me a lesson. But later, when he saw that part of that lesson included you, he was very, very angry."

"What would he have done if Algar had killed you?"

With a shrug, Geir answered, "If that had happened, he probably would have put all of the captives to the sword. Then he would have prayed to the gods, as you were praying, for forgiveness and for them to cool Lid's anger.''

Sure he was laughing at her again, Maida flushed. In a low voice she said, ''But my God will answer my prayers; He will deliver me from you.''

''Let Him try,'' Geir challenged. ''And I will try to deliver Glenna to you. If I succeed and He fails, then which of us, Maida, will be worth more to you?''

''You can not put yourself with God,'' she said. ''You are only a man.''

''There are many, many gods,'' he told her. ''I have been with the people who follow Allah and with those who worship the sun and—''

''They are all false gods!'' she cried.

''If they are false, then why does your God allow them to be worshiped by the people? All of those people should bow down to Him.''

''They are in the hands of the Devil,'' she answered, thinking that might be what Father Quinell would have said.

Geir shook his head, and that brought an end to the conversation.

Of course Maida thought all the things she might have said to him but that was after they had stopped talking. She knew about the followers of Allah; her father, when he had been much younger, had fought many battles with those who came to raid the shores of Cornwall. Paige had told her stories of some of those encounters. After listening to them, she would be too frightened to sleep in her place and sought safety next to Paige.

She glanced at Geir. That he had challenged God was blasphemous beyond anything she had ever heard. She fully expected God to strike him dead, or at least punish him in some obvious way.

The sun was far down in the west and the sky was filled with soft yellow light. Geir steered the ship closer to the shore, and soon they were making their way into a small cove.

The oars were shipped and as the ships ground themselves on the sandy beach, the Viking went over the sides and immediately took up defensive positions. Fire pits were dug and food was cooked on the beach, but everyone slept in the ships.

As Geir settled down next to her under the sheepskin robe, he said that he would not want to cut his way out of the cove. He slipped his hand over her breast and wished her pleasant dreams.

"Were you surprised by what the Franks did?" she asked.

"No . . . I knew the rope had been placed there," he answered. "I watched them putting it across yesterday. The skill was in finding it from the deck of the ship and then cutting it. It is something that will be remembered by those who saw it done. And by doing it," he chuckled, "I taught Bjorn a lesson."

Maida sighed deeply. She would never understand Geir. Except when it came to what he did with her in his passion, he was not like any other man. She did not know whether he was braver or more foolish than Christians or even his own kind. But their respect and love for him was obvious. He was a good leader, or chief, as they called him.

The night was sharply cold and moving closer to him, she asked him in a whisper not to stir her nipples. Then she closed her eyes and sleep took her.

For five more days and nights, Geir's small fleet of ships worked their way north along the coast. Each day was filled with bright sun, blue sky and wheeling, darting flight of sea gulls, terns, and skimmer birds.

The cottages on the shore became less frequent and for all Maida could see, she and the Vikings were the only beings on the face of the earth. Such an idea gave her a strange feeling. She felt even more peculiar when she spoke to Geir about it and he answered, "There is some truth in that. Those that do not see us do not know we are here, and we cannot be sure that those we do not see are here."

Her only real delight was in the ready way she was able to speak and understand Norse. She could speak to the men and they to her. From each one, though more from Einar and Geir than any of the rest, she learned the words of the new language and how to put them together. To her surprise, she no longer found it ugly and harsh. It had its own fluidity, its own cadences.

Einar had memorized whole portions of the sagas and recited them to Maida. Each saga was a story of a hero and his encounter with the heathen gods or his battles against other people. The savagery of these people was no less in their stories than it was in their lives.

She asked Geir if he was a follower of Odin.

He leaned back, and looking up into the blue of the late afternoon sky, he said, "As he protects me in battle, I honor him; but I am not a berserk. I fight when I must; I do not fight because there is nothing else I can do."

"Your gods are all so cruel," she commented.

"As is everything else," he answered, rubbing his wounded shoulder.

"And what about love?" she questioned.

"I have heard that your God is a god of love." he said with a shake of his head. "I do not understand that kind of love. I have known only the love of a woman."

"That is a different kind of love," she said, suddenly coloring.

"It is what I know. Have you known it?"

"You were the first to—"

"Do you know it with me?"

"No," she answered in a low voice. "You have taught me passion and have conjured lust where before there was only innocence."

Geir nodded and then he asked, "Would you still rather drown than come with me to Gottland? Those were your words the night of the raid."

"Since then you have taken me many times," she answered.

"But you gave yourself to me as well," he said.

"God will call me to account when the time comes," Maida told him. "I know that I sin with you, but as God is my judge, I am defenseless against your conjurations."

"Given the choice between life and death," he asked, "which would you choose now?"

Prickles raced down Maida's spine; there was that look in his blue eyes and that expression on his face that made her wary of her words.

Before she could answer, he said, "Do not tell me now. Tell me later."

"But how can I answer that question?"

He gestured to the sea and said, "Tell me when the choice lies with water and not with you. It is easy to speak of death when death is not near, but when it stands next to you, ready to take you into its arms, then speak about it; then tell me that you would prefer its embrace to life here and now until the day when Heimdal, the god of hunting, blows his war horn to signal Ragnarok, the battle between the gods and the end of the world."

"I will tell you," she told him haughtily.

"Yes," he answered, "I am sure you will."

"Christ will stand with me."

Geir shrugged.

"Has death ever been close to you?" she asked.

90

"Many times."

"And he never tried to take you?"

"He did but I always fought him off. I love life too much to let him just whisk me away. I knew he was trying to take me before time—it is a game that we play with one another."

"A game?"

"By playing with death, life becomes more interesting," he told her.

Maida did not understand, and the converstaion ended with her being confused. Death was God's way of bringing all to His reckoning. The struggle between life and death was not a game but a matter for the Almighty to decide. That night she slept fitfully and awoke several times from the sound of her own cries. That Geir was close by provided her with some comfort, especially when she felt his hand on her breasts.

XII

GEIR'S WOUND HEALED quickly and Einar became strong enough to row several hours a day. The two Franks and the Saxon carpenter, whose name Maida learned was Elton, quickly adopted themselves to their new roles. Except at night, when Geir put into a cove or the mouth of a small river to make camp, they were unfettered and had as much freedom aboard the vessel as any other member of the crew.

Some days the crew did nothing, and the large square sail billowed out with wind, making them skim over the top of the water. Each day was like the one that had passed. The sunlight glinted off the waves while the sky was very blue and almost cloudless.

Maida lost track of time; she no longer knew how many days had passed since she had become Geir's woman. The rhythm of her life was now so different from what it had been formerly and what it would have been if Geir had not taken her. Then she would have been the lady of Algar's castle and she would have had many servants and many comforts befitting her station. But now her once-beautiful gown was in tatters and her lovely black hair was unkempt and filled with salt spray.

Whenever Maida fell to musing about what had been denied her by Geir, she hated him with a passion equal to the one he could conjure in her body at night, when he found the secret places of her body that made it possible for him to play her, as though she were no more than a lute in his hands. For robbing her of the will to deny his lust, she would never forgive him, never permit her heart to soften against him, and always pray to God for her rescue.

The weather remained good. But the men of the *Sea Bird* soon refrained from mentioning it, for fear that the gods might suddenly decide to snatch the sun and calm seas away from them.

"Gods are like that," Geir told Maida, when questioned about the attitude of the men. "They give and they take at their whim and not our convenience. It is always wise not to remind them about what they have given."

"The Lord giveth and the Lord taketh away; blessed be the name of the Lord," she said in a low voice.

Geir shrugged and went forward to examine the lines holding the sail. He loosened several and told one of his men to tighten other ones on the opposite side of the ship, thereby altering the position of the sail. Then he stopped to speak with the two Franks. He spoke their language as well as he spoke Saxon. He asked them if they thought ransom would be paid by their kinsmen for their return.

"We are humble men," the elder of the two said. He was a small man with brown hair and brown eyes. "My brother owns the mill; I help him at harvest time; otherwise I tend the horses of the lord."

Geir looked at the other Frank. He was thin and narrow-shouldered. He coughed a great deal through the night.

"I am the son of a farmer," he said. "All my father has is one cow and three sheep."

Geir nodded. He was not convinced that either of the men told him the truth. But he would not press them anymore. They would doubtlessly be more truthful once they reached the stronghold and realized they would be sold.

He turned to the Saxon and asked him the same question.

The man was about Geir's own age but at least a head smaller. His eyes were green and his hair black. He looked up at Geir. "Viking, I am a carpenter. I own nothing but my tools and they are back in the village."

"A carpenter," Geir repeated, and asked what he could build.

"Anything of wood. Even a ship like this one, now that I have seen it."

Geir asked about the man he had killed.

"He was one of Algar's officers," Elton said. "Fighting and killing was his trade as it is yours."

"So you could build a boat like this one, eh?" Geir questioned.

"That I could," Elton responded without flinching from the Viking's hard look.

Geir explained to his men what the Saxon captive said and they nodded their heads approvingly and suggested the Saxon not be sold but he be kept to repair the ships and make furniture for them.

Geir told them he would think about it. Then he returned to the stern and sat down next to Maida.

"The carpenter belongs to Alrek, one of the men on Thorkel's ship," he told her. "I do not know if he will sell him."

"Then you are considering buying him?" Maida questioned. She had followed the conversation between Geir and Elton with great interest.

Geir shrugged and did not offer any more of an answer than what was contained in his silent gesture.

Immediately after they had put to sea the following morning, Geir went forward to the bow. He scanned the sun-drenched sea. When he came to sit next to Maida, another man took his place at the bow.

Even though Geir was no longer scanning the sea,

Maida saw he continually searched the water. She also realized the crew did the same. She asked him what they were looking for.

He shook his head and told her that she would know soon enough if they found it.

All through the afternoon, Geir and his men were on the alert. And when night came and they made camp, Geir ordered that no fire be lit and the guard around the encampment was doubled.

It was well into the night before Maida felt Geir's hand on her breast.

Before dawn, they were at sea. The sky turned red before the sun rose. Geir frowned when he saw it and said that it was not a good sign.

The day grew lighter but the sun never shone The sky was covered by gray clouds. The sea and the sky were the same color. Then the wind dropped off and the men began to pull on the oars.

Geir climbed up the mast and sat astride the heavy spar that held the sail.

Maida could see that there was also a man on the mast of the other two ships, though she could not make out whether it was Bjorn and Thorkel.

"Ships," Geir suddenly shouted, pointing to the dark mass of the coast. "Ships—there, off the headland!"

Bjorn immediately took up the cry and from the distance Maida could hear Thorkel echo it.

Geir ordered his men to stop rowing and when the other two ships came close, he told them to come alongside of the *Sea Bird.* "Let them think we are only one," he explained to his other captains. Then he added, "Perhaps if Odin does not want any new warriors in Valhalla today, they will not see us." He motioned Hougen away from the tiller and he took over the task of steering the ship.

The men were grim, and when Geir ordered them to begin rowing again, they worked until sweat poured down their faces.

Maida looked toward the headland. At first she could see nothing. The dark coast looked like a rent in the solid grayness of sea and sky. Then very slowly she saw the square shape of a sail materialize out of the dark coloration of the land.

"Is that what you see?" she asked, pointing to it.

"They must have a slight offshore breeze behind them," Geir said.

"Who are they?" she questioned.

"The men who follow Njal," Geir answered through his teeth.

"Are they not like yourselves Vikings?" she asked.

"They are sharks," he told her. Then he urged his men to row faster.

The other two ships kept pace.

Then suddenly the wind freshened from the east. Almost at once, Maida realized there were four sails in the distance.

"They have seen us!" Geir shouted to his other captains. He ordered his men to stop rowing.

"But why not raise your sail and run from them?" Maida asked, her heart beating so loud she was almost certain that everyone on the ship could hear it.

He shook his head. The skin around his jaw was tight and his eyes were a cold ice-blue.

The three ships turned their bows toward the oncoming enemy. Under the sweeping hand of the wind, the sea became ruffled.

All too soon, the marauding ships drew close enough for Maida to see the black dragon on their sails and on their bows.

"Stay very low," Geir cautioned her.

"But there are four ships to your three!"

"Four, five or even fourteen would make no difference," he said. "We would fight them no matter what their number. Njal's berserks are to us what we are to you. They raid us, take what is ours, and destroy what we have. It was during one of Njal's raids on my uncle's stronghold that my father was killed."

Suddenly Maida realized that to fight Njal's berserks was a matter of honor with Geir. He could no more flee than the waves stop running before the wind.

Geir called to the two Franks and asked them if they would fight.

"We do not know how to use a blade," the elder one said, "but we could manage a battle-ax."

He told one of his men to give them each a good ax and then he said, "Should you use it against us, none of my men would hesitate to kill you. But if you should be taken by those Vikings, you will quickly wish to die."

Each one of them told him that they would not lift their weapon against any man in the boat.

Then Geir asked Elton if he would fight.

"With a blade," the carpenter said.

"Do you know how to use it?"

"Yes," he said. "And I also give my word that I will not use it against any of your men."

"So you understand the language of the Franks, too?" Geir questioned.

"And something of your own," Elton answered.

"We will speak of these things later," Geir told him and turned his attention to the oncoming ships.

The four vessels separated and came toward Geir's three ships in a straight line. They were using their oars as well as their sails.

Suddenly Geir ordered his men to begin rowing and within moments the ship was underway, rushing toward the center vessel. His action caused the opposing ships to alter their course and denied them the use of their sails.

Geir's ship bore down on the side of one of the vessels. His men pulled as hard as they could against the movement of the sea.

The marauding ship tried to swing away from the bow of the *Sea Bird* but could not manage a full turn. The ship shuddered as she struck the other vessel. The air was filled with the sound of cracking timbers and the yells of angry men.

Geir shouted to his men to backwater. The *Sea Bird* moved away. The other vessel's side was stove in and she was sinking rapidly. The crew was scrambling to stay out of the water but the ship turned over on its side, pitching all of its men into the heaving sea. They screamed at Geir and shook their fists at him.

Geir swung his ship around and brought it against the side of another one of the enemy ships. By now Bjorn and Thorkel were too engaged in fierce battles of their own to know what was happening to Geir.

As soon as the *Sea Bird* was alongside the enemy vessel, the ships were made fast to each other with grappling hooks. But even before this, the berserks from each vessel met each other in a wild orgy of shouting and slashing of swords.

Iron clanged against iron. Spears whistled through the air. Several found their mark in the chests and stomachs of many of the men, and some of the spears flew into the sea.

Shouting was fearful. The smash of shield against shield or crash of ax against ax sounded like the crack of thunder.

Geir fought from the stern deck. He cut several men down with his sword and threw one man into the sea.

Terrified, Maida crouched low on the deck. A head dropped from a man's shoulders and rolled to her feet. She tried to draw away from its accusing eyes but could not.

The desperate fighting swirled in front of her. The men were merciless with one another. She saw Einar spear a man and with all his strength hurl the man with a spear still in him into the sea.

A man came screaming over the side of the ship and tried to grab hold of her. Skled shouted to the attacker, and the two of them swung wildly at each other with their battle axes until Hougen drove his sword into the man's back.

Not far away, she could see the men from the other ships hacking away at each other but she could scarcely hear anything other than savage din around her.

The fray moved from Geir's ship to the other vessel. The carnage on the *Sea Bird* was fearful to look at. Men from both crews lay dying on the deck of the ship. Many were bleeding from stumps where their arms and legs used to be. Others lay with their heads cracked open, their gray brains splattered over the sea-worn deck.

Maida looked for Geir; he was no longer standing on the high stern deck. He was aboard the other ship, hacking at a man with such a savage stroke that it clove the man apart from his neck to his waist.

Stained with blood and breathing deeply, Geir pressed the enemy until those that were left threw down their arms.

"Kill them!" he ordered.

They died shouting Odin's name.

Geir called his men back to the *Sea Bird,* cut her loose from the enemy vessel, and went to aid Bjorn. But the other marauders freed themselves from Geir's ships and made their escape as fast as possible.

XIII

MORE OF THE ship's crew were dead and wounded than were fit to man the oars. Skled was badly slashed across the chest; Hougen was bleeding profusely from the right side of his head. The two Franks lay with their skulls smashed open and their brains splattered over the side of the ship. Miraculously Einar survived and so did Elton.

Geir looked down at the remainder of his crew and sadly shook his head. He was wet with sweat and breathing very hard. His eyes found Maida's and for the briefest instant the terrible grimness left his face. He nodded to her and said, "There are many of my men who need tending."

"I will see to them," she answered but did not move.

"Are you hurt?" he asked.

She shook her head and then she cast her eyes down to the head that still lay at her feet.

Geir jumped down from where he stood and lifting up the head by its bloody hair, he looked at it for a moment. His eyes went to slits, and speaking to the grisly object, he said, "Let your spirit walk in Njal's dreams and tell him that Geir one day will come to him. One day Geir will come!" Then he threw the head into the sea.

Horrified, Maida watched its arcing flight, saw it splash into the leaden water, bob on the surface and then vanish beneath the waves.

By the time Geir was back at the helm, Maida had moved to the wounded and the dying. Einar helped her and so did Elton, who said nothing to her, though she tried several times to speak to him.

When the dead were thrown into the sea and the wounded patched up, Geir found he had lost half his crew and of the half left, several would not be able to man an oar for a long time.

The men on Bjorn's ship and Thorkel's fared no better. All of the livestock had been killed. But none of the captives were dead, though two of the women had received slight sword wounds.

The ships moved together, and all the men captured by Geir were put at the oars of the three vessels. But even with additional help, all of the crews were below strength.

"I think you will lose two more men by nightfall," Maida said looking up at Geir, when she returned to the stern.

He nodded and told her that in such a fight they were lucky not to have suffered more casualties. "But we will not attempt to row tonight," he said.

"It might be better for everyone if we could make camp," she responded. "The dead livestock will supply the meat."

He shook his head and pointing to where the land was, though by now it was completely obliterated from sight by low lying banks of very dark clouds, he explained that Njal's ships were somewhere off the coast. "They would like nothing better than for me to come to them. No, we will spend the night here. And perhaps Njord, the god of wind and sea will not become too angry at us, though it seems," he said, looking at the sea and the sky, "he grows angrier and angrier."

Indeed, the wind was now blowing much stronger from the south east and the waves were larger, some of them even had white tops.

Geir ordered food to be given to those who could eat. Then all the oars and everything else that could be lashed down was tied securely. The men, too, slipped ropes around themselves and then looped the end around their oars.

"We will keep within hailing distance," Geir told his other captains.

"How long do we wait if we are separated?" Thorkel asked.

"A day at the most," Geir answered. "Then sail for the stronghold."

The wind began to sigh and moan. The crests of the waves grew higher.

Geir held the ship in the direction of the wind. He called to Maida and he beckoned to her to join him. When she was near him, he took a length of rope, wrapped it around her waist, then around his and finally tied it to the dragon tail that formed the stern of the ship. There was enough line between them that allowed Maida to move around and even sit down if she wanted to. But she stood close to Geir.

The wind whistled and roared, making it impossible for them to understand one another unless they shouted.

Geir pointed to the waves. They had grown much, much higher, and the *Sea Bird* rode up to their crests and then slid down into the troughs between them.

"They will become much worse," he shouted.

That hardly seemed possible; already the crests of the waves covered with a white froth that blew over them.

Now and then Maida caught a glimpse of one of the other ships, especially when one of them hung for an instant on the very top of a wave before it plunged out of sight.

The sea broke over the *Sea Bird*. The water swirled over the deck and round Maida's feet like a hissing snake.

She had never been so cold or wet in all of her life. The wet and cold seemed to be inside of her as well as outside.

The sky turned black. And the waters, too, were black, except for ragged patches of spume that came off the tops of the rushing waves.

The saltwater soon felt like sand against Maida's hands and arms. Her skin became raw; then cracked and bled.

The wind shrieked and then suddenly the black under belly of the sky was rent by a jagged streak of lightning. Moments later the whole of the sea and the sky trembled under the heavy pounding of thunder.

The sea grew wilder. The waves rose up like huge mountains in front of the *Sea Bird*. She struggled to reach their tops and then plunged down, down, into the depths between two walls of black water.

Lightning tore the sky apart. The sea and the sky trembled with each crash of thunder.

"Thor!" Geir shouted, after one burst of lightning and roll of thunder. "Thor and his hammer." And he pointed up toward the black sky.

Maida shook her head. The sea and sky had gone wild. They were demons trying to tear her away from the ship, trying to smash the ship to pieces.

"Dear God," she shouted, "I do not want to die; I do not want to drown!" But a wave came up over the ship and plunged her so deep underwater that she was sure she would never again breathe air. Then the ship broke free. Coughing, Maida gasped for air and filled her lungs.

Twice she was swept back over the ship and held to it only by the length of rope that Geir had secured around her waist. Once a breaking wave drove her into Geir, knocking him over the side.

She screamed his name and she pulled with all her strength to bring him back on the deck. Finally he regained his place. But the bow of the ship had swung away from the waves, and the vessel was in danger of foundering under the torrents of water that fell over it.

"The oars!" Geir shouted, above the cry of the wind. He gestured to his men.

They understood, and those who could worked desperately to free their oars. Soon many of them were pulling. The ship began to swing toward the waves.

Geir fought the sea and the wind to hold the vessel into the wind. More and more waves broke over the craft.

The night passed but the sky was still dark.

Maida saw one of the ships and pointed to it.

Geir nodded. He was numb with cold and very, very tired. He desperately wanted to sleep. His eyes closed but he forced them to remain open. Sometimes he held his arm tightly around Maida's waist. Her nearness gave him a strange kind of warmth. He could see she was frightened, but he could not drive her fear away.

Sometime late in the day, the wind abated somewhat and the waves became less mountainous.

"It will soon be over," he shouted at her and then he pointed to the sky to indicate that it was becoming lighter.

Maida was too weary to answer and she nodded. Never had she experienced such a storm; never had she thought that the elements had conspired to kill her; never had she thought that God had in every way deserted the world and had left it to the Devil.

Patches of blue appeared in the sky; the leaden clouds lifted from the sea and became white. Then the wind lessened and the sea moderated.

Geir searched the sea for the other ships. He saw them; they were practically on the horizon to the west, silhouetted against a red sunset. He turned the *Sea Bird* toward them and asked the men to row.

"Here," he said to Maida. "Hold the tiller this way.

Look at the ships and at our bow. Keep our bow to them. . . ." He untied himself from her and went down to the deck. He put the two dead men over the side. Then he sat down at one of the oars and began to pull with the rest of them.

The clouds gave way and the first stars showed themselves before the *Sea Bird* joined with the other ships.

Geir took the tiller from Maida and with a tired smile, he told her that if she were a man, he would make a fine Viking out of her.

"No, thank you," she answered. But nonetheless, she was pleased with the compliment. In the past days, she had survived much hardship and, to her surprise, she found herself strengthened by all that had happened to her.

The night came. The sky was full of stars and it was very cold. Even under the sheepskin robe, which, like her own clothes, was wet through and through, she could not find the slightest bit of warmth. Geir slept next to her, and he, too, trembled from the cold. But he was too exhausted, too numb to feel anything. He did not even bother to put his hand on her breasts, and though it was hard for her to admit it, even to herself, she missed it.

When she awoke the following morning, Geir was already inspecting the damage done to the ship by the storm. Some things had been smashed, but nothing that would render them unseaworthy.

He spoke with Bjorn and Thorkel.

From what they said, Maida realized that they had been blown far off-course.

Geir said, "I think we must be somewhere near the Faroe Islands."

"Closer to Norway," Bjorn said.

Geir said he might be right and suggested they sail east. "In any case, we can sail around the southern tip of Norway and make for the Baltic that way. With the gods smiling at us, we can be home in ten days or so."

The ships swung eastward and slowly began to move. Sometimes the men pulled at the oars; other times they used a sail.

During the day the sun shone bright but it was never really warm, and Geir showed Maida that it spent less and less time each day above the horizon. The nights were cold enough for their breaths to steam.

After several days they sighted land and moved along the coast.

Then one evening, Geir sat down next to Maida and said, "By tomorrow at this time we will have reached the stronghold."

She did not know what kind of a response he wanted her to make, so she kept silent and nodded.

"I have been thinking about us—about you," he said.

Again he seemed to be waiting for her to speak and again she remained silent.

He said nothing more to her then but when he settled down next to her for the night and put his hand on her breasts, he whispered that he had fallen in love with her, that he wanted to make her his wife.

"I am already married," she answered him.

"But I have you now," he said.

"In the eyes of God, I am still Algar's wife."

"Your God has no power over my people," he told her harshly. "His eyes never see where we are and what we do."

"I am a Christian," she said.

"I love you."

"And I cannot love you," she told him. "You use the Devil's ways to bring passion and lust into my body, but you cannot touch my heart with them."

"Then you will be my thrall," Geir told her angrily. "Nothing more."

"I am that now," she responded.

Geir withdrew his hand from her breast and he left the shelter of the sheepskin robe. He went to the bow of the ship and stood there looking out over the black water of the Baltic Sea.

He did not understand why he wanted Maida to be his wife; he did not understand why he felt differently toward her than the two women in his house who were only too eager to share his bed, one at a time or both together. They did all a woman could do to satisfy a man's lust but his feelings to Maida were very different than—

Suddenly Elton called to him.

He turned and went to the man.

"Will you sell me when we reach the stronghold?" Elton asked.

"Would you serve me?"

"Willingly."

"To what end?" Geir questioned.

"To be a free man," Elton said.

"Then you expect me to buy you and then give you your freedom?"

"Yes," Elton said. "You will find I am worth my freedom."

"Are you sure that you are no more than a carpenter?" Geir asked. "I caught sight of you fighting and have my doubts."

"I am a carpenter with many talents."

"And a ready tongue?"

"That, too."

"I will buy you," Geir said. "But to gain your freedom, you will have to render me some great service."

Elton reached out his hand and Geir took it.

"We have made a bargain," Elton said.

Geir agreed and started back toward the stern; then he suddenly changed his mind and returned to Elton. "Tell me," he said, "do you, too, believe in the Christian God?"

"Yes," Elton told him with a nod.

Geir looked at him for several moments; then he returned to the stern, to Maida, and slipping under the robe, he said with disgust, "Elton believes in your God, too, and I thought he was a clever man."

But Maida did not answer. She was already asleep.

XIV

THE DAY CAME bright with sunshine. With the exception of the captives, everyone at the oars bent their backs to the rowing. But soon the sun was hidden by clouds and a wind came out of the west.

Geir ordered the sail raised. The ship moved rapidly through the sea, while he stood at its helm. Now and then he glanced down at Maida.

Their brief conversation the previous night stayed with him, making him uneasy. He had revealed himself to her, and he was now uncertain how much power she had over him. He was almost certain that Freyja, the goddess of love, was laughing at him. She was wont to do that whenever a woman managed to make a man declare himself as he had done. He shook his head and wondered what the outcome of his folly would be.

By afternoon, the first dark mass of Gottland appeared in the east. To Maida it looked no different from any of the coasts she had seen. But as soon as the men in the ships saw it, they began to boisterously shout across the open water to one another.

They were so obviously pleased about going home that Maida found it hard to believe they were the same men who raided Algar's village. And for the first time she heard them speak about their wives, mothers, and sweethearts. With the exception of Einar's mother and Bjorn's father, none of the men ever mentioned their kinsmen. And often it seemed to Maida that the men had no earthly ties other than to Geir, to one another and to the ship; that they were truly the Devil's spawn!

Maida clambered up to where Geir was. The wind whipped her long black hair out in front of her. She was forced to hold it down with her left hand and use her right one to grasp Geir in order to keep her footing on the slightly tilted deck of the ship which ran before the wind.

"It will be strange to remain on land after all this time at sea," Maida commented.

With a shrug, Geir said, "It is always good to return home. The men know they have done something and they are proud of themselves. They have fought bravely and have taken rich booty."

"They have plundered, raped, and killed," she responded, looking straight at him.

"It is our way," he told her. "Otherwise why would we go to sea? We would all be farmers and never go a vi-king. But then others would come against us. No, it is better we do it than others do it to us."

She shook her head but did not answer.

The shore in front of the ships became much clearer. Steep cliffs came down to the very edge of the sea, where huge waves smashed themselves against boulders.

The cliffs were black, though here and there on their tops Maida was able to see the gnarled, naked limbs of some trees. Gulls and other sea birds winged their way over the waters around the island.

Geir swung the ship slightly toward the north. By late afternoon the sail was lowered and the men began to row.

A strange hornlike sound came from the island. It echoed and reechoed several times as countless birds took flight.

"We have been sighted," Geir told her, explaining that Lid's lookouts had seen them and were signaling their approach.

110

"But how do they make that sound?" she asked.

"By blowing into a huge shell," he answered.

Again the sound came across the waters. And its echo followed.

Geir raised a red shield to the mast and he explained to Maida that the shield showed they were coming in peace.

"But they must know you," she responded.

"All ships are enemies until they are fully recognized." He pointed to the shield at the top of the mast. "They now know we come in peace."

Maida could see nothing but she knew somewhere on those black forbidding cliffs there were men watching her.

Three short blasts were sounded on the shell.

"They have seen the shield," Geir said.

The three ships turned east, moved closer to the shore. As they rounded a headland, the cliffs fell back from the sea. There, on a wide strip of land, Maida saw Lid's stronghold.

Her heart suddenly began to race; her legs felt as if they would give way. She realized there was where she would live. It was a larger place than she would have thought. There were many buildings made of stone and wood with high thatched, gabled roofs. The shore was crowded with ships; several of them were much larger than the *Sea Bird* or any of the other vessels in Geir's fleet. People were already shouting and running down to the beach to greet the homecoming men.

The ships moved in closer to the shore. Several small boats were launched and came toward them.

Maida saw the men in the stronghold were dressed like the men in the ships with leggings and loose-fitting blouses, over which they wore cloaks.

The women ranged behind the men. They did not wear gowns but were attired in shifts on top of which were large rectangular pieces of cloth in the front and rear held

111

together with brooches. Many of the women wore a shawl on their shoulders and several had a cloth covering on their heads.

The men in the small boats drew along side of the *Sea Bird.* They hailed Geir, asking him if the raid was successful. Then, pointing to Maida, they wanted to know who she was.

Geir told them he brought back rich booty, many captives, and that she was his thrall.

They said that gods smiled at him. Then they kept pace with the ship as it moved closer and closer to the shore.

Suddenly Maida saw there were carcasses of various animals on platforms above the doors of some of the houses. She asked why they were placed there.

"For the gods," Geir answered.

Maida shuddered.

"Over there," Geir said, pointing to a tall gray-haired man on the shore, "there is Bjorn's father, Lid."

One by one the ships ground ashore. The men leaped over the sides, while others came running down from the beach to help with final grounding of the vessels.

There was a great deal of shouting and calling of names between the people in the stronghold and the men in the ships.

Geir went over the side of the *Sea Bird* and walked up the beach to where Lid stood.

His uncle said, "Tell us, what success you had." Lid was a man in his middle years. He was as tall as Geir. He wore a blue woolen cloak and held himself very straight. His eyes went to Maida, lingered for a few moments, and then moved to the men of the other ships. When he saw Bjorn, he nodded with satisfaction and again asked Geir to tell him what had happened.

Geir answered, "Many of my men have gone to Valhalla. We plundered Algar's village and took booty and captives from it. Later we fought with the Franks and after them we did battle with Njal's men. Then, storm-tossed, we were driven far out to sea and had to make our way back to the coast of Norway.''

The crews of the three ships and the other two captains gathered behind Geir as he told his uncle that the wife and mother of every one of the men who had been lost would be given that man's share of the booty.

"Half would have been generous enough," Lid told him. "But a full share does credit to the spirit of the man who is dead and to your standing as their chief."

The people shouted their approval.

"Tonight we will feast in my hall and pay tribute to those warriors who did not return," Lid said.

Maida was surprised that none of the mothers, wives, or sweethearts cried out for the men they had lost.

Almost at once the ships were unloaded by the crews.

Geir returned to Maida, saying, "I will take you to my house. I have two other women there . . . Karinia is from a land in the east, where the Rus live; the other is a Norse woman taken in a raid. Her name is Thyri. They will see to your needs."

She responded hotly, "So am I to be used when you tire of your other women, or will you use them when you tire of me?"

"If you do not come with me without giving me trouble, I will sling you over my shoulder and carry you," he told her sharply.

Maida did not want to be humiliated in front of all the people, and with a nod, she consented to go with him. When they came to where Lid stood, Bjorn was already with him.

Maida saw Lid's eyes were even grayer than those of his son. He looked at her and told Geir she would bring a good price.

"She understands what you said," Geir told him and then he added, "I do not intend to sell her."

Lid raised his eyebrows but said nothing.

Bjorn said to Geir, "The matter of the woman must still be settled between us."

Lid's eyes went from his son to his nephew and then back to his son.

"We have just come home," Geir said. "Let us not—"

"No more of your cunning words, cousin," Bjorn shouted loudly, so that those nearby turned to look at him.

Geir said quietly, "You do your father a dishonor of which I want no part. Maida is mine; she is my thrall."

Lid's brow contracted.

"My cousin has not yet learned to be a man," Geir told his uncle.

"I would have what is mine!" Bjorn stormed.

"What is yours, yes. But what is mine or any other man's, no," Geir answered. Then, without waiting for a response from his cousin or words from his uncle, he took hold of Maida's hand and pulled her away.

"It is not my fault that your cousin wants me," she said, stumbling after him. "There is no reason for you to be angry with me."

Geir slowed his pace.

Maida looked around the stronghold. There was a high wall with several small towers on the land side of it. And the dwellings were far better made than she would have suspected; indeed, they showed a great deal of craftmanship. Many were decorated with images of their gods and of wild animals.

Geir's house was at the far end of the stronghold. The bottom part of it was built of stone, and the upper portion of wood formed into a high gable roofed over with thatch. There were no decorations on the outside of it, but on the platform was a carcass of a ram.

Geir pointed to it with pride and said, "That was done by my women to keep me safe from harm."

Maida pulled an ugly face and told him, "It does nothing more than stink and grow flies."

He shrugged and explained, "It is very strong magic, especially when a ram is slaughtered by a woman and she rubs her breasts and thighs with its blood."

"I do not want to know anything about it," Maida said.

The door opened. One woman came out and then the other. The first was olive-skinned, black-haired, and sloe-eyed.

The second was blonde and fair. They were good-looking women, with ample breasts and good hips.

Maida guessed the darker of the two was Karinia.

She said, "I told Thyri that you would be bringing another thrall to your bed. I dreamt the night before last. I saw you on your ship with a woman at your side."

"It was a true dream," Geir answered. Then he pointed to the ram on the platform above the door and thanked them for their concern about him.

The four of them entered the house.

It was gloomy inside, and it took a while for Maida to see everything around her. There were several benches to sit on, a table, a large hearth on the far side of the room, and near it a sleeping place.

"Her name is Maida," Geir said. "She understands and speaks our tongue, though not every word of it. She is a Saxon lady, the daughter of a duke and the—" He was going to say the wife of an ealdorman but since she was his thrall, he decided not to say she was anyone's wife.

"Will you sell her?" Karinia asked.

"Perhaps in time," he answered evasively. "But while she is here, you are to treat her with respect; neither one of you will beat her, for if you do I will use the birch on you."

"Will she sleep on the pallet with us?" Thyri asked.

"Yes."

"Then you will use her as you use us?"

"Yes."

Maida started to object but then changed her mind for fear that any objection she might voice would anger Geir.

"See to getting her proper clothing," he told his women. "And give her a hot bath. She has been at sea a long time and smells like a herring."

The two women laughed and moved toward Maida.

She shrank away from them and with her eyes pleaded to Geir for help.

He said, "When I return, have some meat ready."

Thyri answered that there was meat now if he wanted it.

He waved her offer aside and said, "Later." Then he left the house, leaving Maida alone with his two women.

She shouted after him, but he would not turn back.

"Do not be frightened," Thyri said. "We will not harm you."

"Dear God," Maida cried aloud, "help me!" Her plea was useless. Geir's two thralls were at her, ripping off her clothes and making obscene comments about her naked body.

XV

GEIR VISITED THE families of the men who had not returned. As he had said he would, he gave them a full share of the booty and he spoke highly of the dead men, assuring each family that their husband or son had surely entered the great hall of Valhalla to be with Odin until the day of Ragnarok, when the world would come to an end. He did not invent too much, but he always left the impression with those he visited that the husband or son they had lost had given his life to save the other members of the crew and the ship itself. If there was a young man in the family, he made sure that the boy would always remember that his father had died a hero's death.

By the time Geir finished visiting the families of the dead men, he was filled with the gray mist of sadness. Almost half his men had been lost; men he had known all his life.

He paused for a few moments to look toward the west, where the setting sun put fire in the sky.

Someone said, "The gods take what they must take and give only what they want to in return for what they take."

Geir turned around and found himself looking at the misshapen body of Kar, the soothsayer. For a man bent over with a hump on his back, Kar was surprisingly tall. His voice was deep, almost as if he were speaking out of a deep cavern. He was very old. Some people claimed that he had been vomited out of the earth more than a hundred years ago. His face was seamed with countless lines, but his blue eyes were very bright. He carried a stout ashen staff, the top of which was carved into the head of the world-circling serpent.

"The voyage is not yet done," Kar told him.

"I am home," Geir answered. "My ships are beached."

"The voyage is not yet done," Kar repeated. "It will not be done until you recover your sword Bluetooth."

Geir's hand went to the hilt of the weapon he wore.

"You see," Kar said, "I knew from the very beginning that your voyage was ill-advised. Had you listened to my warning, many men would still be alive. The gods spoke but you chose not to listen. And now they speak again." And pointing to the beach where the ships stood, he repeated, "The voyage is not yet done." The moment he finished speaking, the light went out of the western sky and darkness covered the earth.

Geir shrugged, and saying nothing more to Kar, he went his way. He had never put much faith in Kar's words, or for that matter in the man. His preference, when it came to knowing what the gods might do, was to have Gruden, the old spaewoman, who lived up on the high cliffs, tell him. He decided he would pay a visit to her within the next few days and ask her if his voyage was done or not. But he was disturbed that Kar knew about his loss of Bluetooth. . . .

Geir stopped at Alrek's house. He was a member of Thorkel's crew. He owned Elton and Geir came to speak with him about buying the Saxon.

Alrek was a big, red-bearded man, who was very good at the oars and fought as well as any man. His family was large, with four sons and three daughters, his wife's father and mother as well as his own. He invited Geir to sit at the table with them and at least drink a cup of ale.

After observing all of the courtesies demanded by the

situation, Geir said, "I have come to ask you if you would sell me your Saxon thrall."

Alrek pulled on his beard and considered the request.

"I will give you two gold coins and ten silver ones for him," Geir offered.

"Are you going to let him breed with your Saxon woman?"

Geir shook his head.

"He is a carpenter, I was told," Alrek said.

"I will let you use him without charge," Geir answered.

"I might be able to sell him for more—"

"Three gold coins and five silver ones," Geir said.

Alrek nodded and offered his hand to seal the bargain. "Come, I will give him to you. He is locked up for the night with the animals in back of the house."

Geir placed the gold and silver on the table.

Alrek tested each of the coins with his teeth and nodded with satisfaction that they were pure. Then he called his wife and his oldest son to the table and let them handle the coins. Each of them bit into the round pieces of metal and held them close to the wavering flame of the oil lamp.

"There is Moorish writing on the gold," Geir told them. "And some Frankish markings on the silver."

"I do not think I would have gotten more for the Saxon if I sold him to someone else," Alrek told his wife and son.

They agreed with him.

A short while later, Geir and Elton were walking side by side. "Now," Geir told him, "you will have to prove your words. I paid a high price for you."

Elton explained that the following day he would show him how to make better use of the sail aboard the ship.

"That will be a good start," Geir answered, as he led him through the darkness. Here and there the light of a pine torch sent its wavering yellow light against the sides of the houses and revealed the person carrying it as no more than a dark form.

Geir brought Elton to his house. He found Maida freshly dressed in the garb of a Viking woman. Her black hair was loose around her bare white shoulders. She stood near the hearth and held a large iron poker in her right hand. There was as much fire blazing in her black eyes as there was in the hearth.

"She would not take the gold cross from her neck," Karinia explained.

"Its power is useless here," Geir responded. Then to Maida he said, "Put down that poker. Put it down or I will take it from you and—"

She dropped it into the holder next to the hearth.

Geir said, "Elton belongs to me now. He is not to bed with any of you. Should I find that he has, he and his partner will be killed. He by being made to fly with the blood eagle and the woman by being thrown to the crabs and fishes in the tidal pool. I want no bastards of his in my house—is that understood?"

One by one each of the women told Geir they understood. Then he looked at Elton and received a nod of acknowledgment.

Geir sat down at the table and devoured half of a roast chicken before going off to the feast in Lid's great hall. When he finished eating, the three women and Elton helped themselves to what was left.

Maida ate very little. Her appetite suffered greatly from the dire circumstances in which she found herself. The chance for her return to her rightful husband was so slender as to seem nonexistent. And the thought of being in bed with Geir and his two thralls frightened and embarrassed her.

Geir chided her for not eating and laughingly told her

hat if she continued not to eat, she would soon be skin and bones and fit for no man's bed.

"Better no man's bed," she unhesitatingly told him, "than be brought to sin by the lust of a heathen."

"Better to be brought to sin," Geir shot back, "than to become a hag with no other use than to keep other people's tables clean of dung." He stood up and said he was going to Lid's great hall to enjoy the feast.

"We will be waiting for you," Thyri said.

"Sleep," Geir answered. "I will wake you if my passion should need draining."

"When a man drinks spiced mead," Karinia said, "his passion needs draining."

Joined by Geir, the two women laughed. But Maida did not even crack a smile though her skin colored red with embarrassment. She did not enjoy the coarseness of the conversation and was ashamed that a man from Algar's village saw fit to take part in it. And in their own language told him so.

Elton replied in Norse. He saw nothing wrong with his actions. The Vikings were the sinners, not he. And what they said about spiced ale was perfectly true. As everyone knew, it roused the passion, though it sometimes played tricks on the drinker by filling him with fire but then denying him the wherewithal to satisfy it.

"I will leave you to speak about such things," Geir said and he left to go to Lid's feast.

When he arrived in the great hall of the stronghold, all of the men who had sailed with him were there, and many of those who had remained home came to toast and eat with those who had returned.

The great hall was part of Lid's house. It was as long as several of the longest ships set in a line bow to stern, and as wide as one good ship was long. The high gabled roof was supported by many triangular rafters, and it was covered

121

with lengths of woven wattle over which were laid a thick thatch. It was lighted by many torches.

Lid and Bjorn were seated at the table nearest the hearth. Bjorn was on his father's right side. The chair on Lid's other side was left for Geir. After stopping to speak to many of the men, he finally sat down alongside of his uncle.

Before the platters of roast meat and birds were brought to the table, several toasts were made to the spirits of the men who had been lost. The ale was very good and soon many of the men were singing or reciting passages from the old sagas that recounted the deeds of warriors greater than themselves.

But Lid did not drink much, though he seldom did. He drank enough to satisfy his guests but never so much as to lose his wits.

From time to time, Geir saw his uncle's gray eyes looking at him, measuring him in a way that he had not done before.

Each man from every ship spoke about the adventures that befell them. And all of them praised Geir for his skill in battle and at sea.

And Lid said, "It pleases me that my nephew has so much praise heaped upon him by those who have returned. That praise does honor to me and every man in this stronghold. But would the praise be half so great if the dead could send their voices to us?" His slate-gray eyes went to Geir and with a hint of a smile on his full lips, he recounted his own past glories, adding, "I always managed to return with most of the men who sailed with me."

The unseen barb went straight to its mark, and Geir's face suddenly reddened. But he did not come to his own defense. It was clear that Bjorn had spoken ill of him to his father. But he had not really expected anything more;

Bjorn had been angry from the time he had not been made chief of the raiding party.

"I would have rather had less booty," Lid said, "and more of our men sitting at the table with us tonight."

"Most of them were lost fighting Njal," Geir said.

"Perhaps it would have been better to run—"

"I will not run from Njal's berserks," he told him in a loud voice, "or from any other man.

"When you lost Bluetooth," Lid said, "you should have known that the gods did not want you to fight."

Geir bolted up.

"Sit down, nephew," Lid ordered sharply.

Geir obeyed. At a word from Lid, a dozen spears would be in him.

"There is much to be sorted out about what has happened on your raid," Lid said. "But I will leave that for another time. Now we are here to enjoy ourselves."

"It is hard for a man to enjoy himself when the praises given to him by those who were with him is lessened by one who was not." He spoke softly, but his eyes never left his uncle's face.

A thin smile passed over Lid's lips, and with a nod he said, "Your skill with words is almost as good as my own. But you are there and I am here, and because of the difference between where we sit, my words carry more weight than yours and in the end, whatever it might be, what I say will prevail."

Geir did not answer either with words or by gesture. He drank and ate in silence, though the drink no longer pleased him and the meat lay heavy in his belly. He did not look at his uncle or his cousin for the rest of the night, and when it was time to go, he did not go to them and bid them good night. He left the hall and walked into the cold, overcast night.

Thorkel hailed him and he stopped to wait for his captain. They walked together for a while before Thorkel said, "Your uncle must favor his son."

"But not by ridiculing me," Geir answered.

"It is only because Bjorn wants the Saxon woman." Thorkel said.

"He will not have her."

"Then he will drive a keen blade between you and your uncle."

Geir shrugged.

"Many of the men were angry at Lid for what he said," Thorkel told him, "and would have drawn their swords had you drawn yours."

"It will not come to that," Geir responded. "Lid will not let Bjorn spill blood for a thrall."

"But should it," Thorkel said, "know that there are many who felt the insult as keenly as yourself."

"Are you among them?"

"I would be on your right side if it should come to a fight."

Geir thanked him, and placing his hand on the captain's shoulder, he assured him that in a few days Bjorn would have found some other woman to please him and Lid would find a way to apologize for being rude. "My uncle sometimes lets himself be swayed by his son too easily." Geir said. "But he is a wise and reasonable man."

"Let us hope that he remains that way," Thorkel commented.

The two men shook hands and parted, each going to his own house.

XVI

GEIR WALKED SLOWLY. He was of two minds; one made full of desire by Lid's strong ale and the other full of anger over Lid's strong words.

His uncle had not liked it when the ship's crew had chosen him as their leader instead of Bjorn. But then Lid could not go against the will of the men.

Now Geir knew it was different. His uncle had made that difference all too clear when he had explained the disparity between their positions at the table.

Geir sighed deeply and looked up at the sky for the North Star, which was a fixed light in the sky that he had used to guide himself home from sea many, many times. He could not see it. The clouds covered the sky.

He would have felt better if he had been able to see the star, and with a shake of his head, he quickened his pace. He did not like what had happened in Lid's hall. His uncle had been good to him and Bjorn had always been his friend.

His anger against him did not sit well with him and he almost suspected that Loki, the demi-devil, was playing with them for his own amusement. Loki always did things to make men miserable and anger the gods; that was his way.

When Geir came to the door of his house, the passion in him raged up and drove all else from his thoughts. He flung open the door and entered the main room.

When Maida had heard his footfalls outside, she had

made herself very small at the side of the large bed, while Thyri and Karinia giggled with anticipation. Previously, they had stripped themselves naked and had put sweet-smelling essences all over their bare bodies.

"He is here!" Karinia exclaimed in a whisper the instant the door burst open.

"Pretend you are asleep," Thyri told her.

Maida held her breath. From under the heavy bearskin that covered her, she peeked at Geir.

He stood framed in the open doorway. The night behind him was lighter than his form. He hesitated. He took several deep breaths; then he closed the door.

The darkness of the room and of his form became practically one. He came toward the bed, stopped, and took off his clothing.

Naked he was much more visible. Maida had never seen a man that way before.

His body was almost as white as her own. His arms, shoulders, and legs were corded with muscles. And his organ, though she had fondled it and had felt its heat inside of her, was also something she had never seen. She was somewhat surprised by the difference between its size now and when he had thrust it into her or when she had held it.

Unable to hold her breath any longer, Maida exhaled deeply.

Geir turned his head toward her.

She could feel his eyes stab at her through the blackness of the room. She remained very still. Her heart beat with drumlike loudness.

Geir laughed softly; his senses told him that Maida was looking at him. And for a moment he considered going to her. But then he changed his mind; Karinia and Thyri had to be given the opportunity to satisfy their passion after all the months they had been without him. And they had honored him by sacrificing the ram and spreading its blood

126

over their breasts and thighs. Besides, it was time for his Saxon woman to see what she had probably never seen before and to be touched in a way that she probably never before had been.

Geir sniffed at the air and in a loud voice, he said, "Such fine scented women should not waste their time sleeping." And pulling back the deerskin robes that covered the two women, he uncovered their nakedness.

Both of them bolted up and laughingly pulled him down to them.

"Not too much noise," Geir told them, "or we will wake our Saxon friend."

"I asked her if she would join us," Thyri said, "but she would not."

"She even refused to remove her shift," Karinia commented, "but I told her it was a foolish woman who denies herself pleasure."

"And what did she say?" Geir asked.

"She crossed herself three times and mumbled something about the Devil," Karinia answered.

Then all three of them laughed.

Maida slipped deep under her bearskin cover and put her hands over her ears. She did not want to hear their blasphemous chatter or listen to them laugh at her for following the dictates of Christian virtue, though in truth the passion with which she had met Geir's embraces had nothing of Christian or any other kind of virtue about it.

To isolate herself even more, Maida closed her eyes, making darker the darkness of her shelter under the robe.

Yet in that blackness she saw Geir in all his splendid nakedness and though she prayed for the vision to leave her, it would not.

Geir suddenly remembered about Elton and asked about him.

127

"Asleep in the back of the house," Thyri said, pressing her breasts against him.

Maida took her hands from her ears; she heard nothing. She opened her eyes. There was some movement, but she could not tell which one had moved. She listened intently.

Geir caressed Thyri with his left hand and Karinia with his right. Thyri's breasts were large, almost pear-shaped and her nipples were very light pink.

Karinia's breasts were more like the shape of a crescent moon. Her nipples were larger and darker than those of Thyri.

Geir enjoyed the difference between them immensely.

Thyri stroked his chest while Karinia played her hands over his stomach. Each of them pressed their breasts against him.

He kissed Karinia's breasts, taking time to roll his tongue over her nipples.

She moaned.

Maida heard the low sound.

Then Geir took Thyri's breast into his mouth, and he made her cry out with delight.

Maida broke free of her bearskin shelter.

With Thyri's other breast in his mouth, Geir saw her. She was staring at them. He pretended not to see her. He said nothing to the other women for fear they would look at her and frighten her back underneath the bearskin cover. It gave him a strange kind of pleasure to know she was watching.

For a few moments Maida could not differentiate Geir or any of the women, though she knew he lay between them. But then she realized he was at Thyri's breast the way he had sometimes been at hers. And she saw their hands stroke his body, even to one rubbing the palm of her hand over the head of his organ, while the other used her fingers along its length.

Geir rolled slightly up on his back.

Maida's breath caught in her throat as she watched a hand—she could not tell whose—slip under the sac of his manhood and do to it what she herself had done.

Geir made a deep throaty sound of pleasure and in a low voice, he said, "Move up some so I can play my fingers over your sex."

The women instantly obeyed and splayed their thighs to give him easy access.

Maida's hand flew to her mouth. She squeezed her eyes shut and she shook her head. Geir was doing to them what he had done to her. She could hear each of the women utter whimpers of pleasure. She started to sink down and pull the cover over her but could not resist the Devil's temptation and opened her eyes to look at what was happening.

The women were writhing with ecstasy; he had unerringly found that special place between the lips of their sex that he had also found between hers.

"Ah," Geir commented, "Karinia is already wet with passion. I once had a woman in Miklagard, who would become that way the moment I touched her breasts. But she was very young."

"Geir," Thyri asked, "do you want me to nibble on you?"

"But not drain me?"

"If she does," Karinia said, "I will beat her myself."

"She would have you kiss her bottom before she nibbles on you," Thryi responded.

The women argued with each other for a few moments about which one would do what to Geir before he ordered them silent and said, "I will throw the two of you out of bed and make you sleep on the floor if you do not stop bickering with each other over nonsense. I want to enjoy myself and not have to worry about what each of you wants to do. Thyri, nibble on me, if that suits you; and as

129

for you, Karinia, come and spread yourself over my face so I can do what pleases you. Then, when each of you have had enough, change places.''

Maida watched them with absolute fascination. She had never seen a woman place a man's organ between her lips or a woman offer her sex to a man's mouth. But she remembered having heard about it years before when her monthly blood began to blow. She had come up behind Glenna and Paige; they had been sitting on a bench under the shade of a large oak . . .

Paige said, ''The man asked me to mouth his organ.''

''And did you?'' Glenna asked.

''It is the way of those who serve the Devil,'' Paige answered.

''You mean you never served the Devil that way,'' Glenna chided, ''or let the man serve you and the Devil by mouthing you?''

''When I lay with the duke,'' Paige admitted, ''he would sometimes—''

Glenna laughed and said, ''Often it would be better than being harshly mounted and more harshly ridden.''

Paige laughed and said ''I could swear to that . . .'' Then they heard her and quickly shifted the conversation. But Maida was already worldly-wise enough to know what Glenna had meant when she had said, ''Harshly mounted and more harshly ridden.'' And though she had asked them to tell her what they had been talking about, they refused, though Glenna said, ''You will know when the time comes . . . You will be the second to know.''

''Why the second?'' Maida said.

Glenna and Paige laughed heartily and speculated about whether or not she would be the kind of woman to take matters into her own hand, so to speak.

''More like her own mouth,'' Glenna said.

Maida watched Geir and the two women with intense

130

curiosity. She could tell that from the various sounds each of them made that they were enjoying themselves greatly.

Geir pushed his organ deep into Thyri's mouth or she moved her lips and tongue over it in such a way that made him pause at his effort and utter deep throaty growls of pleasure.

Karinia straddled Geir's face. She rocked back and forth while he applied his mouth to her sex with great avidity. Now and then the woman reached down and spread the lips of her womanhood, moving in whatever way gave her more pleasure.

Several times Maida wanted to pull the cover over her head and hide from the iniquitious sight. She knew she was committing a mortal sin by watching. But she was too weak-willed to move her eyes away from what she saw; or even to close her eyes. Indeed, as Geir had told her, God was absent from the land of the Vikings; he surely did not see what was happening. Here in this place the one God was powerless against the many gods. Powerless as she herself was powerless to stop looking at abominations being committed by Geir and his two thralls.

Even as she watched them, their bodies began to move. The women changed places. Thyri now had Geir's mouth against her sex, and Karinia was lovingly swirling her tongue at the root of Geir's organ.

Maida suddenly realized that her own nipples were hard and there was much fluid oozing from her sex. She touched her nipples. Tendrils of warmth went from them to the depths of her body.

She shook her head. She wanted to free herself of the magic that Geir and the two women had woven over her but she could not. She could not take her eyes off the sinuous movements of the three bodies, nor could she stop her hands from moving over her own. She had not touched herself since she had been a girl and had been scolded by

Paige and then by Father Quinell for having played with her sex. But now what else could she do to bring some measure of relief?

Geir had somehow managed to change their positions. He was now astride Thyri and Karinia was lying off to one side with her hand slowly moving over the sac of his manhood.

Thyri was thrashing from side to side and making small cries of delight. Suddenly her legs clamped around Geir's back and she swore by the god Thor that the world was whirling under her. She heaved herself up against him, and then her body was shaken like a leaf in a strong wind, before she fell away from him with a contented sigh.

Geir laughed, and leaving Thyri, he went to Karinia.

She greeted him with open arms and immediately began to undulate under him. Thyri extended her hand and played with Karinia's bottom.

Geir's movements with Karinia were more vigorous than they had been with Thyri, and very quickly Maida found herself caught up in them. She could not stop fondling her own body. Suddenly Maida gave way to the impulse to lie down and spread her thighs. The ministrations brought the tension to life in her; she culled it to its full expanse until her body felt as if it were ready to snap in two. She was oblivious to the sounds she heard coming from Geir and Karinia; all she could hear was the roaring in her ears.

All at once she felt a weight, Geir on her body; she could not fight against him. She let him possess her. . . . Her body was lifted up and then flung down; lifted up again and flung down, and for a third time it was lifted up and flung down . .

When Maida opened her eyes, she found herself looking up at him. He was bending over her.

"Sleep," he said. "Sleep!"

She wanted to ask him if he took her as he had taken the other two women. But when she started to speak, he put his finger across her lips. She nodded, sighed contentedly, and closed her eyes. Sleep came very quickly.

When the first cock crowed, Maida opened her eyes. Geir was sleeping next to her, his hand on her breast. She turned toward him. He looked very peaceful. She glanced at the other women; they were asleep together on the far side of the bed.

XVII

By AFTERNOON A pallid sun shone through a covering of milk-white clouds. A strong cold wind blew from the north, and the sea continued to smash against the rocky coast.

Maida stood by the shore and looked toward the west. She did not want to think about either what she had witnessed or what happened to her the previous night. She had no doubt that some time during the final frenzy of her own lust Geir had taken possession of her. But she did not want to remember either her ecstasy or the Devil's play she had seen, for fear that even in memory it would stir her once more into that state of lustful excitement.

That morning Geir had told her she had complete freedom of the stronghold; she could go wherever she wanted to without fear, though he had cautioned her about wandering too far beyond the walls. She had accepted his words with a silent nod.

But now as Maida stood and looked out on the open sea, she realized that regardless of her freedom to move as she pleased about the stronghold, she was still a prisoner. She was still Geir's thrall. She held no more of a place in the society of the stronghold than did either Thyri or Karinia.

Again her thoughts went back to the previous night. It was clear to her from what had happened that he could and would use her to satisfy his lust whenever it pleased him. She no longer possessed her own body; it belonged to

Geir. All she owned was her soul, and that she feared would soon become the Devil's!

Her throat tightened and tears blurred her vision. "My true home," she said in a choked voice, "is somewhere out there!"

Several gulls flew low over the water and cried out to one another, wheeled, and flew off to the west.

Maida watched them until they vanished where the sky and the sea came together. Had she been able to take wing, she would have flown with them across the sea to where she would be truly free!

She wiped her eyes. Tears were useless. She would find strength in prayer and hope that God would see her and deliver her from the heathens. She was certain that there must be a way for her to return home and that with God's help she would discover it.

Fortified by her resolve, Maida walked through the tall reeds until she came to where the ships were beached. There she saw Geir and Elton; they were standing near the *Sea Bird* and were so deeply engaged in conversation that neither of them saw her.

Elton was gesturing toward the ship. He no longer looked like a Saxon. Except for the sword, he was dressed like a Viking. That he would so readily become what he had not been born completely mystified Maida. She had no respect for a person who was so eager to serve the enemy of his own people. And from what little she had heard him say about Algar, she knew he bore no love for her husband.

Maida called to Geir.

He turned to her and said, "Elton has just been telling me how to rig the sail so that I can alter it when the wind shifts."

She responded venomously, "Elton must love his new master better than he did his old."

135

Geir looked at Elton.

"Algar," Elton said, meeting Geir's ice-blue eyes without flinching, "was not loved by many of those who tilled the fields or did other work in the village."

"Men like Harold loved him," Maida snapped back.

"Men like Harold lived off our sweat," he answered. "They did nothing but beat and rob us to meet Algar's demands and take something for themselves."

"Liar," she screamed, striking out at him. "Son of a whore!"

Open-palmed, her hand slammed across his face.

Elton's head went to one side and blood sprung from the corner of his mouth.

"I speak the truth," he said slowly. "By the holy blood of Christ our Savior, I speak the truth."

"Lying dog!" she shouted and would have struck him again, but Geir caught hold of her hand. "Beat him!" she yelled at Geir. "Let me beat him until he begs for mercy!"

Forcing her hand down, Geir said, "I have known Algar; he had me on the end of a rope and treated me like a dog. I have nothing but hate in my heart for him."

"He is my lawful husband," Maida responded angrily.

Geir shrugged.

"He did not take me by rape!" she exclaimed fiercely.

Geir ignored her, and facing Elton, told him to do what was necessary to rerig the sail. Then taking hold of Maida by the arm, he said, "We will go now and attend to other matters."

She pulled away from him and said, "You take me by night, but during the day, you let other men insult me."

"Elton spoke against Algar," Geir told her. "He said nothing against you."

"Algar is my husband!" she cried.

"No," Geir said quietly. "You are my thrall."

She stopped and shook her head. She tried to speak but her lips trembled. Every time he reminded her that she belonged to him, she was overwhelmed by a huge wave of desolation that took her breath away and robbed her of speech.

Geir said after a while, "We are going to Jon to find out if he would be willing to sell Glenna."

Maida's eyes opened wide. She had hardly dared hope Geir would honor his word after the trouble she had caused between him and Bjorn by going to Glenna without him having spoken to Jon first.

"Do you think he will sell her?" she asked.

"I do not know."

"I would even be willing to give him one of my silver bracelets," she said.

"Make no mention of it," Geir told her. "The price—if there is one—will be arrived at between Jon and myself. He is a good man and will deal fairly with me."

Jon's house was not far from Lid's great hall, and when they arrived there, Jon was outside mending a leather harness. He and Geir greeted each other warmly, and Geir said, pointing to Maida, "Your thrall Glenna was her serving woman."

Jon nodded, set his work aside, and said, "I will need a new harness by spring."

"Perhaps some trader will come before winter does," Geir offered.

Jon said he thought that was possible; then he stood up.

Maida looked questioningly at Geir. Her heart beat very rapidly. Geir suddenly sensed something was wrong; his right hand went to the hilt of his sword. Jon's eyes went wide and he gave a slight shake of his head.

Geir removed his hand from the sword. For a moment, he considered leaving, but he was too aware something was amiss to do that. Ordinarily, Jon would have invited him into his house and give him ale and now he just stood there apparently waiting for something to happen.

Maida was unable to contain herself any longer. "Might I speak with Glenna for just a moment?" she asked.

"The truth is," Geir said, annoyed that Maida had spoken out of turn, "I have come to make you an offer for your thrall, if you are willing to sell her."

Jon scratched his beard and he answered, "I have already had one offer."

"Dear God, no!" Maida exclaimed. She said nothing more when she saw Geir's scowl. "What is the offer?" he asked in a low voice.

The door to Jon's house opened and Bjorn stepped out. "Three gold coins and twelve silver ones," he said.

Geir knew how useless it would be to bid against Bjorn. Only Jon would benefit from that kind of foolishness.

"Oh, please let me see her," Maida implored.

"It would be a kindness to me," Geir said, looking at Jon.

The man nodded and called to Glenna.

She came out of the house, took one look at Maida, and ran weeping into her arms.

The three Vikings were made uncomfortable by the women's open display of tenderness and private feelings and moved away from them.

Maida spoke rapidly, in her native tongue. She told Glenna that Geir had come to buy her but Bjorn had previously made a substantial offer for her.

"What will happen now?" asked Glenna, trying to control her tears.

"I do not know," Maida replied, and directing Glenna's attention to the three men, she whispered, "There are bad feelings between Geir and Bjorn."

The men shifted uneasily. They waited until the women had finished embracing each other before they continued to speak.

Geir said, "Suppose I match Bjorn's offer. Would you consider selling her to me?"

Before he answered, Jon scratched his beard once more, "I would consider it," he said, "but only because of their former life together. I am not against giving happiness to thralls. . . . I am thankful that the gods put them in thralldom instead of me."

"In that case, I make the same offer," Geir said. "I will give you three gold coins and twelve silver ones for Glenna."

Bjorn became livid.

Jon separated himself from Geir and Bjorn. "I would have sold her for less," he said.

"My offer is firm," Bjorn said.

"And so is mine," Geir said.

"She is not worth more than two gold coins and half the number of silver ones you offer. I have lain with her several times. She gives good sport and enjoys all that a man can do to her, but she is not good for hard work . . . . My wife complains she is lazy."

"All the more reason to sell her," Geir said.

"I will give you one more gold coin," Bjorn offered.

Jon shook his head.

"Let it be," Geir said.

"Will you offer more gold, too?"

"No," Geir replied. "But I will give you Thyri."

Maida uttered a cry of surprise. She did not understand how Geir could have lain with the woman the previous night and the very next afternoon barter her away as if she were no more than a cow or a horse. Very quickly she said to him in her own language, "But she lay with you last night; she even put the blood of a sacrified ram on her

139

breasts and between her thighs for your safe return. She will die—"

"I am doing what must be done," he answered harshly, "so that you might have your serving woman with you."

Maida looked at Glenna and said, "I did not want to be the cause of another woman's sorrow; God in heaven knows all of us have our own sorrows to bear."

"Maida," Glenna said quietly, "do not interfere or we will lose each other forever."

"God forbid!" Maida exclaimed, suddenly clutching Glenna to her.

"Do you love Saxons so much," Bjorn questioned, glaring angrily at his cousin, "that you would own all of them and breed a line of bastards from them?"

Geir winced, but he answered calmly, "I came here to buy Jon's thrall; I did not come to speak with you about my love for Saxons or any other people. To your offer you added another gold coin; to mine I added Thyri. Jon must choose between them."

"Jon cannot sell her to you," Bjorn shouted, his face turning red with anger. "I made him a fair offer and I made it before you came."

Jon threw up his hands and he said, "Now, wait a minute, Bjorn. Do not tell me what I cannot do. The thrall is mine and I will do what I want with her."

"He has one Saxon woman," Bjorn responded in a fury. "What does he want another for?"

"I did not ask him," Jon said, "I do not have to know that."

"Another gold coin," Bjorn raged. "And another one after that?" He took the money from his pouch and dropped it on the table. Even in the waning sunlight, the gold and silver gleamed brightly.

Jon looked down at the coins and then at Geir.

"That is more than I will offer," Geir said.

"Then she is mine!" Bjorn laughed. "The Saxon bitch is mine." And he started toward her.

"I think not," Jon said.

Bjorn stopped and whirled around. His red face was taut and there was a strange look in his eyes.

Terrified, the women shrank away.

"I respect a man who gives gold and silver," Jon said. "But I respect a man even more when he does not try to tell me what I can or cannot do."

Bjorn's hand went to his sword.

Geir was ready with his. "I am willing to die," he said quietly, "if it comes to that." He had drawn his weapon so swiftly that none of those present realized it was out of its scabbard until they saw the glint of the naked blade in the pale light of the late afternoon.

Bjorn hesitated for several moments. Then he gathered up the coins and put them back in his pouch. As he walked slowly away, he said nothing.

Geir took a deep breath and put up his sword. He gave the gold and silver to Jon and said he would send Thyri to join him by nightfall.

The two men shook hands and Jon asked Geir if he noticed the wildness in Bjorn's eyes.

"Yes, I did," Geir said.

"He is working himself into a killing time," Jon told him.

Geir shrugged and said, "I hope it does not come to that. It would not sit well with me if I had to be the one to stop him."

Jon nodded understandingly.

XVIII

EACH DAY THE sun's path across the sky shortened. The nights were very long and so very cold that the wolves howled on the cliffs. When the sky was clear of clouds, white, blue, and green lights flickered across the northern rim of the world.

The people in the stronghold said the lights foretold a long, hard winter. Maida would not believe such heathen talk. Only God knew the future; men and women could only know the past and present.

Glenna was less positive about the matter. She would not entirely discount what the Vikings were saying. "After all," she pointed out, "these people know many more things than we do about the sea and lands that we have never heard of."

Maida would concede nothing, though in the few days since her arrival, she could not help but notice that the Viking craftsmen worked metal, wood and stone far better than the Saxons did. The women wove well and lacked nothing in the way of metal pots and pans for cooking.

Most of Maida's time was spent with Glenna and Karinia. Between the three of them they maintained Geir's house and cooked for him and Elton.

On some days Maida and Glenna walked around the stronghold. Sometimes they came across Thyri, but she always ran back into Jon's house whenever they approached her.

At night Geir would more often than not satisfy his

passion with Karinia. He would seldom go to Maida, and when he did, she would not willingly embrace him. It was only when he worked his devil craft on her that she would finally surrender herself to his lascivious embraces. After she met his passion with her own, she hated him for having such absolute power over her; yet she realized that he did not use it as often as some other man might have.

One day Einar came to see Maida and they sat at the table talking and drinking ale. He told her sooner or later Geir and Bjorn must come to some sort of a settlement. "Every man here knows that," he said.

Maida had difficulty finding her voice but when she finally did, she told him that Bjorn seemed to be intent on picking a fight with Geir.

"Only to win you from him," Einar answered.

After the young Viking had left, Maida sat by the fire a long time and tried to think of a way to turn the enmity between Geir and Bjorn to her advantage.

If the two men fought and killed each other, Maida's position would not be any better, perhaps it would even be worse. She might be sold to some trader or given to another Viking in the stronghold. None of these prospects was worth the risk of encouraging a fight between the two men. Geir at least protected her from those who might do her harm. If nothing else did, that alone made her realize it was best to leave the matter alone.

But Lid could not let the situation alone; it was drifting dangerously close to open combat between the two men, and he was not in the least bit sure which of the two the gods would favor.

From the beginning of the expedition, Lid knew that Bjorn had resented having to take second place to his cousin. And he had also discovered from Thorkel and some of the other men that had Bjorn come to Geir's aid on the beach, where Algar had attacked, they would have

143

been able to capture or kill Algar and many of his vessels that very afternoon.

Lid took counsel with Kar the soothsayer many times. And from Kar he had learned that Geir's voyage—indeed the voyage of most of the men who had been on the raid—was not yet done.

But when Lid pressed Kar to learn more from the fates, Kar tried and he failed.

"There are things," Kar said, as they sat together near the hearth in Lid's great hall, "that are beyond a man's knowing."

Lid fretted. In a low voice, he said, "I must try to protect my son."

Kar nodded and suggested that he might visit Gruden, the spaewoman. "Often," Kar explained, "what is hidden from a man is easily seen by a woman."

Lid frowned with displeasure. Gruden had once been his thrall; he had taken her in a raid and forced his will upon her. When he had finally brought her to the stronghold, the gods had robbed her wits and had given her the falling sickness. One day she had run away from the stronghold and had taken to living in a small hut.

"Even the Wendols fear her," Lid commented.

Kar said, "I have heard tell that when they have more meat than they need, they leave some on the roof of her hut. I have never seen them do it, and it is hard to believe that they would not eat her. But she is there. Just this morning I saw the plumes of wind-blown smoke from her hearth."

Lid uttered a snort of disdain and said, "No hearth is there. Only a fire pit, nothing more."

Kar made an open gesture with his hands. "I have done all I could," he said. "The gods may have shown her more."

Lid stood up and paced halfway down the length where Kar was seated and said, "I will go. Will you go with me?"

"As far as a dozen paces from her door," Kar replied. "Then whatever she tells you is for you alone to hear."

Lid agreed and said they would go the following morning just as the sun came up.

"It would be better just as the sun goes down today," Kar told him.

"If that is the way it must be," Lid said resignedly, "then that is the way it will be. I know the cliffs well enough to find our way back. We will go armed—"

"*Without* swords or battle-axes," Kar interrupted. "A torch to light our way and signal our coming."

"Signal our coming?" Lid questioned, resting the weight of his body against the table.

"She will want to be sure it is us," Kar told him.

"But who else would go to her?"

"Geir has already gone," Kar said. "She knows you will come but not when. The torchlight will tell her that."

"You never told me that Geir went to her."

"I have answered all that you have asked," Kar said. "You never asked whether Geir went to her or not."

Lid made no reply. He was angry with himself for not having put the question to Kar. But it was impossible for any man to know all the questions he must ask if he is to know something about the future. Questions about the past were easy to come by; all the events were there to look at. Even questions about the present were not too difficult because what was real a man saw. But the future was too immense—or too small—for a man to even know where to begin and end. . . .

"Do you know what Gruden told Geir?" Lid questioned.

Kar shook his head. "But if you ask her, she will tell you," he said.

"I will take two dogs with me," Lid told him.

"That will offend no one," Kar responded.

145

Lid grimaced but he did not speak again. After a while, Kar took his leave and Lid stood by the hearth staring into the flames. He did not want to see either Bjorn or Geir enter Valhalla, but if it had to be one of them, he prayed that Odin would take Geir.

Thorkel and several of the other men were with Geir that afternoon as they tried the *Sea Bird* with Elton's new rigging. The ship could sail closer to the wind than ever before, and by chaining the lengths of the lines that ran from the sail spar to the sides of the ship, the wind could be used to more advantage than ever before. It was a good afternoon's sail, when the sea was raging and the wind blew at various times from practically each of the four corners of the earth.

When *Sea Bird* was safely beached again, Thorkel, in his slow, easy manner, made mention of his conversation with Lid. "I would not speak of it," Thorkel said, "but Lid seems uneasy with the truth. He did not press me for details when I told him that Bjorn did not come to your aid when you summoned him. I think he already knew most of what I said. But nonetheless I told him that Bjorn's actions sent men—good men—to Valhalla, and some of them while their hands were tied behind them."

Geir nodded.

"If I were you," Thorkel cautioned, "I would avoid Bjorn or give him the Saxon woman."

"I can do neither," Geir responded. Then he added, "Bjorn has a strange look in his eyes."

"Yes, I have seen it there these past few days," Thorkel said.

"I cannot give him Maida," Geir told him. "Besides, if I did give her to him, of what use would I be to the men? They must know I will hold what is mine or they will never again trust me to defend what is theirs."

146

"That is true," Thorkel admitted. "If you broke faith with yourself, they would never believe that you would keep it with them."

The two men did not speak again until it became time for them to separate and go to their own dwellings. Then Thorkel repeated what he had said to Geir the night of the feast in Lid's great hall. But this time he added, "There are many swords that would join mine to defend your right to keep the Saxon woman."

"Lid will never let it reach that point," Geir said. "He would not want his own men fighting against his own men. Nothing but sorrow can be gained from such a contest."

Thorkel agreed and went to his house.

When the sun turned the western sky yellow and red, Kar came for Lid. They walked with two large hunting dogs that were held in check by strong ropes, against which they strained. Kar carried a torch and the fire implements for lighting it.

The dogs pulled on them once they were in the open field beyond the wall and in front of the base of the cliffs. Neither of the men spoke. The wind slammed hard against them and their breaths steamed in the cold air. Overhead the gray clouds sealed off the coming of the night sky with all its bright stars.

Kar moved slightly ahead of Lid and found the very steep rocky patch that led to the top of the cliffs. To keep from being blown off the ledges, each of them was forced to push his body close against the rocky wall.

Lid was sorry he had brought the dogs with them. They were difficult to control, and more than once each animal seemed determined to pull its master and itself off the rocky escarpment.

Breathless and weary from the perilous climb up to the top of the cliff, Lid and Kar paused to rest. The light in the west had long since faded, and everything was in darkness. Kar struck the flint against the metal. Sparks flew. He struck it again and suddenly the torch burst into flame. He lifted it above his head and they made their way over a narrow twisting path to the spaewoman's hut.

They came upon it after a few minutes. It was not much of a dwelling place, made of a wattle covering bent around a triangle of three stout boughs. Smoke was coming from a small opening in the roof. But it did not have the savoriness of meat about it.

Kar silently gestured Lid forward. He said he would hold the dogs and the torch.

Lid gave him the rope to his hound and slowly made his way to the hut. He could see the light of the fire through the opening in the wattles. It was truly a miracle that she could survive the wind and snow of winter in such a fragile dwelling place. There was a heavy sailcloth covering in front of the opening. He reached out at it and he was about to draw it aside when Gruden cackled and bid him enter.

Lid did not move. He would have not been half so much afraid to face a berserk in mortal combat than he was to face this spaewoman, with whom once he had taken pleasure. He gathered his courage, and pulling back the curtain, he stepped inside the hut.

The spaewoman was not the Gruden he remembered. She was old; her skin was dirty and her blue eyes wild with an inner light far brighter than the fire in front of her. She looked up at him and gave a toothless smile. With her hand she bid him sit down by the fire opposite her. Then she said, "You already know the voyage for those who went with Geir is not yet ended."

148

"Yes," he answered with a cough. Whatever was in the fire was making his eyes burn and his throat ache.

The wavering light of the fire played tricks; all at the same time he seemed to see her and not to.

"Your son will also continue the voyage," she told him. "But not with Geir and the others."

"Where will my son voyage to?" Lid questioned wiping the tears from his eyes with the back of his hand.

"To an old, old land."

"And where will Geir voyage to?"

"To those places he has never been and to where he has already been before he finally returns."

"Will my son return?" Lid asked, trying to hold her in his eyes.

"I can say no more," Gruden cackled. "All I had to say, I have already said."

"To come such a long hard way for so little," Lid told her, "is less than satisfying. I came to find—"

"How to protect your son," she said, "And I can only tell you what I can, no more and no less."

"And what did you tell Geir?" he questioned angrily.

"What Kar had already told him."

"And no more?"

"No more, no more, no more," the spaewoman repeated over and over again with a cackling laugh that made Lid's blood run cold and caused prickles of fear to rise on his back. He stood up and looking down at her, he said, "The gods have told you nothing, old woman —nothing."

"They have told you everything," she answered with a high-pitched laugh. "They have told you everything, but you will not see it or understand it until it happens."

Lid hurried out of the hut. Once again in the presence of Kar, he felt more at ease. Together the two men made the treacherous journey down from the top of the cliffs. Now and then a wolf bounded over the rocks, but the dogs and the torch kept the beasts at bay.

"She said nothing," Lid grumbled to the soothsayer when they reached the safety of the stronghold. "She told me absolutely nothing."

Kar did not answer.

XIX

A COLD THIN rain was falling. Maida and Glenna sat at the table with Karinia, who was telling them about the long night that was rapidly approaching. According to her, the sun rose above the earth but was quickly chased over its rim by a black dragon.

Maida did not like Karinia because she always gave herself so willingly to Geir and then boasted about it. There were also times when she aroused Geir when he had no need for a woman.

"And what happens to the dragon when summer comes?" Glenna asked.

Karinia shrugged and said, "He spends more time in his cave under the earth."

"What do you think about this?" Glenna asked, looking at her former mistress.

"To be sure, there are dragons," Maida answered, "but Father Quinell has said that God's angels armed with swords keep them from ever venturing out of their lairs."

Karinia was about to take issue with the priest's explanation when suddenly she was distracted by the sound of arguing outside of the house. "Geir," she said, "and . . . and Bjorn."

The three women ran to the door. Maida flung it open.

Geir and Bjorn were standing no more than a pace from each other. Several other men were close by.

"You must hear me out, cousin," Bjorn said.

"I must . . . I must!" Geir responded harshly. "Who

151

says that I must do anything? I am no man's thrall. Like yourself, I am a free man.''

"I came to you in peace," Bjorn said brittlely.

"You came to bargain for what I will not sell," Geir told him.

Maida sucked in her breath and slowly she let go of it. She could not control the wild beating of her heart. In her native tongue, she said to Glenna, "He has come to buy me."

"Oh, dear God, no!"

Maida nodded.

Geir looked toward the doorway. He motioned the women back into the house, but they did not move.

Bjorn cast his eyes toward the doorway. With a sudden running movement, he placed himself between the women and Geir. Then pointing directly to Maida, he said, "I will give you my share of all the booty for that Saxon woman."

Geir's eyes became gimlets. In a low, flat-toned voice, he said, "Do not stand between me and what is mine."

"She is not yours!" Bjorn replied with controlled fury. "When I came into Algar's great hall, she was—"

"I would not have been in Algar's great hall," Geir told him, "if you had fought at my side."

Bjorn's face turned very red. "You needed to be taught a lesson," he answered. And gesturing toward Maida, he said, "You were Algar's prisoner, held by him on the end of a rope like a dog. I freed you and won the woman—Algar's woman. She is mine by the right of my sword."

"Then you will have to use it to gain her," Geir answered, drawing his weapon.

Bjorn's sword came out of its scabbard.

The men gathered silently around the two combatants. Maida saw Thorkel. She called to him to go to Lid before blood was shed.

152

Thorkel hesitated but then he ran toward Lid's great hall.

Geir and Bjorn circled one another. Now one struck at the other and now the other. Each slashing stroke was fended off. Metal clanged against metal.

Everyone in the stronghold gathered to witness the fight.

Bjorn was forced away from Geir's house. Despite the cold rain, each man was sweating profusely.

Bjorn's thrusts were numerous; each was deadly.

But Geir blunted them.

The people began to murmur; it was obvious to them that Bjorn's movements were becoming wilder and wilder. He was soon slashing more frequently at the air in front of Geir or at his sides than he was at him.

Then suddenly the edge of Geir's blade rode against his opponent's hand. Bjorn's fingers opened; he dropped his sword.

In an instant, Geir had Bjorn's neck on the point of his blade. "Move one way or the other, cousin," he said, "and blood will flow."

Bjorn's face was very white. His breath came in short, ragged gasps.

"Kill him!" cried several of the men. "Kill him!"

Many began to call for Bjorn's blood.

Then Lid came. Breathing hard, he pushed his way through the circle of men. When he saw where Geir's blade was, he stopped short, his eyes wide with terror.

The men who shouted for Bjorn's blood fell silent. Only the soft rustle of the rain could be heard.

Lid moved slowly around to where Geir would be able to see him. In a steady voice, he asked, "Would you kill him, Geir?"

Geir's eyes flicked to where his uncle was standing.

"Once you were the best of friends, and now you have drawn your swords against one another."

"For all that you have given me, uncle," Geir said, "I give you his life." And he lowered his sword.

A sigh of relief could be heard from the people who had gathered.

"As I love you, uncle, I must tell you Bjorn has much to answer for; but I leave him to give you those answers. I want only to live in peace."

"The woman!" Bjorn shouted. "The Saxon woman should be mine!"

"Enough," Lid roared. "I have had enough for one day, for a week, a month, a year. I have had enough for the rest of my life!"

"I offered to buy her and—"

"I will hear no more, Bjorn!" Lid raged. "Pick up your sword and return home." Quickly he called the names of six men and told them to see his son returned to his hall. Then Lid dispersed the people, telling them that the dispute would be settled between him and Geir.

"There is no argument between us, uncle," Geir said, when all the people had gone.

"When you lift your sword against my son," Lid answered, "you also lift it against me."

Geir said nothing.

"We will go into your house and reach some conclusion about this matter," Lid told him. "I speak now not as your uncle but as your chieftain."

Geir sheathed his weapon. He started for the door where the women were waiting for him. Fear marked all of their faces, even Maida's. He motioned them back and he courteously allowed Lid to enter first. He followed and closed the door after him.

"Bring something hot," Geir called out.

The two men sat down at the table and looked at one
154

another across the small yellow flame of an oil lamp.

Karinia brought a stone crock of mead to the table, heated an iron poker until it glowed with the red of a fire sunset, and then plunged the hot poker into the mead. It hissed like a serpent and steamed like a caldron.

Maida and Glenna sat down on the far side of the room.

"Bread?" Geir asked.

Lid nodded. "It would be unfriendly of me to come into your house and refuse your bread but drink your mead."

Geir ordered Karinia to bring the bread. He broke the piece she gave him in half and gave one piece to his uncle and kept the other for himself.

"To your safe return," Lid toasted, lifting his cup of mead.

Geir accepted the toast humbly. The two men drank, took time to eat some of the bread, and drank again before Geir said, "It would have made me very sad if I had killed Bjorn."

"I know that," Lid responded.

Geir gestured to Maida and said, "He wants her."

"I know that, too." Lid told him.

Geir drank more mead. Then he said, "Had he wanted any other woman, I would have given her to him. But that one is mine."

Suddenly Maida rushed to the table and cried, "I am not his! I am lawfully wed to Algar. Geir took me the night of my wedding."

Geir was up on his feet. Before she realized what was happening, he struck her so hard across the face that she dropped to the floor.

"Let the woman speak, Geir," Lid said, reaching down to help Maida regain her feet.

There were tears in her eyes and an ache in her throat, but she did not give way to weeping. She took several moments to compose herself and then she told Lid who her

155

father was and the circumstances of her capture by Geir.

Lid rolled his eyes up to Geir, who was still standing. "She might bring a large ransom from her father and from her husband," he suggested.

"Oh, yes," Maida cried, suddenly realizing that she had found the way to be returned to her husband. "They would pay for my return; they would give gold and silver—a great deal of gold and silver." And she went down on her knees before Lid.

Filled with disgust that she should be on her knees, Geir turned away and angrily ground his teeth together. He had thought her to be above begging for anything, even her freedom.

Lid rubbed his beard. He had not expected the woman to enter into his conversation with Geir. But he silently thanked the gods she had. "Geir," he said, "she is worth more in gold and silver than the pleasure she gives you in bed."

Geir faced Lid and told him, "I take no more than she is willing to give and she gives no more than I am willing to take."

"Then you will be glad to have gold and silver to buy a woman who will give you more than you can take. There are such women . . . in my life I have known several." Then, pointing to Karinia, Lid said, "I wager you have no trouble with her. She is willing to give more than you can take. But with this one, gold and silver will give you more pleasure than she ever will."

"I will not give her up," Geir said.

Lid shook his head.

"She is mine," Geir said.

"I will send word to her husband and to her father."

"Do as you wish, uncle," Geir told him in a hard voice, "but I will kill any man who tries to take her from me." His hand went to the hilt of his sword.

"She will return with me to my house," Lid said.

"You are wrong," Geir responded, drawing his sword halfway out of its scabbard.

Lid was furious, but he knew it would be foolish of him to attempt to fight his nephew. He took a deep breath and waited for his anger to subside before he said, "I will see if the woman's husband and the father will pay gold and silver for her; if they will, I will then decide what to do."

Geir did not answer.

"I will not take her from you now," Lid said. He stood up, threw the bread to the floor, and poured the mead over it to indicate according to the custom that he was leaving the house in anger.

Geir was in a rage, and grabbing hold of Maida, he beat her until she cried for mercy; then he beat Glenna and Karinia. But his fury was in no way assuaged. He rushed out of the house and ran down to where the sea smashed itself against the rocks. There the combination of wind and spray finally cooled him.

By nightfall he returned to the house. Karinia and Glenna were up and around but when he entered, they cowered against the wall.

"Maida?" he asked.

"There," Glenna said, pointing to the big bed. "Under the bearskin cover."

"Get out!" he told the two women.

"But where—" Karinia started to object.

"Out!" he roared.

They opened the door and went into the night.

Geir moved to the bed and when he reached it, he pulled back the bearskin cover.

Maida looked up at him. Terrified, she made herself into a small ball.

Slowly he lifted her face. There was dried blood at the

157

corners of her mouth and bruises on her cheeks and head. He lifted her in his arms and held her very close to him.

"I will always hate you," she wept. "Always . . . always!"

Geir moved his hands over her body.

Several times Maida winced and cried aloud. But he was working his devil magic on her, and soon she was breathing very fast.

Geir stripped her naked and wherever he bruised her, he put his lips. Finally, when his organ was deep in her, he told her he loved her and asked her to marry him.

"Dear God," Maida cried, thrashing under him, "dear God, I am already married. I am already married!"

"You are mine, Maida," Geir growled. "You are mine!"

The gush of his fluid was ecstasy to Maida, and she sank her teeth into his bare shoulder and raked his back with her nails.

"Oh, Geir," she wept, holding him tight to her bare breasts. "Oh, Geir, if I could, I would love you—I really would!"

XX

"SUCH A MAN is worthy of any woman's bed," Glenna commented, referring to Geir late the following morning, when she and Maida went walking in the field beyond the wall of the stronghold.

Maida uttered a deep sigh but did not speak.

"He is a man—"

"I will be ransomed," Maida told her suddenly, stopping. "I will be returned to my rightful husband and take my place at his side." Her tone was sharp and her black eyes blazed with anger. "I will not remain Geir's thrall!" She began to walk again, only this time her pace was quicker.

Glenna went after her and said, "He loves you, Maida. That much should be clear to you."

"He loves—he loves what he takes by force or by conjuring the Devil's lust in me."

"He conjures no more than any man conjures in the body of a woman," Glenna said softly.

"Lust!" Maida exclaimed with disgust. "Perhaps you have forgotten what Father Quinell said about lust, but I have not."

"The good father," Glenna responded, "was often too much taken with what the Devil was about than what men and women were about. It is hard for me to believe God would have given us the means to enjoy pleasure and then consigned all those who used those means to His archenemy."

"I do not give a tinker's pot for what you believe," Maida cried. "I was taken against my will, I was brought here against my will, and now if I can use my will to regain my proper place, I must, or I am neither a Christian nor Algar's wife."

After a short pause, Glenna said, "I think you are a Christian and you are Algar's lawful wife."

"There—then you see why I must bend every effort to see that Lid sends word to my husband and to my father."

"Notwithstanding either your belief in Christ or your marriage to Algar, I also think it is possible for you to love Geir."

"Never," Maida raged, stopping again. "Never!"

They did not speak again until they returned home.

Glenna was wise enough not to mention she had heard her mistress say to Geir that she would love him if she could. And experience had shown her many times that *never* existed only when death put an end to a person's life, otherwise *never* was just an expression which came either from the heart, or from the blood but not from the head.

As for Maida, she was too upset with Glenna to speak. The woman, having been in servitude so long, first to Maida's father and now to Geir, could not begin to understand how a woman who had been free all her life could feel about not only having been forced into thralldom but also into whoredom, for that was her state no matter how she looked at it. To call it anything else would be self-deception beyond her capability.

When they reached Geir's house, they found it empty except for Elton, who was at the hearth heating what was left of the previous day's fish soup for himself.

Maida was never pleased when he was nearby. She felt he was a traitor to her husband and did not even merit her notice. She pretended not to be aware of him, though he and Glenna spoke easily with one another.

"There is an uneasiness in the stronghold," Elton commented, blowing on the bowl of soup to cool it, once he set it down on the table. "The people are taking sides between Geir and Bjorn."

"And no doubt you would side with whoever offered you more," Maida said, breaking her silence in order to indicate how little she thought of him.

Elton cocked his head to one side and asked her whom she would follow.

The rapid turn about of the question took her aback.

"It was you who pleaded to be ransomed," Elton said, using a well-carved spoon to lift the soup to his mouth.

"Did Geir tell you that?" she asked in exasperation.

He pointed to the wall behind which he slept and told her that it was impossible for him not to have heard her entreaties to Lid.

"A man with true honor would not have listened," she said.

"A woman with honor," he answered, looking straight at her, "would not have begged."

Flushed with anger, Maida cried he was against God and country.

"Not against God," Elton said, finishing his soup. "And most definitely not against the *people* of my country. But I will tell you this and you make of it what you will. Here a thrall of a Viking, I have more freedom than I ever had as a freeman in my own country." He stood up, and washing his bowl and spoon in a large bucket, he set them to dry on a place near the hearth. "Consider yourself fortunate, Maida," he told her, "that Algar did not have you on your wedding night."

"I was raped by Geir," she shouted, stamping her foot. "Raped in the stern of the *Sea Bird!*"

Elton nodded.

"Everything that should have been mine was taken from me," she railed.

"And much has been given to you in return," he answered.

Shaking her head, Maida told him that he understood nothing of a woman's feelings.

"That is true enough," Elton responded. "But you fail to see the bond between you and Geir.

"There is none!" she shouted. "There is absolutely nothing between us."

"Let her be," Glenna told him softly.

Elton nodded and said he spoke only out of his deep feelings for Geir. Then, pointing to Maida, he added, "If she withdrew her petition to be ransomed—"

"I will not . . . I will not give up what is mine!"

"My words have been wasted," he said. "But let her pray to God," he went on, looking at Glenna, "that she never have cause for regret, if all that she wants comes to pass."

"Let me lie next to my lawful husband and sit opposite him at his table," Maida responded haughtily, "and I will know true happiness."

Elton said no more and he left the house.

"The impudence of the man!" Maida exclaimed resentfully. "He speaks to me—calls me by name—as if he were my equal."

Glenna softly reminded her, "Here we are all equal; we are all Geir's thralls."

"Yes . . . Yes." Maida acknowledged in a choked voice, "He owns all of us. . . ."

XXI

GEIR COULD FIND no peace in his heart. The men who came to him and said their swords would be one with his should the matter between him and his uncle become a fighting one, distressed him greatly. He did not want to bring bloodshed to the stronghold. But he could not give up Maida; either to Bjorn, who certainly had no claim on her, other than his own lust for her; or to Algar, who according to the Christian God had the right to use her body.

Geir had almost decided to go to Lid and discuss the situation. But to do that in his eyes and in Lid's would have been a form of supplication that he could not make. He could not ask Lid to refrain from sending word to Maida's father or to her husband.

As chieftain, Lid had that right whenever the prisoner taken was a highborn man, or if the captive was a woman married to a man of rank. Whatever gold and silver came to Lid from such an exchange, every man in the stronghold would receive an equal share.

Geir could not measure Maida's worth in terms of how much gold and silver her father and husband would be willing to pay for her return. He loved her, though by Freyja, the goddess of love, he did not know why his feelings tended that way. But from the moment he had seen her looking down from Algar's keep, he had wanted her. And those times when he had possessed her, it had required more patience and skill than he had ever before needed with a woman.

He was beginning to understand that he was her captive

as much as she was his. The difference between their thralldom was that she would happily relinquish her hold on him and be returned to her husband, while he would not let go of her, even if it meant his death. With such thoughts in his head, Geir went up the steep cliffs to once more speak with Gruden, the spaewoman.

Geir arrived at the hut when the short day was just drawing to an end. He carried no torch to light the way, but in his hand, he held a battle-ax, whose length was half his own and whose edge was so finely honed that it would easily slice through the silk from Miklagard.

The wind was stronger up on top of the cliffs than it had been in the stronghold and he bent his body into it, pausing to look around before calling out to her. There was smoke coming out of the hole in the roof. But it was rapidly carried away by the wind. There were several chunks of meat left on the roof by the Wendols. And his senses told him that from behind the rocks he was being watched by either the Wendols or the wolves. The presence of either made him uneasy. He shifted the battle-ax from his right shoulder, where it rested during his climb, to both his hands, so that he would be ready to use it should he have to.

He approached the hut cautiously and called to the spaewoman by her name several times.

"Come, come," she responded, in a thin reedy voice that trailed off into a high-pitched cackle.

Geir pulled aside the deerskin covering and entered the hut.

The spaewoman sat on the far side of the fire pit and motioned him to sit down opposite her.

The smoke from the fire was more blue than white; it went straight up to the hole in the roof. And in the wavering yellowish-red light of the fire, the smoke looked like the sapling of an ash tree.

Gruden nodded and said, "It is not the great ash tree Yggdrasil, whose branches touch the limits of the sky and cover the earth upon which we live, and whose three roots reach out to the realm of the dead, the home of the frost giants, and our world, where men and women live. It is no more than what you see—smoke."

"Smoke," Geir repeated.

The spaewoman cackled softly and said, "We will all be smoke when the day of Ragnarok comes and Surt the giant will come forth spouting flames."

Geir knew the prophecy but when she spoke of it, the end of the world seemed more imminent, more certain. By comparison to that pending catastrophe, his own difficulties seemed puny.

She apparently divined his thoughts and said, "But those of us who are here must tend to our lives and carry out our destinies. Yours, Geir, will not be easy."

"Will I be forced to give up the woman?" he asked hastily.

Gruden shook her head. "You will leave her."

"Leave her?"

"It is all in blood," the spaewoman said. "The secret is in blood and the answer is in blood. . . . one leads to the other. . . . they are but parts of the chain of life."

Geir shook his head, "I do not understand," he said. "Whose blood do you speak of?"

The spaewoman began to chant. Her voice was low and dark; the words barely audible. She closed her eyes and reached toward the smoke.

Geir scrambled to his feet. He had enough of Gruden's magic, and he rushed from the hut. The night was black; not a star shone in the sky and wind stung him with its sharp bite.

He hurried along the narrow twisting trail to where he would begin his descent. Suddenly from behind him came

165

a wild screech. Holding his battle-ax low on its shaft, he swung around and struck.

A scream of agony pierced the blackness.

Geir ran. He felt the warm stickiness of blood on the handle of his battle-ax.

Another screech!

He stopped, whirled, and swung again. This time he saw the Wendol's head roll from his massive shoulders.

Geir ran!

A wolf suddenly leaped in front of him.

He sliced it in two and breathlessly made for rocky ledges that would bring him off the cliffs. Hurriedly, he leaped from rock to rock. Twice he lost his footing and fell a distance before he could break his fall. But he held on to his battle-ax. When he reached the bottom of the cliff, he ran toward the wall of the stronghold without looking back.

"Open the gate," he shouted up at the guards, whose dogs were barking furiously. "It is Geir. . . . It is me, Geir."

The men opened the gate, Geir rushed into the safety of the stronghold, quickly mounted the parapet, and looked out toward the dark base of the cliff. There were many shadows moving there.

The dogs on the wall caught the scent and barked wildly.

"Wendols?" asked one of the guards.

"Yes, Wendols," Geir answered, breathlessly. He held up his blood-stained ax and said, "I killed two of them on the cliff there." Then he shouldered the weapon and started for his house.

XXII

THE SNOW CAME swirling down from low-hanging dark gray clouds. The cold was so intense that ice formed along the shore of the cove in front of the stronghold and in those places where the water was very still. The wind blew all the time, changing its voice from a wail to a demonic shriek; then to a continuous moan of agony and back to a wail.

Maida grew more and more restless; even Geir prowled the confines of his house like a caged animal. He drank a lot and spent long hours sleeping, regardless of whether it was night or day; though sometimes it was difficult to tell which was which.

Geir fornicated with Karinia, doing what Maida had watched him do with Karinia and Thyri the first night she had been in the house. He smilingly invited her to join them, but she would have none of it.

By the third day of the storm, Maida felt as if her skin would split. She desperately needed to breathe fresh air and cleanse her lungs of the foul smells that filled them. Her thoughts were full of her father and of Algar.

She wanted to be away from where she was; she wanted to be free, the lady of her own table and not the thrall of a Viking. More than ever before she hated Geir and loathed his wild sensuality. Now, whenever she could muster the strength to resist his devil conjurings, she let him have his way with her but did not respond.

"I am going out," she announced.

167

Geir, who was in bed with Karinia, lifted his head to say, "You will come back soon enough."

Maida dressed herself in her warmest clothes, and on top of them, she wrapped a robe made of the white fur of a bear that Geir had killed two summers before far to the north of Gottland. She left the house with the sound of Karinia's passionate cries ringing in her ears.

She hurried away from the house. Her breath steamed in the cold air, and the wind cut through all of her clothing. But she was determined to walk at least as far as the shore. She took several deep breaths and nodded approvingly. But the cold brought tears to her eyes, and these quickly froze on the side of her face.

From the shore, she could see beyond the cove to where the sea was almost black. She glanced at the stronghold. It was white, and here and there above it were windblown puffs of smoke. The cliffs in the distance were hidden by the swirling snow.

The wind was too fierce for her to remain at the shore. She moved away, taking shelter for a short time on the lee side of a grounded ship. She pulled her bearskin robe more securely around her. She tied it so the wind would not be able to get inside of it as it previously had. She stamped her feet to drive the numbness from them and decided she had enough of the cold and the wind. She was about to return to Geir's house when she suddenly saw Bjorn.

He was standing several paces from her, saying nothing.

Maida remained motionless. Her heart skipped a beat; then it raced.

Bjorn came toward her.

She shook her head and ran toward the shore.

He was swifter than she and soon caught her.

She fought him off but he held onto her. She screamed for help but her words were tossed away by the wind.

168

Bjorn forced her down in the snow and began tearing at her clothing.

Maida clawed at his face.

He ripped open her bearskin robe and tore her outer gown from her body. The cold seared her body and made her nipples hard. She screamed and screamed.

Bjorn ripped her shift and began to force himself between her naked thighs.

As the snow fell on her face and mingled with her tears, she fought not to take his organ into her body. She clamped her thighs together and tried to twist away, but his strength finally prevailed. Suddenly her right hand clutched at a small rock. She lifted it and with what force she could muster, smashed it against her attacker's head.

Bjorn uttered a low cry of surprise.

She struck him again and blood flowed from the gash she inflicted on his forehead. Confused, dazed, he shook his head.

The third time she hit him, he rolled off to one side.

Maida leaped to her feet and hurled the stone at him. Crying, she ran to Geir's house where she collapsed on the floor, and sobbed out her story.

"Where is Bjorn now?" Geir asked, his voice flat with anger.

Maida shook her head.

Geir grabbed hold of Maida's hand and pulled her after him.

"Please!" she cried. "Please let me be!"

Geir let go of her and calling to Karinia, who was still naked in bed, and to Glenna, he ordered them to take care of Maida.

"And where are you going?" Maida wept. "He has lost his wits."

"Then I will go to Lid," Geir said. "He must control his son." He went for his sword. Then, changing his mind, he commented aloud, "It will be better if I go without any weapon."

"Let me go with you!" Maida asked.

Geir shook his head. "This will be settled between Lid and myself," he told her. "I do not want you to say anything more to Lid."

"But—"

Geir pointed his finger at her and said, "Lid is a fair and a just man."

"What will you ask in recompense for the injury done to your property?" she asked scathingly. "Perhaps a cow or even a horse?" She started to laugh hysterically.

"See to her!" Geir shouted to the other two women. "The trolls have taken hold of her." Then he turned and left the house.

First he went to the shore, where Maida had escaped from Bjorn. Bjorn was not there. But the beaten-down snow was evidence of the struggle that had taken place.

Geir then followed the footprints back to the lee of the ship and he saw where Maida had paused to stamp her feet and where Bjorn had stood watching her. When he was sure he read all there was for him to read in the snow, he went straight to Lid's great hall.

Many men were there, and he was warmly welcomed by them. They offered him drink, but he said his business was with Lid, who was seated in a huge oaken chair near the hearth, where it was warm.

Geir approached Lid courteously.

Lid nodded and asked Geir to enjoy the hospitality of his house. "Many have asked for you these past few days," Lid told him, "But most agreed you were well entertained by your Saxon woman.

Geir agreed. He looked at the men in the hall. Several were playing at dice, or moving various pieces of carved wood on boards marked out in squares. These were games that had come from Miklagard, and they served to pass time away when it was impossible to do anything else.

Geir faced Lid. In a low voice he said, "I have come to lodge a complaint against Bjorn."

The slight smile on Lid's lips vanished. His face became very hard-looking. His eyes blazed but he waited for Geir to speak.

"He tried to rape my thrall," Gier said.

Lid took a deep breath, and when all the air had left his lungs, he shouted for Bjorn. The sound of his voice rang through the great hall and every man there turned his eyes toward their chieftain.

Bjorn came into the great hall from another part of the house. He had cleaned the blood from his face, but the side of his head was bruised where Maida had struck him. He went straight to where his father sat. He did not look at his cousin.

Geir moved slightly to the right.

"Your cousin has lodged a complaint against you," Lid said.

The men in the hall left their places and moved close to where their chieftain, his son, and Geir were. There was an unfamiliar tension in the hall.

Bjorn did not speak.

"Your cousin claims you attempted to rape his thrall," Lid said.

"And I say," Bjorn told his father, "that his thrall uncovered herself to me."

Lid looked at Geir.

"And I also say," Bjorn said, "that my cousin comes crying to you like a woman when it was his thrall who put herself before me."

"You lie, Bjorn!" Geir exclaimed.

Bjorn's face crimsoned; his hand went to his sword; he drew the blade from its scabbard.

171

Geir threw up his hands to show he was weaponless. "I came for Lid's justice," he said, "not to fight you."

"It is time we fought," Bjorn answered. "It is time one of us sent the other to Hel or Valhalla."

The men moved away to give the combatants room.

Geir looked up at Lid and he asked, "Is this what you will have?"

"Bjorn," Lid shouted, rising to his feet, "he came without a weapon."

"Then my killing of him will not take so long," Bjorn answered, thrusting his blade at Geir.

Geir darted away.

"See how he runs, father," Bjorn laughed. "See—and you always thought that he was better than any of the men, even your own son." He ran at Geir, but again his cousin avoided a killing stroke. Bjorn cursed him.

One of the men shouted to Geir and tossed him a sword. The blade clattered on the hard wood floor. Geir rushed to it.

Bjorn went after him. He brought his weapon down with such force that it sent splinters flying in all directions.

But Geir had grabbed hold of the weapon that had been thrown to him, and he rolled clear of his cousin's stroke. In an instant, he was on his feet. The sword felt good in his hand, and he began to move in a slow circle.

Bjorn rushed his cousin with such swiftness that he was able to drive the point of his blade into Geir's left side. "First blood!" Bjorn shouted in triumph. "First blood!" The wildness of his cry echoed through the great hall.

Geir staggered; Bjorn's blade brought fire into his bowels, and he backed away from Bjorn's savage attacks.

"Enough," Lid shouted. "Enough! I order the two of you to put up your weapons."

"No," the other Vikings answered. "Geir must be

172

allowed to fight. Bjorn drew his weapon first . . . Geir must be allowed to fight."

Lid pursed his lips and watched his son and nephew stalk each other.

Geir continued to move away from Bjorn. Suddenly he stopped, but Bjorn could not leap back. Geir struck hard at the base of his cousin's weapon. The blades came together with a great ringing clang.

Bjorn's fingers sprung open. His weapon fell to the floor.

The two men stood and glared at each other. A dreadful silence came into the great hall.

Geir was wet with sweat. His left side dripped blood on to the already blood-stained floor.

Bjorn looked at his sword and then at Geir.

Everyone in the great hall knew the instant Bjorn moved, Geir would cut him down.

"Put up your sword, Geir," Lid said in a strangled voice. "For the love you have left for me, put up your sword."

"Speak to your son, Lid," Geir answered. "Ask him if he wants to live or die."

Lid looked at Bjorn.

"The woman should have been mine," Bjorn said. "I tried to take what should have been mine to enjoy."

Lid shook his head; his son had lied to him in front of everyone in the hall, but Bjorn was his son and he could not let him die at Geir's hands. He had hoped that some day Bjorn would take his place as the stronghold's chieftain. All his other sons had either been killed in battle or had died when they were no more than children.

"I will offer fair recompense," Lid said to Geir.

"It is Bjorn who must make the decision," Geir answered. "I want nothing from you, uncle, but from him I want an apology to me and to Maida in front of every man, woman, and child in the stronghold.''

"Never!'' Bjorn shouted.

"Give him what he asks,'' Lid pleaded.

"Nothing,'' Bjorn roared. "Nothing!'' And he ran forward, taking the blade of Geir's sword into his stomach. He staggered, dropped to his knees, and tried to shout Odin's name but the word would not come; the god would not come. He died, kicking and screaming in fear as death took him.

Lid cradled the body of his son in his arms. Looking up at Geir, he cried out against him.

"You betrayed me,'' he shouted. "You betrayed me as I always knew one day you would. By blood you belong more to Njal than to me; that blood has shown itself here today, as I was told it would.'' Then he bent over his dead son and wept.

XXIII

To APPEASE THE gods and assure his son's entry into Valhalla, Lid had ordered a special funeral for him that would take place in ten days. In the meantime, Bjorn's body had been laid in the ground. But despite Lid's efforts to have Odin accept his son, many of the people believed that Bjorn had already entered Hel, the place where criminals, outlaws and cowards went after life.

Lid was inconsolable over his loss. He spent hours praying to the gods for their help; he wanted to understand why Geir had betrayed him when he had been nothing but kind to his nephew."

And as for Geir, he was in a truly dark mood. He saw no connection between himself and Njal, yet his uncle had said most definitely there was one. Several times he had thought about going back to Gruden, the spaewoman, to ask her if she knew what his connection to Njal might be. But the Wendols were seen daily on the cliffs, sometimes even climbing halfway down their rock faces. The Wendols could always sense when there was trouble in the stronghold.

Maida was terrified by the turn of events. She knew there were many people who believed she was responsible for Bjorn's death; that in some way she had managed to bewitch him and Geir so they would fight over her. She spoke to Glenna about it.

And Glenna answered, "Elton says all the men who

sailed with Geir would stand with him if it came to a fight."

"God in heaven," Maida cried, "I want no more blood spilled."

She tried speaking with Geir, but he neither spoke or lay with her anymore. And at night, when the house was dark, except for the red glow in the hearth, she missed the warmth of his body next to hers and his callused hand on her breast. It gave her small comfort to know he did not lay with Karinia either, but spent most of the night staring into the red glow of the fire. And during the day, he stood alone, where the sea smashed itself against the black rocks along the shore.

Three days before the funeral, Geir stopped Kar and asked after Lid.

"His grief is grayer than the sky," the old soothsayer answered.

Geir told him, "My sorrow is no less than his grief. Bjorn was a brother to me."

Kar leaned very close to him and said, "You must make new plans."

"I have been thinking the same thing," he responded in a low voice.

Kar nodded and went toward the ship that was being prepared for Bjorn's last voyage.

On the afternoon of the funeral, a blustery wind blew from the north. The sky was covered with swirling gray clouds, and every so often the air was filled with snow.

Maida stood on Geir's right. Karinia was to his left. Elton and Glenna were behind them.

Everyone in the stronghold came down to the shore where the ship was. It had been hauled ashore and held by four posts. Around it was piled a great deal of wood.

Snow whipped across Maida's face, and she brushed it

off her eyebrows. Geir's face was set. From time to time she realized that many of the men and women looked at him and then at her.

A wooden bench was placed aboard the ship. It was covered with beautiful silks and cushions from Miklagard. Then an old woman came into view. She began to arrange the cushions.

"That is the angel of death," Karinia whispered. "She will dress Bjorn and will provide him with a woman."

Maida looked back questioningly at Karinia.

In a low growl, Geir ordered Karinia to be silent.

Maida gave her attention to the old woman. She was very tall and her face was seamed with wrinkles. Several times the woman changed the position of the cushions. Then, when she was finally satisfied, she stepped back and raised her right hand.

A few moments later several men came down toward the shore. Between them they carried Bjorn's body. It had turned black during the ten days it had lain in the ground.

Maida stifled a cry; she closed her eyes and held them shut until the body was aboard the ship.

The angel of death dressed Bjorn's body, and when that was done, it was carried into a tent set up in the stern of the ship. The body was surrounded with food, jugs of ale and beer, sweet-smelling herbs and some of Bjorn's personal belongings. Meat, bread and onions were flung before the corpse.

Suddenly the silence was rent by the fearful yelping of a large dog.

Even before Maida could ask what the dog was doing about the ship, the two men who had carried Bjorn's body aboard took hold of the yelping animal and with a single stroke of the sword, one of them cut it in half. Blood flew up and drenched their faces and chests. The two pieces of the dog were thrown into the ship, near the body.

Maida's stomach churned; the food she had eaten earlier seemed ready to spew out of her mouth.

The men laid Bjorn's weapons next to his body.

Afterward two horses were run around the ship until their hides glistened with sweat and foam came from their mouths. Then they were cut to pieces with swords and the meat was flung into the ship. Two cows were slaughtered in the same way. Then a cock and a hen were killed and their bloody bodies thrown into the ship with the rest of the flesh.

Maida felt sick. She did not want to witness any more Viking barbarities. Truly, God could not possibly see what was happening here and still allow it to happen!

Then suddenly Lid stepped up to the prow of the ship and cried out, "All this I do for my son so that Odin will take him into Valhalla."

And the people shouted, "Odin, take him into Valhalla."

Then Lid cried out, "What woman will go with my son to Valhalla?"

For several moments, only the wail of the wind could be heard. Then a woman answered, "I, Thyri, will go with your son!"

Geir started forward but stopped and Maida cried out, "Oh, no!"

All eyes went to her. Some were filled with surprise while others burned with anger.

Thyri went toward the prow of the ship and repeated three times that she was willing to make the journey with Bjorn.

Lid took her by the hand and led her to the tents of his kinsmen, where she lay with each one of them. When she was done, she called out, "Tell your master I did this out of love for him."

"Please, Geir," Maida whispered, "I cannot watch what will follow."

"We will stay," he answered.

"But Thyri—"

"She will die!" he exclaimed sharply and looked away from her.

Thyri was lifted into the ship and she cried out, "I see my mother and my father." She was set down on the ground again. And a second time she was lifted into the ship. "I see all my dead relatives sitting around." Once more she was set on the ground, and for the third and last time, she was lifted into the ship. "Look," she cried. "I see my master, I see Bjorn; he is in Paradise and Paradise is beautiful and green. With him are men and young boys. He calls me. Let me join him then!"

Thyri removed her bracelets and gave them to the old woman.

Many men carrying wooden shields and sticks arrived. Thyri was given a drink of strong beer. She sang softly about death.

Prickles rose on Maida's skin. Her breath steamed in the cold air, but it was so very hard for her to breathe. She looked at Geir. His face was expressionless.

"If you had not brought me here," Maida whispered, "Thyri would not be going to her death."

"It was her destiny to do what she is doing," he answered in a choked voice.

"She looks bewildered—something was put in her drink."

Geir nodded.

Suddenly Thyri turned toward the tent and put her head inside of it. Then the old woman pushed her into it.

The men of the ship began to beat their shields with their sticks.

179

Six men entered the tent, and when they came out, they proclaimed that they had possessed her.

Then she was set alongside of Bjorn. The angel of death put a cord around her neck and gave an end to each of the men. The old woman took a small dagger and plunged it between Thyri's ribs, moving it back and forth while the two men strangled her.

Maida grabbed hold of Geir's arm; she buried her face into it. She could not watch. Silently she prayed for the Holy Mother of God to have mercy on Thyri!

"Lid comes," Geir said.

Maida raised her head and looked toward the ship again.

Lid held a burning faggot in his right hand. With a hand on his buttock, he walked backwards toward the ship. Despite the wind and the bitter cold, he was stark naked. When he reached the wood gathered around the ship, he turned and plunged the burning faggot into the pile. Kinsmen came and did the same. Then Bjorn's friends added their burning faggots to the funeral pyre.

Maida saw Thorkel and many of the men on the ships place their torches with the others.

Then Geir picked up a faggot and went to where the fire was.

Lid blocked his way and said, "You were not his friend."

Geir looked around him. He could easily see some of the men were ready to draw their weapons either for or against him. But he would know which of them would be for him and which would be against only if he challenged Lid's authority. His eye caught Thorkel's and he knew he could depend on him. But Geir did not want to see him or any of his friends enter Valhalla. With a nod, he threw the torch aside and walked back to Maida.

The wind fanned the fire under the ship, and in a short

180

time the ship itself began to burn. A cloud of smoke rose into the sky and air began to smell of burnt flesh.

"Hell must smell like that," Maida said to Glenna.

"It was a terrible way for Thyri to die," Glenna said. "If Geir had not bought me—"

"I do not want to hear any more about Thyri from anyone," Geir told them angrily. "Not one word more!"

The sky turned darker and the snow began to fall more steadily. The wind dropped off and the smoke went straight up.

Lid, now dressed, stood watching the burning ship. There were tears in his eyes. He asked Kar if he could read the signs.

Kar studied the smoke. It was very black and it lay pressed under the clouds. The old soothsayer shook his head. "The doors of Valhalla are shut," he said. "See how the clouds trap the smoke."

"Then it was all for nothing?" Lid asked, his voice broken with grief.

"Who can answer that?" Kar responded.

Lid faced Geir; there was more hate in his uncle's eyes than he could bear to look at, and he turned away.

"He will kill you," Maida said in a tremulous voice. "As God is my judge, he has murder in him."

"Come," Geir said, to those with him, "it is best that we go home. We are not wanted here."

When they reached the house, Geir lingered with them only long enough to drink several large cups full of strong beer before he went out again. He needed to be alone. He went to the far shore where the rocks broke the back of the sea into swirling white roaring water.

The snow came down steadily. Through it Geir could make out the burning funeral ship, but the smoke was lost in the falling snow.

He turned again toward the sea. Only the rocks and the

white water could be seen, but he fixed his eyes on the impenetrable grayness beyond the surge of the sea, where he saw nothing more than himself. If anyone was to blame for Thyri's death, he was; he had sold her to satisfy Maida's wish to have her own serving woman with her again. Thyri had been loyal to him and she willingly gave him her body in whatever way pleased him.

Geir shook his head. It had been foolish of her to choose death, and he remembered that Maida had said she would die without him.

He took a deep breath. Then in a loud voice he called to the gods to keep Thyri from being angry with him and to prevent her ghost from coming to visit him in his sleep. Then he said a special prayer to Freyja, the goddess of love, asking her to soften Maida's heart toward him.

His words were lost in the roar of the sea, but Geir was sure that the gods would have been able to hear his prayers, especially since he was seldom given to asking them for anything.

He looked toward Bjorn's funeral pyre and said, ''I did not want you dead, but I could not let you take my life without fighting for it. . . . I am sorry that you—''

There was another blaze of fire off to the far right of where Bjorn's funeral ship lay smoldering. The roar of the sea prevented him from hearing anything. And yet another burst of red came from out of the snow.

Geir ran toward the center of the stronghold. He drew his sword, and when he came to where the ships were, he saw the Wendols. They had broken through the wall and they were already killing anyone they could find.

He rushed toward them shouting Odin's name over and over again.

182

XXIV

To DULL HER senses, Maida sat at the table drinking strong beer. Bjorn's funeral was like nothing she had ever seen, and Thyri's death filled her with remorse. And now Karinia was telling her that Lid would not rest until he avenged his son's death.

"If I were you," Karinia said, as she stood by the hearth and looked at Maida, "I would make sure I was ransomed before Lid kills Geir, or you might be sold to another man—or worse, be called upon to die with him."

Maida shook her head and whispered, "Never . . . Never . . . It is against the will of God."

"Not *their* Gods," Karinia answered with a laugh.

Maida knew that was true and she silently sipped her beer. Then she asked where Glenna was.

"No doubt with Elton," Karinia said. "Those two have become very good friends."

Maida raised her eyebrows.

"Yes," she responded, "they lie with one another."

"Does Geir know?"

"These days," she replied with a shrug, "who can tell what Geir knows or does not know?"

After a long silence, Maida asked, "Do you love him, Karinia?"

"He is good to me," she answered, moving closer to the table. "And he gives me much pleasure, as I am sure he gives you, when you let him."

Maida flushed.

"I am his thrall and he is my master," Karinia told her.

"But do you—"

"Do you love him?" Karinia questioned, interrupting her.

The two women looked at each other and for several moments neither of them spoke. Words were not necessary; their silence said all that had to be said between them.

Maida looked down at her cup and she said, "I am married; in the eyes of God I am married." She looked up at Karinia. "I am caught between—"

Karinia whirled around and faced the door.

"What is wrong?" Maida asked, rising to her feet.

Karinia waved her to be silent.

Maida hurried to Karinia's side.

"Outside," she whispered. "People are running."

Maida listened. At first she could only hear the low moan of the wind; then she was able to catch the hissing sound of the snow falling and then heard the quick, heavy footfalls.

Karinia shook her head and went quickly to the side of the room where Geir kept many of his weapons. Without hesitation she picked up a battle-ax and hurried back to where Maida was standing. After taking a deep breath, she whispered, "I did not think Lid would have sent his men so soon."

Maida was wide-eyed with fright. She tried to speak but could not form the words on her trembling lips.

A few moments passed. Then from somewhere in the stronghold a man shouted, "Wendols! The Wendols have come!"

The next instant the door was smashed open and two short heavy-jawed, snow-covered men came toward the women.

Maida screamed.

Karinia rushed forward, and swinging the battle-ax, she smashed it against one of the Wendols. It crunched down on his shoulder and sent him sprawling to the floor. But before Karinia could swing at the other Wendol, he had flung himself at her. He drove his huge fist against her head with such force, the blow broke her neck and crushed the side of her skull.

The Wendol on the floor struggled to his feet, and leaving a trail of blood, he made his way out of the house.

The second Wendol went toward Maida.

She shrank away from him. He stank. His thick black hair was matted with dirt and blood. His jaw thrust out and his teeth were filed to points. He made strange low growling sounds as he came closer to her.

She rushed to the hearth, and picking up a burning faggot, she thrust it at him.

He shouted at her in a language she did not understand. His small black eyes glowed with anger.

Maida waved the fireband in front of her. Several times she made the sign of the cross.

The Wendol growled; then suddenly he leaped at her. Grabbing hold of the burning faggot, he wrenched it from her and tossed it back into the hearth.

His hands were on her.

She screamed.

He pushed her down on the floor.

Another Wendol shouted to him from the doorway. He hesitated and then lifting Maida up, he swung her across his shoulder. Within moments he was outside of the house and running toward the wall.

There were many fires in the stronghold. In their red wavering light, Maida could make out the bodies of many men. There was fighting still going on, and the sounds of shouting and clanging of blades against blades could be heard from every quarter.

185

Several times Maida tried to wiggle free, but the Wendol was far stronger than she.

He ran toward the wall; part of it was burning. Once he was out of the stronghold, he raced toward the rock cliffs.

Maida suddenly realized that men from the stronghold were behind her. She shouted at them.

"Maida, is that you?" Elton called out.

"Yes—hurry!"

The Wendol quickened his pace. He ran in a low animal crouch and several times called to the other Wendols with a strange kind of voice, almost like the bark of a dog, or the yelp of a wolf.

Through the falling snow, Maida caught sight of the men. She shouted to them.

A spear whirred through the darkness. It thudded into the earth somewhere in front of the Wendol. He looked over his shoulder. With a growl of rage, he tossed Maida to the ground. He whirled around to meet his attackers.

Maida lay in the snow. She was too frightened to move or even cry out.

The Wendol shook his fist at the Vikings who were coming at him.

Elton shouted to Maida.

"I am here," she cried out. "Here!"

Elton ran toward her.

The Wendol saw him.

Before Maida could shout a warning, the Wendol had grabbed hold of Elton. With one swift motion of his right hand, he tore Elton's head from his shoulders. Then he picked up Elton's sword, and giving a terrible animal yell, he charged into the Vikings who were running toward him.

The melee that followed was fierce and swift; other Wendols came running to join the fray.

186

Many of them were armed with swords and spears. They uttered terrifying yells that rose above the Viking shouts of "Odin . . . Odin . . . Odin!" The falling snow deadened the ringing sound of metal crashing against metal.

Maida saw several of the Wendols stagger away, their hairy bodies covered with blood. She crawled toward the stronghold.

Several times she was forced to stop and lie still in the snow, hoping not to be discovered by the Wendols who passed her.

Soon the din of the fight was behind her and the hiss of the falling snow completely obliterated it. She stopped and stood up. She was very cold—so cold that the nipples on her breast hardened. In front of her glowed the fires of the stronghold. Several buildings were burning, and more of the wall was now on fire than had been previously.

She began to run toward the stronghold. Here and there she saw the mangled body of a Viking. Twice she thought she recognized Geir and stopped to make sure it was not him.

By the time she was back inside of the stronghold, her breath came in short bursts. She was wet with sweat and terrified that Geir might have been killed.

Maida hurried toward the house. There were bodies in the pathways between the houses. Several women lay dying. They were naked and blood oozed on the white snow from their wounds.

Maida came to the house and ran inside, calling for Glenna. No one answered. She went to Karinia and bent over her.

"Dead!" she cried. "Dear God in heaven, she is dead . . . Dead!" Hiding her face with her hands, she wept.

Outside she could hear the sounds of men, the barking

of dogs and the weeping of children. And then, without seeing him, she sensed that Geir was standing in the doorway.

He came to where she was and stood alongside her. He said nothing.

Then Maida felt his hand gently touch the top of her head. She took her hands away from her face and with tear-stained eyes, she looked up at him. He was stained with blood; his leather jacket was ripped and there were huge bloody gashes on his chest.

Slowly he raised her to her feet. His eyes went to Karinia. He made an effort to speak but did not say anything.

"She fought bravely," Maida told him softly.

He nodded and swallowed hard.

She led him to the fire and washed his wounds.

"I fought with one of them," he said. "It took a long time for me to kill him." Then he looked at her and asked if she had seen Elton or Glenna.

She told about Elton.

Again he asked about Glenna.

"I have not seen her," Maida answered.

Geir took some bear grease and spread it over his wounds. Then he picked up Karinia's body and put it in the shed next to the house. "Tomorrow," he told Maida, when he returned, "we will look for Elton. The man was true to his word; he said he would do me a great service and he did. I had much respect for him."

"As he had for you," she said.

Geir went to the smashed door and closed it as well as he could. Then he poured a cup of beer for himself and one for Maida. "On the way back from the spaewoman the last time, I killed two Wendols."

She drank most of her beer before she asked, "Who are they, or what are they?"

188

"Men," he answered with a shrug.

"But like no other men I have ever seen."

"They eat the flesh of other men," he said, pouring more beer for himself. "When I was younger, I went with several of the older men on a raid of their stronghold. We found the bones of many men and women. They raid us for our women and our weapons—they only know how to make things of stone . . . Some of the old people here say that the Wendols never die, that Hel will not take them and the gods have abandoned them, so here they stay—in the forests on top of the cliffs."

Maida shivered and told him that the Wendol who had carried her off had his teeth sharpened to points.

"They all do that," he commented. "They use their teeth like a dog or a wolf."

She asked him if he thought that Glenna might have been carried off.

"Pray to your God she is still here," he answered. "Wendols use our women to give them sport and pass her from man to man until they kill her."

Maida closed her eyes and immediately began to pray for Glenna's safe return. When she was finished, she asked Geir what he intended to do about Lid.

"Nothing now," he answered. "Neither one of us has any strength left after this night." He went to the bed, unbuckled his sword, and placed it next to him against the wall. Then he lay down and drawing one of the heavy bearskin robes over him, he called to Maida.

She looked at the blood-splattered floor. With a shake of her head, she set her empty cup down on the table. Then she went to the bed and stretched herself out next to Geir.

"Hold me, Geir," she whispered. "Hold me!"

He put his arms around her and drew her to him.

"God forgive me, Geir, but I want you to make love to me."

Slowly his hands moved over her body until she was on fire, until the great tenseness began to coil itself deep in her body.

Maida moaned with pleasure and felt for his organ, and when it was in her hand, she found herself desperately wanting to know its taste. She moved down his body.

"Take your shift off," he said.

She obeyed.

He stripped, and when they were both naked, he shifted her over him until her mouth was on his organ and his mouth against the lips of her sex, the way she had seen him go at Karinia and Thyri.

The thrust of his mouth at her sex was enough to make her bolt, but she quickly repositioned herself and then as she took hold of his organ with her lips, she quickly surrendered herself to the torrent of new and deliciously pleasurable sensations that coursed through her quivering body. Just with his tongue he brought her to several tempestuous moments of exquisite delight. And when he finally entered her, the pleasure was more intense than it had ever been.

"Oh, Geir!" she cried out, when her body thrashed under his. "Oh, Geir, I am helpless in your hands; helpless to stop myself from wanting you inside of me!"

When it was over, they slept naked in each other's arms through the remainder of the night. And when morning came, Geir was the first to wake. He saw Glenna sitting at the table. Her shift was soaked with blood and her left arm dangled from its socket.

Geir called softly to Maida and when she opened her eyes, he put his finger across his lips and pointed to Glenna.

"God in heaven!" Maida exclaimed, and disregarding her nakedness, she ran to her former serving woman.

Glenna nodded and weepingly, said, "I was ill used—ill used, my lady." Then she fainted.

Maida called to Geir and together they carried Glenna to the bed and set her down. Geir pulled on her left arm and it snapped back into place. He looked at her other wounds and assured Maida that they would quickly heal. "Unless she is carrying a Wendol child," he said, "she will be fine in a few days."

"If she is carrying a child," Maida said, "it is more than likely to be Elton's than that of a Wendol."

Geir nodded approvingly and then he suggested they put on some clothes.

Maida flushed and in a moment of wild abandon, she threw herself into his arms and taking hold of his manhood, moved it wantonly over her own sex.

XXV

THE VERY NEXT day, the men began to rebuild the wall while the women went out to gather the dead.

Maida performed the grisly task of finding Elton's head and matching it to his body. With the help of several other women, she brought Elton's remains back to the house.

Glenna bathed and dressed the body. When she was done, she turned to Maida and quietly said, "Of all the men I ever knew, he was the only one I truly loved. I shall miss him very, very much!"

Maida had never before heard Glenna speak that way and she acknowledged her serving woman's sorrow by praising the man for his courage.

When Geir returned, he stood looking down at Elton's body. For a long time, he said nothing. Then, moving to Glenna, he told her that Elton would be given the funeral of a free man. Geir explained, "He said to me that one day I would give him his freedom because he would have rendered some great service to me. He will go to wherever your people go when they die, for he never forsook your God for ours."

Glenna nodded and said, "He told me of your agreement, and he was certain that when the time came, you would honor it."

"Are you with his child?" Geir questioned.

"It is still too early to tell," she answered.

"Should it be his son," Geir said, "I will raise him as if he were my own; he will be a free man, as you are from this moment a free woman. Should it be a daughter, she, too, will be raised as my own, and I will give her a fair dowry when she becomes old enough to be taken to wife.''

Glenna threw herself on her knees and she kissed Geir's hands.

"Come, come," he said, gently lifting her to her feet. "Elton would have never bowed to anyone."

With tears streaming down her face, Glenna laughingly admitted that the dead man would have been too proud to do what she had just done.

That night Geir carried Elton's body to the funeral pyre on the shore of the cove, and next to him he placed his tools and the sword with which he had fought the Wendols. Before he set fire to the wood under Elton's body, Geir proclaimed him to be a free man. . . .

As soon as the wall was rebuilt and strengthened, many of the Vikings climbed up to the cliffs and raided the various camps of the Wendols. They killed several of the Wendols and wounded many more before they came back to the stronghold, where life was quickly returning to what it had been before the Wendols came.

Geir spent much of his time on the rocky shore, where the sea was always angry. He realized that between him and Lid there was nothing more than ill feelings. Lid no doubt would try to find some way to kill him; if he were Lid, he would do exactly the same thing.

But Geir was not ready to sit back and let his uncle take his life. And one day when the sea was so wild that it would have pulled him down from the rocks, Geir went to Thorkel's house and sitting at the table with him drinking beer, he said, "I have something to say to all the men who sailed with me. Can you gather them together for me tonight?"

Thorkel nodded. Geir finished his beer and told Thorkel, "Bring the men to my house." Then he left and went for a long walk before he returned home to tell Maida and Glenna that there would be many guests at the table that night.

Immediately after nightfall, the men began to arrive. The first to come were Einar, Skled, and Hougen. They were pleased to see Maida and she welcomed them warmly. Other members of Geir's crew came and then crews of the other two ships arrived. Thorkel was the last man.

Maida and Glenna served them beer, ale and mead. Then they prepared several large trays of roasted chicken, a tray of herrings and a tray of roasted goat meat.

When the men were well fed and had not as yet drunk themselves into a stupor, Geir called their attention to himself by mounting a bench so that every one of them could see him. Then he said, "I am seeking good men to go a vi-king and to establish a new stronghold."

His words brought a strange tension to the room, almost as if each man had sucked in his breath and was holding it.

"My time here is over," Geir told them.

Several of the men made loud whistling sounds as they released the air from their lungs. Others moved around to look at the man next to him.

Maida was stunned, though she might have guessed that Geir would not wait for Lid to act before he himself acted. She turned to Glenna and whispered, "He is risking all our lives to save his own."

"He might also be risking his to save yours," Glenna answered.

Maida looked at her darkly; she did not like to be spoken to that way by her former serving woman. Ever since Lid had promised to send word to her father and husband, she hoped to be ransomed, to be returned to her rightful place alongside Algar. But if Geir succeeded in his plan, her expectation would never be turned into reality. She would remain Geir's thrall for the rest of her life.

194

As long as there was the slightest chance she might be returned to Algar, that possibility was intolerable. To safeguard her future, she had to stop him.

Einar stood up and said, "My sword is yours, Geir."

"Good man!" Geir exclaimed.

Hougen said, "I will go but I would like to know where I will go to."

The men laughed loudly.

"If we have four ships," Geir said, "we will have close to two hundred and forty men—more than enough to start our own stronghold somewhere on the Frankish coast. Close enough to the Saxons to raid and—"

"Will we take our women and children?" Skled asked.

"We will take whatever we can," Geir answered.

Thorkel stood up and asked, "How do you intend to do all this, Geir?"

"I have developed a plan," Geir answered, pausing for a moment to take a long drink of beer. "We will take those ships we need and burn the others."

The men became very quiet. To do any sort of damage to another man's ship was a crime punishable by death.

"We must be able to escape without fear of pursuit," Geir told them. "Our ships will be laden with women and children. If Lid should give chase and offer battle, we will not have much of a chance to escape. By burning all the other ships, we ensure the success of our actions. There is no other way."

The men discussed what they had just heard among themselves.

To silence the men, Thorkel held up his hands; then he said to them, "If we stay here, sooner or later we will have to make a choice between Lid and Geir. If we go, we will have made that choice. I would rather leave the stronghold than see us fighting in it."

There was loud agreement with Thorkel's words.

"When will we leave?" one of the men asked.

"The second night of the dark moon," Geir told them.

Every man raised his cup to toast the success of the undertaking.

When they had finished drinking, Thorkel said, "I will speak to Buliwyf about him and his crew joining us. He has no great love for Lid."

"Swear him to silence first," Geir cautioned.

"I do not think he will need much prodding to join us," Thorkel responded. "He has already hinted that he would gladly lend his sword to yours, should you raise yours against Lid."

Geir nodded and drank more beer. It was well past midnight when the men left the house. Geir was flushed by his success, and the strong beer fired his desire for Maida.

But she did not respond to his caresses; she could only feel more abandoned than ever. If Geir took her with him, all hope of being ransomed would be lost forever.

"Geir," she asked, "do you really want to do injury to your uncle?"

"I want to prevent him from doing injury to me," he answered, enjoying the soft warmth of her breast under his hand. "It is not without sorrow that I have made my decision to leave."

"And if you should fail?"

"I and all of those with me," he answered without hesitation, "will die."

His matter-of-factness made her tremble with fear. She still could not accept the Viking's fearless attitude toward death. She was afraid of death, afraid of the hell that would follow life. In just a few days she would be eighteen. . . . Eighteen and she had already experienced more violence than most women—nay, most men—see in a lifetime.

"On the day of my eighteenth birthday," she com-

196

mented in a low voice, "I will either be at sea with you or dead with you."

"Whatever your fate will be, it will be," he replied.

"Were I in my rightful place," she told him, "there would be a feast in my honor and many gifts."

Geir laughed and said, "At eighteen I was fighting on the Don River. Besides, what is the sense of celebrating the day of one's birth year after year?"

"Because it is the Christian way of honoring life," Maida responded, piqued at his attitude.

He moved his hand down her bare stomach.

Angry with him, Maida tried to push it away. She could not. His strength was far greater than hers.

XXVI

Maida spent a restless night. When the cocks in the stronghold began to crow, she awoke. Geir's hand was still on her breast. She looked at him. The expression on his face was relaxed. He was in a deep, untroubled sleep. She was still furious with him for his attitude toward her birthday. Despite the passion he could raise in her body, he was no more than a barbarian. And she, because of her own lust for him, would remain his thrall for the rest of her life, unless she prevented him from taking her away.

"Dear God," she whispered fervently, "I must betray him to save myself. . . . There is no other way. . . .

Lid received her courteously. But it was obvious that he was still suffering much grief over the death of his son.

He ordered beer be brought to the table for them and then he said, "I had hoped you would come to me before blood had been shed."

Maida flushed. She did not know whether he held her to blame for Bjorn's death or if he was moved to make the comment because it expressed the truth of his feelings.

"I did not think the daughter of a duke would long be satisfied with someone less than her own rank."

"I would not have wanted Bjorn to put his weight on my body," she told him bluntly. "For that, Geir is more than sufficient."

Lid's eyes went to slits; his neck and ears reddened with anger.

"I came here to ask if you have sent word to my husband or my father," she said.

He shook his head and told her that the raid by the Wendols delayed his actions. "These last few days have been very difficult for everyone."

Maida agreed.

"But now that you have come here," Lid said, "you have the hospitality of my house; and once you are here, Geir will not be able to take you back without drawing his sword against me."

"He will not hesitate to do that," Maida told him with obvious pride.

Lid cocked his head to one side; he did not understand her reason for coming to him if she did not intend to leave Geir's house, and he told her as much.

"I came to buy my freedom," she answered, avoiding his eyes.

"But you are Geir's thrall," he told her. "I can only arrange for your ransom, and the money from that will be divided up between all the men in the stronghold. I cannot sell what I do not own."

Maida wet her dry lips with a sip of beer. It was hard for her to know if Lid was playing her or she was playing him.

Then suddenly Lid stood up. He began pacing. For a while he remained silent. But finally he said, "I think I know why you have come, though I would rather hear the reason from you."

"I want to be ransomed," she said urgently. "I want to go back to my home and my husband."

"And you have the gold on your person to buy your freedom?"

"I have something worth more than gold and silver," she told him.

Lid returned to the table and he bluntly asked her if she were offering to lie with him.

"No," she answered. "But I am offering you a way to protect what is yours."

Lid nodded, poured himself another cup of beer and told her he was anxious to hear what she had to offer.

"First," she said, "before I tell you anything, I want your word that you will send a message to Algar and to my father."

"That is not easy to do, especially at this time of the year. The ferocity of the storms at sea are beyond your wildest imaginings."

Maida stood up.

Lid bid her sit down and said, "It will be difficult, but I will see that it is done."

"And that is your word?"

"That is my solemn word," Lid answered. "I will swear by Odin and Thor if that would please you."

"Your word is sufficient. . . . you will not go back on it. But now I must have your word that no harm will come to Geir—that once you thwart him, you will not take his life."

"By Thor's thunder," Lid roared, slamming his fist down on the table, "you ask and ask and as yet have given me nothing."

Maida started but within a moment she regained her composure. "I must have your word that you will do no harm to Geir," she pressed.

"Yes . . . yes, you have my word on that, too," Lid told her impatiently. "Now say what you have come to say and let me be the judge of whether or not you played me for a fool."

The words stuck in Maida's throat. To loosen them, she took several sips of beer. Then with a ragged sigh, she began to tell Lid of Geir's plan. As she spoke, she watched his face become grimmer and grimmer. Then she was done and again took several sips of beer.

"I would not have thought he would burn the ships," Lid commented, almost as if he were talking to himself. "All the rest, yes . . . but not the burning of the ships."

"I swear by my God that is what he said," Maida told him.

"You have paid well for your freedom," Lid told her. "I will keep my word, but Geir will wish he were dead. Now return to his house. I will see to the rest."

Maida nodded and stood up. She walked slowly to the door and out of the great hall.

Outside a light snow was falling. She did not enjoy betraying Geir, but she told herself that she had no choice. She could not allow him to take her away and be committed to him for the rest of her life. She was a Christian and he was a heathen; she was a married woman forced into committing adultery and much worse by— She bit her lips, and quickening her pace, she hurried back to the house.

As soon as Maida entered, she ran to the bed, flung herself down, and began to sob.

Glenna came to her and tried to comfort her.

"I have told Lid about Geir's plans," Maida wept.

Glenna moved away from her. She was too horrified to speak.

"Lid has given me his word that he will send a message to Algar and to my father."

Glenna shook her head.

"No harm will come to Geir," Maida wept. "Lid gave me his word on that, too."

"Geir loves you," Glenna shouted at her. "He loves you!"

"He owns me. I am his thrall. He has freed you but has kept me for his pleasure!"

"Your pleasure, too," Glenna shot back. "I hear you moan and thrash with delight."

Maida sprung at Glenna and slapped her across the face. Then, horrified at what she had done, she threw herself at Glenna's feet and begged to be forgiven.

"It is Geir who will have to forgive you and you who will have to forgive yourself," Glenna told her, moving away.

Maida got to her feet and sat down at the table. "Geir would have taken me with him."

Glenna went to the hearth and stirred a huge pot of stew.

"Will you betray me?" Maida asked.

"No," Glenna answered, "there has been enough betrayal here already—more than enough." And balling her fist, she pushed it against her mouth to stop herself from sobbing, but tears flowed out her eyes and down her cheeks.

Maida went to her and taking Glenna in her arms, she, too, wept.

XXVII

As THE DAYS grew closer to the dark time of the moon, Maida became more and more apprehensive. She not only feared for her life, if Geir should discover her betrayal, but she was no longer certain Lid would honor his word.

Glenna made her see the possibility that Lid might not be capable of keeping his promises by patiently explaining to her that Lid's hate for Geir must necessarily reach out to her also.

"He must see you as the cause of all of Bjorn's troubles with Geir," Glenna said. "Geir is the instrument that killed his son. But the cause must be you."

"But everyone knows there was trouble between the two of them before Geir ever took me captive," Maida answered.

"Lid is still Bjorn's father. He will not see any more of the truth than is necessary to justify his actions to himself."

Maida nodded sadly. She had unwittingly put herself, so to speak, between the jaws of two ferocious wolves, who in their savage blood lust to destroy each other, might also tear her to pieces.

The only surcease from her fears came when Geir possessed her. Then to atone for her disloyalty to him, she surrendered herself with a wild abandon that matched his. There was nothing she did not do for him. She let him use her body in any way that pleased him. She learned that pleasure also came from the other opening in her body.

After each encounter with Geir, Maida silently prayed for forgiveness and vowed to atone for the sins she committed by doing whatever penance her father confessor would place upon her, once she was back in her own country and at her husband's table again.

Almost before she realized it, the dark time of the moon was upon them. For several days she and Glenna had been packing the clothes and other things they would take with them, and Geir spent all of his time with the captains of the other ships.

Thorkel was second in command to Geir. Hougen was made captain of the third vessel, and Buliwyf commanded the fourth ship.

Geir and the other captains carefully planned their moves. Hougen and Buliwyf were responsible for firing the ships. Thorkel and his men would hold the beach until Hougen and Buliwyf were at the entrance at the cove. But it was Geir and his men who would protect the flanks of the cove from attack, while Einar steered the ship through the mouth of the cove. Once all the ships were out at sea, Geir and his men would swim out to the *Sea Bird*. Everyone agreed that Geir's part in the escape would be the most dangerous, and they greatly commended him for taking it upon himself.

When the second day of the dark time of the moon came, the wind blew fitfully from the north, bringing with it low, dark gray, scudding clouds. By late afternoon, a heavy rain began to fall. Lid looked out of a window in his great hall and nodded approvingly. Kar had foreseen the coming of the rain days before, and Lid wove his plans to trap Geir around it. He had mentioned nothing about what he knew of Geir's treachery to any of his captains or even to Kar. But what he did do, when the rain started, was to gather his captains in the great hall and pretend he had dreamt the previous night about ships and fire.

"I cannot make sense out of it," Lid commented, turning from the window to the men at the tables. "But I fear that it is a warning to guard what I have, what we all have."

Kar agreed and added, "The dark time of the moon is always full of danger."

"But what are we to guard?" Lid questioned.

"If you saw the ships burning," one of the captains said, "I say we should guard them."

Lid did not answer immediately. He spent a long time sitting in his great chair with his eyes closed. Then he stood up and asked, "Suppose we find those who would burn our ships—"

The shouting of the men to kill anyone who would so much as try to damage the ships prevented him from finishing, and with a nod, he told them to keep a careful watch over the ships. "But do not be too obvious," Lid cautioned. "And if it should be that you do find the men responsible for my dream, spare none."

His captains assured him they would obey his command. And one speaking for all of the others, said, "If they are men, they will surely bleed."

Though they were anxious to go to the ships immediately, Lid restrained them and said, "Let night come as I saw it in my dream; then go and see who seeks to destroy our ships. Now drink, eat, and enjoy yourselves." He sat back, pleased with what he had set into motion until he saw Kar looking knowingly at him. Then he was forced to turn away.

As the rain continued until the gray light of day had slipped into the long winter twilight, Maida and Glenna waited in the house for Geir to come.

Maida was unable to sit still for any length of time. She moved from the table to the hearth and back to the table again. Several times she was about to ask Glenna if she should tell Geir what she had done. But she knew what Glenna's answer would be and she was unwilling to hear it.

"Perhaps," Maida offered, "if we pray, God will hear our prayers and answer them."

"And how would you want Him to answer?" Glenna asked. "With whose victory and whose defeat?"

Maida wrung her hands in silent despair.

"You must tell Geir," Glenna finally said. "At least tell him so that so many good men will not have to die."

"I cannot," Maida wept. "I cannot . . . Lid will keep his word to me. Nothing will happen to Geir and I will be ransomed."

Glenna shook her head.

"He will . . . he will . . . he gave me his word!" Maida insisted, and she left the table to stand by the hearth once more.

"Geir is coming," Glenna said softly.

A moment later, Geir opened the door and stepped into the house. "The night is wild," he said, shaking some of the rain off his heavy woolen cloak. He helped himself to a drink of beer and told the women it was time for them to go to the ship.

Maida did not move.

Geir repeated what he had said.

"I am not going," Maida told him in a quiet voice.

Geir looked at Glenna, saw her shrug, and brought his eyes back to Maida.

"I cannot go," Maida said with a choked sob. "Lid has sent word to my father and my husband . . . I cannot go . . . I want to be ransomed."

"Ransomed!" he shouted. "You will go with me!"

"I want my rightful place," she cried. "I want to be with my husband."

206

Geir's face burned red with anger. "You have no husband," he roared at her. "You have only me!"

"In the eyes of my God," she screamed, "I am married to Algar."

"Your God has no power here" he shouted back at her. "He is blind to us and what we do. Now come!"

Maida shook her head.

"You will come," he roared, "even if I have to pull you to the ship by the hair of your head." And he went toward her.

"You and your men will never leave the stronghold," she blurted out.

Her words stopped him. His eyes went wide with surprise.

"Lid knows," Maida cried out. "He knows!"

"You told him?" Geir asked, his voice flat and menacing.

She nodded.

"Bitch!" he exclaimed in a growl, and leaping to where she stood, he struck her down to the floor. "Bitch!" he shouted and he smashed his hand across her face.

Maida's eyes blurred and blood poured from her nose and the corners of her lips.

"Tell me why." Geir demanded. "Tell me why!"

Maida shook her head and could not form the words on her trembling lips.

"And the love that you gave me meant nothing?" he rasped. "Nothing?"

She would not answer.

"If ever a man was made a fool by a woman, I am that man," Gier said.

"Kill me!" Maida suddenly shouted, baring her breasts to him. "Use your sword and kill me now."

"If I do it," he answered harshly, "I will do it when I

207

choose. You will have no say in that matter. Now you will come with me. If we die, then we will die together.'' Without waiting for her to answer, he slung Maida over his shoulder and rushed into the night.

Glenna ran after him.

He ran straight to Thorkel's house and giving Maida over into the hands of Einar, he told him to take her and Glenna to the ship. ''If one or the other of them attempts to flee,'' he said, ''kill the both of them.''

Einar questioningly raised his eyebrows.

''Will you follow my order?'' Geir asked sharply.

Einar nodded and left with the women.

''We have to change our plan,'' Geir told Thorkel and he quickly explained what Maida had done.

Thorkel's face became very grim and he said, ''Now whether we succeed or fail, we are all outlaws.''

''We will succeed,'' Geir said and asked Thorkel to bring Hougen and Buliwyf to him. ''I will be in my house. I do not expect anyone will look for me there. Tell the men what I told you and tell them that we will do what we must do to assure our success.''

Thorkel hurried from his house and Geir went quickly back to his own. Several times he saw the shadows of Lid's men dart between the houses, but in the dark of the rain-splashed night, no man would call out to another for fear the man might turn out to be a troll or the ghost of a man. Some people in the stronghold had already claimed to have seen the ghosts of those whom the Wendols had slain.

Geir gained the safety of his own house without difficulty. He sat down near the low fire in the hearth and stretched his hands toward it to warm them.

His anger with Maida was great enough to make him gnash his teeth. He could not believe she would eagerly mouth his organ and then betray him. Such duplicity was beyond his comprehension. Though she had never told him she loved him, all she had done to please him had been enough proof of her feelings for him: or could she have been pretending all those times he had possessed her?

Geir left the hearth. He strode around the room. He had never been played false by a woman before, and the experience had given him a sick feeling in the pit of his belly—almost as if he had recently eaten some tainted meat or fish. He continued to walk from one side of the room to the other until his other captains arrived.

"Lid's men are all over the stronghold," Buliwyf said in a growly voice. He was a short barrel-chested man with a broken nose and huge hands.

"I saw them," Geir responded. "But I think we can outwit them—we will take Lid with us."

The other captains looked at each other, nodded, and immediately followed Geir out into the rain. They made their way to the other side of the stronghold and stood in the shadow of a nearby building to look at Lid's great hall.

Yellow light showed through many of the windows, and now and then a man entered or one left.

Geir unsheathed his sword; the three men with him bared their weapons, too. Following Geir, they made their way to the rear of the great hall, paused long enough to slip their heavy cloaks back on their shoulders, and silently rushed into the great hall.

Geir was the first to reach Lid, who was seated in his great chair. He put the point of his sword against the chieftain's neck and shouted for every man in the hall to throw his sword to the floor.

An angry shout came from the men.

"Tell them, Lid," Geir said, putting more pressure on the sword.

"Obey him!" Lid called out, moving his head far to one side and rolling his eyes up to his nephew.

The swords clattered to the floor.

"Lid will come with me," Geir said, "and the rest of you go out into the night and tell your men that I have Lid and I will kill him, if anyone should try to stop us. Now, Lid—up!"

Lid did not resist; he knew Geir was desperate and would not hesitate to kill him or anyone else.

Within a matter of minutes, Geir, his captains, and Lid were racing down to the ships. Lid slipped and fell several times, but Geir always dragged him to his feet.

Geir took Lid aboard the *Sea Bird* and ordered him securely bound; then he and many of the men ran toward the entrance of the cove.

Within minutes Hougen and Buliwyf set fire to the ships on the beach, making sure that each would burn despite the heavy rain.

Thorkel held his men on the shore to let the other two captains get under way. And by the time his men were at the oars, the light from the burning ships glowed red in the night.

Geir posted his men on either side of the cove's mouth. Several times they heard the cries of Lid's men, but none came to attack them. From where they were, the fires were almost wholly obscured by the rain, though now and then a sudden gust of wind made them suddenly very much brighter.

The last ship to clear the cover was Thorkel's and when it did, he called out to Geir, telling him that the *Sea Bird* was coming close to shore to pick him and the other men up. Geir and those with him splashed into the heavy sea. With long, powerful strokes they drove their bodies through the icy water toward the ship. The sea was running very high and swimming was extremely arduous.

Geir could not see the ship, but now and then he heard the sound of the horn and swam toward it. His limbs became tired and his chest ached as he gulped air and then swam below the surface, where he did not have to struggle against the waves so much.

Then suddenly he saw the ship. It was to the right of him. He headed for it. A short time later, his hands were on the lead oar on the left side, and he was quickly hauled aboard.

Gasping for air, he turned around and sought the hand of the man who followed him.

In all, he held out his hand to twenty men. And then he stood at the side of the ship a long time waiting for the other four men before he ordered the men to put to sea.

"The sea people have taken their due," Geir said, moving to the stern. And with a sigh of exhaustion, he sat down in the stern sheets next to Maida and Glenna.

One of the men took his wet cloak off and threw a heavy bearskin robe over him. Another gave him some mead to drink.

Geir ordered Lid to be brought to him. He had seen him in the bow when he first clambered aboard.

"Tomorrow morning I will set you free. You will be able to make your way back to the stronghold. I had to take you with me," Geir said.

"And I will have to hunt you down," Lid answered, "and kill you."

"Yes," Geir told him with a weary nod, "you will have to do that."

Lid remained silent.

"Suppose," Geir said, "I were to ask you to tell me about my father and my mother. What would you say?"

Lid gathered a wad of spittle in his mouth and letting it fly to one side, he said, "Since you are more of Njal's blood than mine and more like him than like me, ask him.

Perhaps he will answer you before he kills you.''

"And you will not answer me?''

Lid shook his head.

"Put him back in the bow,'' Geir told the man who brought Lid to him. "We must stand out to sea for the rest of the night.'' And lowering his head on his arms, Geir quickly fell into a deep sleep.

XXVIII

MAIDA AWOKE WITH a start; for a moment she had no idea where she was. She still possessed remnants of a dream in which she was once again in the warmth and security of her father's great hall. That memory passed in an instant and she became aware of everything around her.

The sea had calmed and the rain had changed to snow. Glenna was sleeping soundly next to her and Geir was at the helm. The crew and the other people were covered with snow. Except for the rhythmic sound made by the oars as they dug into the leaden surface of the sea, all she could hear was the hiss of the falling snow.

Suddenly she realized that during the night someone had thrown the white bearskin robe over her. She glanced up at Geir, knowing it was he.

From her place to his was scarcely two good-sized paces, yet the falling snow rendered Geir more like a phantom than a man. That he had once again altered the course of her life was something she found difficult to accept, and yet she knew she would have to. He had wrested all hope of her ever being ransomed. She would remain his thrall until the end of her days. In her own mind, she was undeserving of such an outrageously hard fate. Closing her eyes, she lifted her face toward the falling snow and prayed to God for His mercy, though deep in her heart she was beginning to doubt He had any power over the Vikings. . . .

The sound of a shell horn abruptly ended Maida's prayers and roused everyone on the ship. Within minutes identical reverberations trembled through the snow-filled air.

Then Geir called out to his captains, telling them he was turning toward the land that lay unseen to the left of the ship, in order to put Lid ashore.

And each of them answered they would follow close behind him, in case he needed their swords.

Geir shouted his thanks; then he ordered his crew to quicken their strokes, while he pointed the prow of the *Sea Bird* to the land. After a while, he gave the helm over to Einar and sent a man to the bow, instructing him to keep a sharp lookout for an opening between two huge rocks that looked like the trunks of trees. He came down to the stern sheets and had Lid brought to him.

"In a while, you will be set free," Geir said, cutting his uncle's bonds. "You will be no more than a half day's walk from the stronghold."

"Am I to thank you?" Lid asked icily.

Geir shrugged. "I could have killed you."

Lid moved his eyes to Maida. There was smoke in them and in a slow voice, he said, "You betrayed Geir and you betrayed me; I think Bjorn was right when he accused you of practicing trollcraft. What you have begun, Saxon woman, only the fates now know where it will end. But because of you I have lost a son and there is enmity between myself and Geir that will not be satisfied until one or the other of us is dead." He looked toward Geir. "You have my word, nephew. I will hunt you down and kill you, even if I spend the rest of life trying to do it."

214

Geir accepted his uncle's threat without rancor and with the simple acknowledgment that in his circumstances he would do the same.

Maida looked questioningly at the two men. She could not believe that they were sitting there calmly talking about how in the future they would kill one another.

Lid said, "The Saxon woman will bring you nothing but difficulty. Why not set her ashore with me? I might be able to dissuade my men from demanding your blood."

Maida drew back toward Glenna. Her heart began to race. After what she had done, she was afraid that Geir would accede to his uncle's request.

"And what would you do with her?" Geir questioned.

"Sacrifice her to the spirit of my son," Lid replied without hesitation. "But first I would see that as many of my men that wanted her, had her."

Trembling now, Maida moved her eyes to Geir.

"She deserves no better," Geir answered.

"Oh God, no!" Maida wailed.

Geir struck her across the face.

She recoiled from the shock and bit her lips to hold back the sobs.

"I will keep her, uncle," Geir said. "Her life with me will not be pleasant, I assure you of that."

"In the end," Lid replied, "she will work her trollcraft on you again."

"Then it is my destiny for that to happen," Geir told him.

"I am giving you the opportunity to change it."

"You should know, uncle," Geir said. "It is even foolish to try to do that."

"And is that your last word on the matter?" Lid questioned.

"Yes," Geir said and he offered his uncle food and drink.

Lid accepted and, as he ate, he asked Geir if he intended to go to Njal.

Geir nodded and said, "A man must know who and what he is, and since you will only tell me I am closer by blood to Njal than to you, I must know how close."

"And then what will you do?"

Geir waved his hand to encompass all the people in the *Sea Bird* and those in the other vessels. "They look to me to lead them," he said, "and I will do the best I can."

Lid drank a full cup of beer before he answered. "Remember, nephew, I will seek you out and kill you."

Geir nodded. And after a short silence, he said, "I am sorry we must part enemies. But be assured, uncle, I do not fear your coming, nor will I run onto your blade as Bjorn ran onto mine. I have done nothing to shame myself in the eyes of other men. I do what I must do in order to survive. I would rather be your friend than your enemy. But if the fates have cast me as your enemy, then know, uncle, I will be as ruthless an enemy as you have ever encountered."

"Then why not kill me now?" Lid challenged.

"I spare your life out of my love for you," Geir explained.

Lid turned away and did not speak again. Even when Geir let him leap free of the *Sea Bird,* he said nothing. But when the ship was just within hailing distance, Lid called out, "Geir, I will hunt you and all those who have followed you and when I find you, I will spare none!"

"It will be a hard fight," Geir shouted back.

If Lid replied, no one was able to hear him.

Geir ordered the *Sea Bird* turned westward; the other ships followed, and then more to himself than to Maida or Glenna, he said aloud, "We will be a long time looking for Njal's stronghold—a long time!'' He reached down, picked up his cup, and drained from it what was left of the beer. A moment later, he leaped up to the stern deck and took the helm from Einar, telling him to eat and drink.

"I was afraid he would give me to Lid,'' Maida said to Glenna in a low voice.

"Then you are a fool!''

XXIX

THOUGH HE WAS tired and hungry when he arrived back at the stronghold, Lid found his way there without any difficulty. Toward afternoon the snow had stopped and the sky was bright with sunshine. Long before he reached the stronghold, he could see the smoke from the burning ships.

As soon as he was seated in his chair in the great hall, Lid was told that the Wendols had struck again during the night and had killed several of the guards and dogs on the wall, but they had not entered the stronghold. Then Kar explained that the Wendols had hung Gruden from the cliffs. The birds were already at her.

"Does she scream?" Lid asked.

Kar shook his head. "She will last a long time up there."

"Do you read it as a good or a bad sign?"

"Changes are coming our way," Kar answered. "Changes are coming our way."

Lid accepted the soothsayer's words with a silent nod. Thus far everything he had predicted had come to pass. Geir was again at sea, and Bjorn had voyaged to the land of the dead.

Lid did not ask Kar for any more information. He turned his attention to appointing several men who would be responsible for rebuilding the ships. As he had guessed, nothing of their hulls could be saved.

"Until we have our ships again, all of us are thralls to the land," Lid told his men. "But once we have them, we will seek Geir and his followers out and kill all of them."

A great roar of approval arose from the men in the hall.

Lid ate, drank, and then he set out with his men to pick the trees that would be cut down and shaped into the ships.

For several days the thwacking of axes could be heard in the forest near the stronghold where the trees were felled. The trunks were stripped and dragged by men and oxen to the shore of the cove. It was slow, arduous work, and while it was going on, the Wendols watched from the cliff, just above the place from where the half-eaten body of Gruden hung.

Then one afternoon, when the sun was low enough in the west to spill the yellow of gold across it, the lookouts for the stronghold sounded the alarm. And pointing seaward, so that the others could see the direction from which the danger was approaching, they shouted, "Ships . . . ships . . . ships!"

Lid and his captains rushed down to the cove. They were fully armed and prepared to defend the stronghold and if possible capture the ships.

"Saxon ships," Lid said, recognizing the difference between those the Vikings sailed and those the peoples of other nations used.

"One came into the cove with the shield of peace on its mast," one of Lid's captains commented.

The ship moved slowly. It was low in the water with a high stern and two small square sails.

A large dark-complexioned man stood on the stern and

when the ship came within hailing distance of the shore, he called out, "I am Algar. I come in peace to speak with the chieftain Lid."

The Vikings looked at each other and waited for Lid to speak.

"I have been told that Lid makes his place here on Gottland," Algar shouted. "And I and my men have traveled all the way from our country with the permission of our king to ransom my wife Maida."

"I am Lid," Lid answered, waving his arm over his head so that Algar might see who was addressing him.

"We come in peace," Algar said.

"Then you may stay in peace," Lid answered. "Your ships will be safe in our cove and your men will be safe among my men. Will you come with me to be my guest in my great hall?"

Algar agreed and in a small boat he quickly came ashore. As soon as he exchanged greetings with Lid, he asked to be allowed to see his wife.

"She is gone," Lid told him, realizing his guest carried Geir's sword Bluetooth.

Kar noticed the sword, too, and nudged him to call his attention to it.

But Lid ignored the soothsayer and told Algar, "Your wife was stolen by Geir and his men."

Algar's face turned red with rage. "Did he know of my coming?" he asked.

Lid shook his head. "It is a long story," he told his guest. "One best told over food and drink."

"And Maida," Algar asked, "what of her?"

"Come," Lid said, putting his hand on Algar's shoulder, "the night has not yet begun and the story is very long."

Lid provided Algar and his vassals with meat, bread, and great flagons of strong beer. They had been at sea for several weeks and were delighted with the opportunity to eat fresh food.

Algar told his host that he had petitioned the king for men and ships shortly after Geir's raid and had been searching for the stronghold for a long time.

"And how did you finally find it?" Lid asked.

"Some days ago," Algar explained, tearing the meat from a chicken leg with his hands, "one of the lookouts saw smoke to the east. We continued to sail until we came here."

"That smoke will be the undoing of Geir," Lid commented with a smile. And then he spun out the story of how Geir had refused to give Maida for ransom and how he used her to satisfy his lust.

Algar listened and several times he swore vengeance.

Then Lid said, "He took her by force and burned our ships to stop us from giving chase."

He said nothing about the fact that he had been taken hostage, or the death of Bjorn, or even that he suspected Maida of using trollcraft on Geir as well as on Bjorn. Later he would give the Saxon reason to think that his wife had bewitched Geir and wanted him between her naked thighs in preference to her rightful husband.

Algar was red with anger. He shouted curses at Geir and cried out that all he asked of God was the chance to kill him. Then suddenly he stopped shouting, and turning to Lid, he asked, "I will pay you well if you will tell me where I might find Geir."

Lid waved his offer aside and said, "We both have reasons to kill him. Suppose we join our forces together? Our numbers will be greater than any he can muster."

"By the living God," Algar shouted, "I will join with you. I will even help you rebuild your ships."

Lid shook the Saxon's hand, and many toasts were drunk in honor of their new alliance.

"And where do you think Geir will be?" Algar asked.

"In Njal's stronghold," he answered. "When we find it, we will find Geir."

His words brought a sudden silence to the hall, as Saxon and Viking alike knew and feared the man whose name was Njal.

XXX

GEIR'S SMALL FLEET made its way along the southern coast of Norway and then turned south to the land of the Danes. Njal's stronghold was somewhere along the coast, but neither Geir nor his captains knew exactly where.

Geir said very little to Maida, and sometimes he even spoke to her through Glenna. But whenever the fleet stopped for the night and camp was made on some deserted island or at the mouth of a small river, he spent the night with her. His lovemaking was savage and most often her response, though she tried to avoid it, was just as fierce.

Day after day, the ships plowed through the sea. Geir used Elton's new rigging to get the most out of the wind. There were many days when the men at the oars did nothing. The weather was brutally harsh, and many of the smaller children wept from the bitter cold. But miraculously none of them died.

Not once was another sail seen, and at night, when Geir chose some rocky island or a deserted strand of beach for a campsite, he surrounded it with many guards. His only respite came when he lay with Maida. But even then he did not seem to be totally at ease with himself.

By his actions toward her, Maida was certain he no longer cared for anything about her. He treated her roughly, sometimes striking her across the face or kicking her shins. He used her for satisfying his lust in a way that was almost brutal. He seemed to want nothing else from her.

One day Maida told Glenna that Geir would probably sell her to someone in Njal's stronghold.

"He is very angry," Glenna answered.

"And I have welts all over me because he is angry," she answered with a cry.

"You must make your peace with him," Glenna advised, "lest he do something that each of you will regret."

Maida spent the entire day thinking about Glenna's words. Many times she looked up to where Geir was at the helm. If he saw her, he did not give even the slightest indication that he had.

But at night when Geir came to her in the tent and began to lift her shift, Maida put her hand on his and stayed its movement.

"Wait," she told him, "I want to speak with you before you take what is not really yours to take."

He slapped her face, but she did not cry out. "Listen to me," she said. "You must listen to me." Maida felt his hand move away from her body. She could see his face hovering in the darkness above her own. His eyes were two bright circles of light and he smelled of the sea.

"I am sorry for what I did," she told him.

He did not answer.

"I ask you to forgive me."

"You betrayed me. If you were anyone else, I would have killed you. Our way is to hold each man and woman responsible for what they do. Bjorn knew that when he ran onto my sword."

"Christ's way is the way of forgiveness," she said softly. "He taught us to turn the other cheek."

Geir shook his head. "I do not understand that. A man must answer hurt for hurt; otherwise he is no man."

"Then why did you let me live?" she asked.

Geir shrugged.

"You are not happy with me," Maida pressed. "Why did you let me live?"

Geir uttered a deep sigh. He lay back and put his hands under his head. "All these days and nights," he said in a low voice, "I have asked myself the same question . . . There is not one man in the crew or any of the other ships who would stop me if I killed you even now."

Maida trembled but she did not speak.

Geir turned his head toward her and he said, "When I first saw you, I wanted you and I still do. That is why I did not kill you."

His words were without guile; he simply told her what he felt and Maida was immensely pleased. He was still as much her captive as she was his. She put her hand on his chest and whispered, "Now I will give you what you want, Geir. I will give you everything you could ever want from a woman."

He turned and passionately embraced her.

Maida met his passion with her own and when she reached the height of her ecstasy, she cried his name over and over again. Later, when they slept, she felt his hand on her breast and she smiled with satisfaction. He had not held her that way since they had left Gottland. She knew she no longer had any reason to fear him.

Whole days and nights were filled with wind-blown snow and rain. But the ships continued moving southward along the coast. There was no sign of life, and more often than not, the land they saw was covered with a deep snow.

Geir was by turns tender and fierce but he was no longer cruel. He never struck or kicked her. Sometimes after he possessed her, he would ask her about Christ.

Though Maida thought the questions blasphemous, coming so soon after their sinful lovemaking, she did her best to answer them.

That Christ would not fight for His life sorely troubled

225

Geir. "If a man does not fight for his life, what right has he to live?"

"He was the son of God," Maida answered, trying to recall what Father Quinell had taught her. "He was born of a virgin—"

Geir burst into a hearty laugh.

"It is true," Maida said solemnly.

But Geir only laughed harder.

"Christ was begotten so that He could die for our sins," she told him.

Geir stopped laughing and said, "No man should die for another's sins."

"But Christ did," she exclaimed.

And Geir answered. "I have yet to meet a man who would willingly die for someone else."

Though their conversations usually ended with Geir saying that her Christ would not survive long among his gods, Maida could tell he was thinking about Him, though she did not know which way his thoughts tended.

On days when the sun shone and the sea was calm, she stood next to Geir at the helm; sometimes it was she who held the *Sea Bird* steady on its course. She soon became as good as Einar, and Geir often teased Einar about it, much to the amusement of the other members of the crew.

Einar would only shake his head and say, "But Geir, you should know the difference between us, since it is she you lie with and me you order about."

Such an answer brought tears of laughter from everyone, and a red face from Maida.

Then one afternoon when Maida was at the helm and Geir was sleeping in the stern sheets, the sky suddenly turned the color of old milk and the sea became agitated. Suddenly the helm was ripped from Maida's grasp. The *Sea Bird* swung sideways.

Geir bolted upright. He tried to gain the pitching stern

226

deck, but the motion of the ship flung him back against the oarsmen.

The wind began to howl and the waves were swiftly transformed into towering black mountains.

Again and again Maida tried to grasp hold of the helm, but each time she reached for it, it whipped away from her.

Geir fought his way up to the deck. He crawled on his belly, finally making it to where Maida was fighting to keep her balance.

"Get down," he shouted above the wild screaming of the wind. "Get down on your belly!" Then he made a desperate lunge for the helm, and grabbing it, he tried to hold onto it. But the ship's movement tore it from his grasp, and the *Sea Bird* wallowed under a wall of water. An instant later the wall broke and poured over the ship.

Geir grasped the tail of the dragon and clung tightly to it. Above the sound of the water and wind, he could hear the screams of the women and children. He wiped the water from his eyes and once more lunged at the helm. This time he was able to hold it. And he shouted to the oarsmen to bring the ship into the wind.

Another wave broke over the *Sea Bird.* The sail crashed down on the ship and Einar was knocked to the deck of the ship by a blow from the spar.

"Cut the sail away," Geir roared.

Several of the men used their swords on the lines. Once the sail was free, it was grabbed by the wind.

The *Sea Bird* made it to the crest of another wave. Geir caught a glimpse of only two of his ships before his own vessel slid down into another deep trough.

The efforts of his men allowed him to gain steerageway, and he was able to keep control of the *Sea Bird* for the remainder of the storm, which passed just as quickly as it came.

When the wind subsided, Geir realized that several

people had been swept overboard. Glenna had been one of them.

Maida stared up at him and shaking her head, she cried, "I tried to hold onto her, but I could not. She was torn out of my hands." And she held them to him. "She was torn out of these two hands."

Geir had no words of consolation for her, and he said, "There are women and children who need your help. See to them."

"But I loved Glenna—"

"And those are my people," he told her sharply.

He did not have to say he loved them; Maida knew that well enough, and with a nod, she moved toward those who needed her help.

A short while later, it was clear to Geir that Buliwyf's ship was lost. There was no sign of it, and though he and the other two captains spent the next two days looking for survivors, they saw only open ocean.

A spare sail was raised and rigged on the *Sea Bird* in a small cove along the coast of the Danes. The survivors of the storm counted themselves lucky not to have met the same fate as those aboard Buliwyf's ship. And they took time to sacrifice several goats to Njord, the god of the wind and the sea.

Though Maida would not take part in the sacrificial rites, she understood how the people felt and she prayed too, giving thanks to Christ for having saved her life. She also prayed for Glenna's immortal soul to finally find peace in heaven.

That night, when Geir held Maida in his arms, he said to her, "I am sorry that you lost Glenna. She was a good woman."

From those few words, Maida understood that Geir was deeply touched by Glenna's death, and she told him, "I prayed for her."

"The sea people have her now," he said wearily, "and they will never give her up."

"But Christ—"

"I do not want to hear about Him," Geir told her. "I am tired and I want to sleep." He put his hand on her breast and almost immediately fell into a deep sleep.

Maida closed her eyes; she silently prayed to God, asking him to keep Geir safe from harm. Then she added, "And forgive me, Lord, for having fallen in love with him. I tried not to, dear Lord, but he has—" She could not tell God how Geir put fire in her body; she could hardly tell herself that what she previously thought to have been the Devil's work was no more than her own passion rising to meet Geir's. . . .

Four days after the storm, Einar was at the helm when from Thorkel's ship came the cry of "Sail landward! . . . Sail landward! . . . Sail landward! . . ."

Geir was on his feet in an instant. He rushed to the bow of the ship. There were two ships, and each of them was sailing close to the coast.

"We will follow them," Geir shouted to Thorkel, who relayed the message to Hougen.

Geir ordered Einar to the top of the mast while he took over the helm. To give himself more speed, he put the oarsmen to work.

"Black dragons on the sails," Einar shouted. "I see them clearly."

Geir called out to Thorkel, telling him that the two vessels belonged to Njal.

"But are they sailing to or from the stronghold?" Thorkel questioned.

"We will follow to find out."

"What if they should turn on us?"

"We will fight and hope to take some prisoners," Geir answered with a shout.

Geir's ships kept after Njal's vessels for the better part of the day.

Just before the sky in the west turned the color of salmon flesh, the two ships lowered their sails and turned into the land.

Geir ordered his men to halt their rowing and lowered his sail. As soon as the three ships were close to one another, he told Thorkel and Hougen that Njal's stronghold might be up the river, or the ships just stopped for the night. He suggested they spend the night where they were. "If we do not see them leave in the morning," he said, "we will turn upriver ourselves."

"With the women and children?" Thorkel asked.

"Yes, with them," Geir said. "We come in peace."

"And should we be attacked?"

"Once we are in the dragon's lair," Geir told him, "we will have to pray to Thor that he believes we mean him no harm."

"We will be putting more trust in the dragon than we would in ourselves," Hougen commented.

Geir agreed. "I think the women and children will convince him we have not come to fight."

"Perhaps one ship should be left at the mouth of the river," Thorkel suggested.

"If we give Njal any reason to think we have not come in peace," Geir responded, "you can be sure he will attack us."

Thorkel nodded.

"We will move closer to the river's mouth," Geir said, "and keep watch all through the night. By daybreak, if the two ships do not put to sea, we will go upriver. Each of our ships will have the red shield of peace at its mast head and our dragon heads will be covered. No shield will be shown on the side of our ships, and none of the men will be armed."

With a wry smile, Thorkel said, "I have always wanted to sail between the teeth of a dragon, and by Thor's hammer, tomorrow I will finally get my wish."

Geir and Hougen laughed heartily, and so did the crews of all of the ships.

XXXI

AT FIRST LIGHT, Geir ordered his ships to sail up river. The sky was dull but the wind had dropped off and except for the ever-present heave of the sea, the water was calm.

Geir's vessel, the *Sea Bird,* was in the lead. Hougen followed with his ship, the *Laughing Bear* and Thorkel completed the line in his, the *Big Seal.* The men rowed silently; their faces wet with sweat and their breaths steaming in the cold air. The women and children held silently to their places in the center of the ship.

Each of the vessels had the red shield of peace on its mast and was sailing with dragon heads covered. No shields were displayed along their sides and all of the weapons were carefully set out so that anyone who saw them would quickly see they were not armed.

Geir beckoned to Maida and bid her stand by him as he swung the *Sea Bird* into the mouth of the river. The banks of the river were heavily wooded.

"Everything is so still," Maida commented, having to clear her throat before she spoke. Though she was terribly frightened, she tried not to show it.

Geir nodded and he was about to answer when the stillness was suddenly slashed by the shrill sounds of a shell horn. With a nod, he said, "Everything is not really so still." With a wave of his hand toward the banks of the river, he told her, "Many pairs of eyes have been watching us."

As the three ships swung around the first bend in the

232

river, the shell horn sounded again. And almost immediately, armed men showed themselves on the banks of the river.

Thorkel hailed Geir and bid him look to their rear.

Geir turned and saw they were being followed by six small ships. All of them were well equipped to give battle and all were fully loaded with berserks, who even from a distance, looked more like wolves than men. He felt Maida tremble and facing the prow of the ship, he said, "To show any signs of fear is to invite death."

Maida nodded and fervently prayed, beseeching God not to abandon her.

Geir ordered the men to slow the tempo of their rowing. As the three ships came around the second bend in the river, they found themselves in the very midst of Njal's stronghold. The river actually snaked its way through part of it. But on every side, it was protected by high walls of earth, so that anyone looking at it from the sea or the land would tend to think it was no more than a hillock that had been cut through by the river.

Geir nodded approvingly. Njal had taken the best features of the land and put them to his own use.

"It hardly looks much different from Lid's stronghold," Maida said.

"See that stone house?" Geir told her, gesturing to the left. "That must be Njal's great hall. It is very much bigger than Lid's."

Suddenly a man from the shore shouted, "What business do you have here?"

Geir answered, "I have come to speak with Njal, if this is where he lives."

"Who are you?" the man called out.

"Geir . . . And my other captains are Hougen and Thorkel. We come from Lid's stronghold on the island of Gottland."

The man who asked the questions turned to another man, who was standing slightly to his rear and he spoke to him.

Maida glanced at one side of the river and then the other. Both shores were crowded with men and women and children.

"That must be Njal," Geir whispered.

"The man who spoke to you, or the other one?" Maida questioned, looking toward the two men again.

The man who Geir said was Njal looked out at them. He was broad shouldered and almost as tall as Geir. His blond hair was almost all gray. His face was weatherbeaten to a dark leathery color. The lid over his left eye drooped. He wore a horned helmet, a heavy black cloak, leggings, good boots, and a sword. He said something to the other man, who then called out.

"Who is the woman standing next to you, Geir?"

"She is Maida."

"Your wife?"

"My thrall."

Maida stiffened.

And Geir quickly told her, "I must speak the truth to him, or none of us will ever leave here alive."

Maida did not answer. A thrall was always negotiable property.

Njal stepped forward and gave Geir permission to beach his ships. "You and your captains will come with me to my great hall. Your men, the women and children with them, and your livestock, will remain on the riverbank until I know more about this visit."

Geir thanked him and ordered the *Sea Bird* beached. Hougen and Thorkel brought their ships on shore, too. Geir told Einar to fire the ships if Njal's men made any hostile move against them, and to fight until none were left.

Njal came to where the ships were beached. The exchange of greetings between him and Geir was guarded. He looked at Maida and said, "She is not a Viking."

"Saxon," Geir said.

"Bring her with you," Njal told him.

Geir called to Maida, and when she joined him, he told her that her presence was requested by Njal.

"You honor me," Maida said, looking at the battle-scarred chieftain. Now that she was close to him, she could see that his dark leathery face was marred with white scar marks and wrinkled around the corners of his eyes, which though blue like Geir's, had a snakelike look about them.

Njal was pleased that she could understand and speak the language of the Norsemen and he commented, "All too many thralls, though they give good sport in bed, can only moan and groan to show their pleasure. But a woman who can tell you about it—ah, that is a pleasure in itself!" A dull light came into his serpentlike eyes.

Maida flushed.

"So you are one of those who cry out in your moment of passion," he laughed with delight. "No wonder Geir had you at his side when he was at the helm."

"I do what a thrall must do to please her master."

The bitterness of Maida's answer went unnoticed by Njal, and with a vigorous nod he responded, "There is no reason for it to be any different." Then, gesturing toward his great hall, he said, "We will go there and talk. It is far too cold to stand here." He glanced up at the gray sky, sniffed the air, and told them that snow was on the way.

XXXII

NJAL'S GREAT HALL was on the right bank of the river. Its walls were made of stone and it was roofed over with stout timbers. Inside there were many tables and benches. To one side was a huge hearth; close to it was Njal's table. He sat with ten of his bravest captains; five to the left of him and five to the right.

Weath, the man who hailed Geir, was something of a counselor to Njal. But he was also a warrior, as was evidenced by his many scars and the good sword he wore at his waist. He, too, sat at Njal's table.

The hall was lit by torches, and thralls ran back and forth between the cooking place, which was outside the hall and tables, with huge platters of meats and enormous cruses of beer, ale and mead.

Seated in front of the Njal's table was a bard who strummed a lute and sang in a pleasant voice about the deeds of Njal and all of the captains that sat at his table.

Maida, Geir, Hougen and Thorkel were guests and therefore they, too, sat at Njal's table, though all were put together on the left of the chieftain.

Njal urged Geir and his men to eat and drink.

"I need no urging," Geir said, tearing into a piece of roasted lamb. "I and those with me have been at sea for a long time and sorely miss hot food."

Njal answered that he, too, was able to recall the sharp longing for fresh meat after having gone without it for a long time.

Maida realized the conversation between Geir and Njal was about everything but the reason why Geir had come to the stronghold. She bent close to Geir and in a whisper asked him why he had not spoken of his reason for coming.

"Njal will ask," he answered. "I am his guest and must give him leave to conduct the conversation as he sees fit."

"What are you whispering about to the woman?" Njal asked, though it seemed he was too busy talking to Weath to notice anything.

Geir told him.

"She is right," Njal said. "It is time for you to tell me what brought you here."

A sudden silence fell in Njal's great hall. All eyes turned toward Geir.

Geir stood up and looked at the men on either side of Njal. They returned his stare with their own. His eyes went to Njal and he said, "I have come to ask you a question."

Njal looked from left to right and then at Geir. "No one has ever come here to do that," he admitted. "You are the first."

"I was told I belong more to you by blood than to anyone else," Geir said.

The silence in the great hall seemed to deepen. Maida looked at the faces of the men at the table. Not one had changed from what it had been before Geir spoke and yet there was a palpable difference in the hall.

"And who told you this?"

"Lid."

"Your chieftain?"

"No longer my chieftain," Geir answered, "but still my uncle."

Njal rubbed his gray beard and asked Weath, "What do you make of this?"

"The ghost of Edgtho came to you not four nights ago," Weath answered, "and told you a visitor would soon be here."

Njal nodded and said to Geir, "Edgtho was slain at sea in a battle between four of my ships and three of—"

"Was one of your ships rammed?" Geir asked.

"Yes."

"I was the one who fought your ships," Geir told him. "I rammed one and my captains and I fought the others off."

A loud angry murmur came from every side of the great hall.

With a quick movement of his hand, Njal silenced them. "You fought well," he said.

"As your men did," Geir answered.

"But not well enough to kill or capture you?"

Geir shrugged.

"Why should Lid tell you that you are more of my blood than of anyone else's?" Njal asked.

"I do not know," Geir answered.

"But surely you did not take three ships with men, women, children—"

"You will better understand me when I tell you the whole story from the very beginning," Geir said.

"Tell it then," Njal responded, leaning forward with his elbows on the table.

Geir took a deep breath and looking straight at Njal he told him about his raid of Algar's village, how Bjorn refused to come to his aid, how he was taken prisoner, and all the events that led up to the taking of Lid hostage and releasing him the following morning.

Njal listened to all he heard with great interest and when Geir was finished, he said, "I fear your uncle has misled you, we have no blood in common, Geir. We are strangers."

Geir rubbed his chin. He knew there was no point to any further questions. He shrugged. "Who knows? Perhaps by sending me into your stronghold, Lid hoped to have me killed."

Njal laughed heartily and said, "Well, we will fool your uncle; you and your men may rest here for the remainder of the winter. When spring comes, you can leave if you choose or stay with us. If you stay with us, you will fight as we fight."

Geir nodded and told his host that he and his men thanked him for his hospitality. "We will stay and in the spring we will put the matter of leaving or remaining with you to vote. If we should decide to stay, the command of my ships will remain with me."

"Are you telling me or asking me?" Njal questioned with a frown.

"When it comes to the matter of my commanding," Geir answered, "I am telling you."

Njal's eyes became slits; his face took on a reddish hue.

"I would just as soon take my chances at sea," Geir told him, "than to remain here without each of us knowing the other's mind."

Njal agreed. Then he said that any captain who fought against his ships as well as Geir had must surely be the equal of his own captains, and therefore he saw no reason to object to Geir continuing in the command of his own ships, should his men decide to stay. He offered a toast to Geir and his men.

Geir toasted Njal's hospitality and the pleasure of coming to know him. Much later when most of the men at the tables were drunk, Maida said to Geir, "Njal knows more than he has told you."

Geir shrugged and said, "If he does, I cannot pull it out of him; he will tell me or not, as he wills."

XXXIII

GEIR AND HIS men were allowed to cut down trees and make shelters for themselves at the far side of the stronghold. The men were permitted to wear their weapons and the women and children mixed freely with those in the stronghold.

Geir spent a great deal of time with Njal, who asked many questions about Lid, but managed to avoid answering any questions about himself.

Then one day when the two men were sitting at Njal's table, Geir said, "I was told that you killed my father in a raid on the stronghold."

Njal shrugged and said, "I might have; it was a long time ago and I do not remember."

But there was something in the tone of Njal's voice that made Geir suspect that his host did indeed remember.

"Are you angry with me because of it?" Njal asked.

"As you said," Geir responded, "it was a long time ago; I do not remember my father." And he continued to drink, until his head was full of fog.

The days passed swiftly. Maida soon realized that Geir was seriously thinking of remaining with Njal, though he never mentioned as much to her. One late afternoon, when she was at the river getting water for the evening meal, she was approached by an old woman whose back was weighted down with a huge hump and whose walk was sideways, like a crab.

"I am called Helga," the woman told her in a scratchy

voice. "And you are Geir's thrall, Maida, a Saxon woman, who speaks our language."

Maida nodded.

"I knew Geir was coming," Helga said. "As soon as Njal asked me to give him the meaning of his dream, I knew it."

"Are you a spaewoman?"

"I am what I am," Helga answered.

Maida crossed herself; never before had she spoken to someone who was a sorceress, a witch.

Helga gave a toothless grin and she said, "Blood draws to blood."

"Whose blood?"

"Geir and Njal's," the hag answered. Then she went off, laughing softly to herself.

That night after Geir made love to her and she cried out her passion, Maida told him of her meeting with Helga.

Geir slipped his hand over her breast and gently fondled it.

She was almost asleep when he said, "Njal is either my brother or my father. But he will not tell me and there is no way I can make him tell me."

"Does it really matter—"

"Yes," he interrupted. "I must know whose blood I have."

"But if he is your brother, then you will have the same blood."

"Speak with the spaewoman again," Geir said. "Perhaps she will tell you more."

"She is one of the Devil's own!"

"Speak to her, Maida—for me?" Geir asked.

"Yes," she answered, moving closer to him. "I will."

The following morning Maida went to Helga's house, which was located upstream but not beyond the earthen walls of the stronghold. The main room was small, neat and smelled of cloves.

Helga offered Maida beer and then she asked why she came.

"I want to know more about the blood that binds Geir and Njal," Maida told her.

Helga shook her head and she answered, "Soon it will not matter; the blood tie between them has brought Geir here; that was its purpose. But as for you, you will be separated from Geir, though not forever."

Maida suddenly felt terribly cold; there was something about the old woman's face that made it look so much like a grinning skull that Maida cried out and ran from the house.

When Maida told Geir of her visit, Geir waved the old woman's words aside.

"She is not as good as Gruden was," Geir said. "I have no faith in her words." Then he added, "If Njal is my brother, then he was carried off when he was very, very young; if he is my father, then he raped my mother."

"Will you not ask him if he is your father?" Maida suggested, aware that Geir did not even mention what Helga had prophesied for them.

"I have. But he does not remember," Geir said.

"Do you think he is your father?"

"Yes," Geir answered. "I think he is my father. I know he is my father and he knows I know."

XXXIV

SNOW CAME. THE hours of daylight diminished until there were very few of them left, indeed. And the people in the stronghold stopped their work to pay homage to the sun and Freyr, the goddess of fertility.

The sun, when it shone, hovered low in the sky and passed swiftly over the earth. For twelve days it stayed in that place between the earth and the sky.

To keep the sun from rolling an ever-greater distance from them, the Vikings lit great fires, sang songs to the sun, and sacrificed many animals to feed its spirit with their flesh and blood.

And to honor Freyr they drank, ate, and fornicated with abandon throughout the twelve days.

Maida was frightened by what she saw and heard. She understood none of it. This was the same time of the year that Christians celebrated the birth of Christ their savior. It is a joyful season, a time of thanksgiving. But what she saw was an abomination! It was as though the people were possessed by a host of devils.

The Vikings raced horses until the beasts dropped from exhaustion and then they skinned them alive, oblivious to the pitiful whinnying of the dying animal. And they lay with one another openly, taking their pleasure wherever their passion came upon them, whether they were indoors or outside in the snow.

Maida found herself caught up in the orgy of unbridled

lust and let Geir do what he wanted with her, wherever and whenever it suited his pleasure. She passed most of the days in a drunken stupor until from the top of the hills she heard the shell horn signal to the people the sun had once again been saved from the abyss at the edge of the world.

Slowly the people in the stronghold revived and the carcasses of the sacrificial animals were burned; the blood-drenched idols were wiped clean and their own lives put into order.

A new year had begun and each day the sun shone it was so obviously stronger that the people congratulated one another on the success of their achievement, for without their prayers, sacrifices and fornication, the sun would have surely died and with it Freyr would have also perished.

Maida realized that with each passing day she was becoming less of a Christian and more of a pagan. There was no way to stop what was happening to her, unless a miracle occurred and she spent hours on her knees praying for one to happen. She did not want to be consigned to hell forever, though she knew she would suffer the torments of purgatory for countless years before she would be pure enough to receive God's grace and enter heaven.

Though Geir watched her pray, he never interrupted her. He was aware of the change in her. He sensed how frightened she was by what was happening to her.

At night after their lovemaking, he could hear her weeping softly, but whenever he would ask her what was wrong, she would shake her head and brokenly tell him that she was lost, utterly lost. To comfort her, he would hold her tight against him and after awhile she would stop weeping and drift off into a deep sleep.

The game of wits between Geir and Njal continued with each of them knowing what the other one knew or suspected. Several times Geir was tempted to call Njal father. But he wanted the admission to come from the old warrior and not be taken from him by trickery.

Despite the fact that Njal was considered an outlaw by everyone, Geir found him to be generous and deeply concerned with the past history of the Vikings. He knew many of the old sagas by heart and to the pleasure of his men he would recite them in his great hall.

"The old ways," Njal once said to Geir, "are better than what we have and much better than what will come. When I was a boy, our gods were stronger than they are now, and because they were stronger, our people were stronger. Now Christ has come among us." He shook his head and drank much of the beer in his horned flagon before he continued. "We have many gods, the Christians only one and yet we seemed to be the weaker." He stopped speaking; his brow furrowed and he seemed to be lost in thought.

A great storm struck the stronghold; it came howling out of the north and brought days of snow. And when it was over, the people in the stronghold dug themselves out of their houses.

The intense cold killed many of the cows, sheep and goats. Several of the animals were frozen solid where they stood. And the women went out with axes to chop their bodies into pieces which they then stored in their larders.

Maida took her share of meat that way and she carried it back to the shelter for future use.

"Not one drop of blood flowed," she told Geir. "It was just as if I were chopping wood."

Geir stretched and rubbed his arms. He stood up. The inside of the shelter blurred. He felt as if he were being sucked into a pool.

"Maida," he shouted, "I am going under!" The next

instant, he was in the swirling vortex and he lacked the strength to fight against it.

Maida turned to see him drop like a stone to the floor. She rushed to him. His head was hot and he was making soft gurgling sounds deep in his throat. She dragged him across the floor to the pallet on the other side of the room. By the time she managed to set him down, his eyes were open again. He tried to lift himself, but the effort was too much for him and he fell back exhausted.

Maida saw that he burned with fever, and she took some snow from the outside and put it on his forehead.

Geir made several attempts to speak. Finally he managed to say, "Bring Helga here. You stay with Thorkel."

"I will tend you," she told him.

He shook his head. "I am sick," he told her. "Save yourself, Maida, save yourself!" He closed his eyes and began to tremble.

She covered Geir with many robes and sat down to watch over him. He was by turns dripping with sweat or trembling with cold. Now and then he would open his eyes, look at her, and slowly shake his head.

By late afternoon Geir drifted off into an uneasy sleep. Maida hastened to Thorkel, but he was already on his way to her.

People were moving all over the stronghold. Some had their belongings on their backs or piled high on carts.

"What is happening?" she asked, fearful of what the answer would be.

"The sickness," Thorkel told her. "They flee from the sickness. Already Njal and many of the people have fallen ill."

"Geir—" she paused and gestured back toward the shelter.

"What will you do?" Thorkel questioned.

"Stay with him," she answered.

Thorkel nodded and said, "Most of the men who came here with Geir will stay." He looked toward those who were leaving. "For many of them it is already too late; they will come down with the sickness no matter where they go."

"Who tends Njal?" she questioned.

"Helga," he replied.

Maida said nothing and returned to the shelter to look after Geir.

For the next few days, death claimed many of the people in the stronghold. Njal died, pleading to speak with Geir, but saying nothing of what he wanted to tell him. Weath died and several of the captains who sat at Njal's table succumbed to the sickness.

But Geir clung to life. Despite the ugly eruptions on his body, despite his black vomit and the times he raved about ships and men, storms and killing, he remained alive.

Maida fed him like a child when he could take food. She washed his sweaty body with water newly made from melted snow.

Day and night merged into one continuous length of time. But she seldom left Geir's side. Sometimes she prayed to God to spare him, other times she prayed for her own soul.

Thorkel came by and so did Hougen. Each of them praised her courage and devotion to Geir.

So many people died in the stronghold that their bodies were left in the snow.

Then one morning Geir opened his eyes. He saw Maida. She was sitting in a chair not more than an arm's length away from him. He slowly reached for her, and when his hand touched hers, she started.

Immediately she was up and bending over him. The

fever was gone, but his cheeks were hollow and his eyes dull with weariness.

"How long have I been like this?" he asked.

"Days," she answered.

"Why did you stay?"

Maida touched his brow and shook her head. Though she wanted to say that she loved him, the words would not come. Instead she said, "Had I been ill, I know you would not have fled from me."

Geir nodded. Slowly taking her hand, he brought the back of it to his lips. "I love you, Maida," he whispered. "I love you!"

She brushed the tears from her eyes and then asked him if he was hungry.

"Very hungry," he answered. And then he asked about the other people in the stronghold.

"I will tell you all I know," she said. "But first you must have something solid in your belly." She silently thanked God for Geir's life.

XXXV

THE SICKNESS PASSED as quickly as it had come. But during its stay, it had taken a harsh toll of Njal's people. For many days and nights the smoke and flames from the great funeral pyres marked the secret place of the stronghold.

Algar and Lid saw the smoke by day and the flames by night. And knowing they had found Njal's stronghold, they beached their ships some distance north of where the river emptied into the sea and took counsel with one another.

The weather was still very cold but the sky was clear. The two men walked up through the snow to some wind-bent trees. Their breaths steamed in the icy air, and they rubbed their hands to keep them warm.

Lid looked to where the smoke climbed up into the sky and said, "The sooner we attack, the more chance we will have of overrunning them."

Algar nodded.

Between them they agreed to send men on foot upriver and strike at the stronghold on its flanks. Neither leader was willing to risk sending any of their ships upriver, or even keeping one or two of them near the mouth.

"They will not expect to be attacked from the land," Lid said. "We will have all the advantages."

"Especially since some of my men will be mounted on horses," Algar added.

Lid again turned toward the smoke and said, "Leave nothing standing. Tell your men to burn everything."

Algar waved his hand in front of him and he answered, "It will look like hell itself when we are through with it."

The two leaders returned to the shore and called upon their captains to unload the ships. Once that was accomplished, the men were assembled and told how and when they would attack the stronghold.

"Women are to be taken, except the very old," Algar told the men. "All the males, regardless of their age, are to be killed."

At twilight the men started off in the direction of the red glow that hung above Njal's stronghold like some strange mist. A thin crescent moon set, leaving a star-filled sky. The men moved silently across the white fields of snow. They worked their way to the north of the stronghold; then half of the force continued to move farther upstream until they found a place to ford the river and double back along the south side of the stronghold.

Lid commanded his men on the north flank and Algar took charge of his force on the south side of the stronghold. The attack would begin when Lid shot a flaming arrow into the night sky.

The two forces climbed up the eastern enbankments without encountering one guard or one watchdog. The night was very still.

Algar looked down at the stronghold and wondered where he would find Maida, or if he would find her, while on the other side of the river Lid touched fire to the head of his arrow and nocked it to the string of his bow. Tilting the bow up toward the dark sky, he shot the arrow.

The next instant the silence of the night filled with wild battle cries of hundreds of men.

Geir leaped from his pallet and grabbing hold of his

sword, he rushed into the night. He could see the attackers coming down the slopes of the embankment. Some of them lost their footing in the snow and tumbled some distance before they were able to stop and leap up again.

Thorkel and Hougen were already out of their shelters.

The attackers came from both sides. From the south, riders were already streaming toward the center of the stronghold.

"We must get to the ships," Geir yelled to his men. And he immediately started off toward them.

Some of the attackers came at them from the north. These were Vikings, and Geir and his men turned to meet them. They charged at each other screaming Odin's name.

Sword crashed against sword. Battle-axes crushed heads. Another crash of swords and then Geir saw Lid. He was leading a group of berserks toward the ships.

"The ships!" Geir shouted. "Get to the ships!" His men whirled away from their adversaries and dashed for the ships.

Four horsemen charged down on them.

Hougen and Skled turned to meet them, felling two of the riders before they themselves were cut down.

Geir heard their death cries but could not stop to look back at them. He and those with him met Lid and his men at the ships. The clang of weapon against weapon was deafening, and its sound rose above the wild shouting of the men.

Geir and Lid found each other and brought their swords into action. Each slashed viciously at the other. Time and time again their blades touched or smashed together.

Old as he was, Lid fought with the strength of a berserk. He wanted to kill Geir more than he wanted to live.

The fighting swirled all around them. In other parts of

the stronghold, Algar's men were already raping the women and putting every male child to the sword.

The snow-covered pathways between the houses were colored red with blood. Everywhere, women and children were screaming.

Geir's breathing came hard. He was still weak from his illness. He knew the longer he fought, the more chance his uncle had of winning.

Their blades locked.

Lid pushed against his nephew, trying to free his sword.

Geir saw the sweat stand out on the old man's brow, and suddenly he drove his knee into Lid's groin. Within an instant, Geir's sword was free. He plunged the blade into his uncle's chest.

Lid dropped to the ground. He died calling for Odin.

"Get the *Sea Bird* into the water," Geir shouted. And with his men, he put his back against the prow of the ship to push it into the river. It took all their strength to move it out of the snow around it. Finally it broke free and began to slide toward the water.

Some of Algar's men saw the ship take the water and ran to stop it.

But Geir and his crew quickly put the ship in midstream. Their breaths steaming on the cold night air, Geir and his men looked back at the stronghold. Theirs was the only ship to be launched. The other two vessels were still on the beach, where their crews were fighting a hopeless battle. Everywhere there was fire.

Men were still fighting and some of the women were already being herded toward the center of the stronghold.

Geir could not make out whether Maida was among them. Too exhausted to move, Geir let the river carry them to the sea, while he continued to look back at the flames that seemed to claw at the sky.

Maida was found crouched in the corner of the shelter by two of Lid's men, who immediately recognized her. They told her that Algar had joined forces with Lid to raid the stronghold.

She did not know whether to fall on her knees and thank God or weep for Geir. And together with the two Vikings, she went in search of Algar.

Outside the shelter the night was filled with the swirl of battle. Everything seemed to be on fire. The wounded and dead were everywhere.

Here and there a woman lay under the thrusting weight of one of the attackers, while another waited his turn.

Children ran screaming from one place to another. She saw small boys run through on the swords of several of the men and then tossed off to one side as though they were pieces of garbage and not a yelling, writhing child.

That the Vikings showed no mercy, she could understand; that was their way. But that Christians showed no mercy was enough to make her rush at several of the men who were just about to drive their swords into the bellies of two children.

But the men pushed her aside and killed the children with a single thrust of their weapons.

Her escort grabbed her and led her from the bodies of the boys.

Maida fought back her tears. A short time later, she found herself looking up at Algar. He stood in front of a group of women. He was splashed with blood.

For a moment he did not recognize her; then he quietly spoke her name.

Maida nodded.

He glanced at the other Viking women and back at her. The disgust showed in his face.

Maida opened her arms to him.

He fended her off and asked gruffly, "Where is Geir?"

She shook her head.

"I will speak with you later," he said. He turned back to the women to see if anyone of them caught his interest. One did—a young blonde girl, who was scarcely a woman. He grabbed her by the hand and pulled her past Maida, then led her into what was left of Njal's great hall and raped her.

Maida heard the girl scream several times. After Algar had his way with her, he told each of his captains to enjoy themselves with the girl.

Most of the night passed before Algar and the Vikings quit the stronghold. Practically all of the fires were burned out. A long line of women walked slowly back to where the ships were beached.

The sky clouded over and a strong wind sprang up from the north. By the time they reached the ships, a violent storm raged.

Algar ordered ships pulled high on the shore and under a tent cover, he forced himself upon Maida, as he had on the young Viking girl. His hands pried open her naked thighs and bruised her breasts.

He jammed his organ into her body and made her cry out in pain.

She tried to throw him off.

"I will have you any way I want you," he told her harshly. "Any woman who let herself be a Viking's whore has no need to think I will treat her as anything more than a whore."

Maida clawed at his face.

He grabbed hold of her hands. Holding them down, Algar exhausted himself in her body. Then he rolled off of her and fell into a deep sleep.

Maida listened to the howling of the storm, and without tears, she remembered how she had prayed for a miracle to save her.

Her prayer had been answered. She looked at Algar and nodded. She had gotten what she had asked for. She was no longer in the hands of the savage Vikings; she had been delivered into the savage hands of her husband.

She shook her head, and despite her resolve not to weep, tears came from the corners of her eyes and ran down her cheeks.

Silently she prayed to God, asking Him to keep Geir safe, though she did not know whether he was alive or dead and would never know.

Maida closed her eyes. She tried to find a comfortable position for her bruised body. But no matter which way she turned, she ached. Finally she settled on her left side.

Sometime before the first light, Maida fell asleep. But she was rudely awakened by Algar's hand on her breast.

He wanted her again.

Without a word, she rolled on to her back and spread her legs. She closed her eyes and hoped she would feel something. But she felt nothing, and when he was finished with her, he left her without saying a word. Maida uttered a deep sigh, turned back on her side, and let sleep claim her again.

Algar went to look at the sea, huge waves of gray water. He had learned from one of Lid's men that Geir and several of his berserks had escaped down the river by ship. Algar hoped the sea would do what neither Lid nor he had managed to do.

He glanced back to the tent where Maida slept.

She was more Viking than he had been led to believe by what Lid had told him about her. That she had been Geir's thrall was something he could have accepted, if he had not also learned from Lid that she had been Geir's willing whore.

Algar hated Geir and wished him dead, but he hated Maida more and prayed that he never show any weakness to her, or any love. He would use her as he would use other women who pleased him, and no man would call him to account for his actions.

Algar turned from the raging sea and he went to where some of the men were already busy preparing something to eat.

Like some giant fist, the storm closed around the *Sea Bird* and snapped most of her oars. The winds drove her far from the coast and to the south of where the river emptied into the sea.

There was neither food nor water aboard the ship. By the time the storm blew itself out and the giant fist released the *Sea Bird,* the men were too weak to raise the sail. They drifted under a blue sky and a blazing sun.

Whenever Geir closed his eyes, he could always see Maida; sometimes he spoke to her but she never answered.

One day when he opened his eyes, he found himself looking up at a dark face.

"Here is another one alive," the man said.

The man bending over him was a Moor. Geir knew Arabic, the language of the Moors, from the many voyages he had made to Miklagard.

"The others are dead," the man said. "With some water and food, the rest of them will make good galley slaves."

Moments later, Geir felt himself being lifted up and passed from one pair of hands to another. . . .

XXXVI

AFTER THE STORM had blown itself out and the spoils from Njal's stronghold had been divided between the Vikings and the Saxons, Algar sailed for home. But not before he brought two Viking women to his bed and forced Maida to lick their sex and have them do the same to her. When she tried to run from his tent, he caught and beat her savagely, shouting that she would do all he demanded or he would give her to his men for their pleasure.

Alone, Maida stood on the stern of her husband's ship. With deepening sorrow and a fearful anxiety about her future, she looked back at the receding coast. Nothing she could do would please Algar. He took her more to satisfy his pride than to satisfy his pleasure and when he lay between her naked thighs, she could not pretend to enjoy what she despised. With her husband she quickly discovered that she was more a prisoner than she ever had been with Geir. That she could have ever prayed to be with Algar was a source of constant sorrow to her.

But within a few weeks of her return to Algar's castle, Maida knew she was pregnant. She told Algar.

And he said, "Have my son and I might someday learn to forget you were a Viking's whore."

But Maida could not be sure whose spawn the child would be, and for the sake of the unborn babe, she prayed to the Holy Mother of God that she would bear Algar his son.

Spring quickly passed into summer. The crops in the

fields ripened and Maida grew big with the child. At summer's waning, when the harvest began, she was brought to bed to deliver her firstborn.

Her whole body was wet with sweat. She lay in her bed breathing hard. On her left was a small table with an oil lamp. The light from the lamp was yellow and wavered in the slight breeze that came through the casement window.

Standing at the foot of the bed, she saw Algar. Angrily he looked at her but said nothing. Astrid, the village midwife, was just to the right of him.

Maida closed her eyes. She was very tired. The previous day the birth pains had begun, and still she had not born the child. The coming of the child, like everything else during past months, was hard. Her life with Algar was miserable. She would not have believed she could be so wretched and yet she was. Whatever meager happiness she experienced came from her memories of the time she had spent with Geir and the love he had given her.

Suddenly the pain tore at her; she screamed and thrashed around, only to feel Astrid's strong hands holding her down. More sweat poured out of her.

"How much longer?" Maida asked in a weak voice.

"God will bring it forth," Astrid said, "in His own good time."

Maida neither accepted or rejected the midwife's words. She opened her eyes and saw that Algar was gone.

The midwife bathed her head with cool water.

"Is it always this hard?" Maida asked.

"With the first," Astrid answered. "The others will drop from you as easily as the cat gives kittens."

"There will be no others," Maida said harshly.

"The master—"

"There will be no others!" Maida repeated with a cry.

"There, there," the midwife said, soothingly. "Later

259

there will be time enough for that . . . let this one be born first."

Maida did not answer. The physical pain she was suffering was a fitting climax to the anguish she endured since she had been reunited with Algar. She did not love him and he did not love her.

Maida did not doubt that she was being punished for the sins she had committed with Geir, nor did she doubt that God would continue to punish her for as long as she lived. But she did not cry out against His will, and she often prayed that in the life to come, she would come to know something of the happiness that was to be denied her in this one.

Maida watched the light in the window grow stronger as the dawn came. She had often stood at that window where she had first seen Geir and had stared out to sea, thinking about him. She never dared to believe he might be alive, though she clearly remembered Helga's prophecy that they would be reunited. But the words of a spaewoman were the words of the Devil!

Another slash of pain cut through her vitals and she could not hold back the scream in her throat.

The spasms of pain became more and more frequent.

"Bear down," Astrid told her. "Bear down and help your child into this world."

Maida pressed her body downward.

Astrid was between her splayed thighs.

Maida could feel the woman's hands on her body.

"The child is coming," Astrid told her. "Press harder!"

The pain made her clench her teeth and ball her fists. She wanted to be free of the pain.

And then, except for the after-hurting, the pain was gone.

A moment later the room was filled with the lusty bawling of a child.

"A boy," Astrid said, handing the naked baby to his mother. "A fine sturdy-looking boy."

Maida clutched the child to her breasts. Almost immediately his lips closed around her nipple. As he began to draw milk from her, Maida uttered a deep sigh of satisfaction. She closed her eyes and gave herself up to the pleasurable sensation that flowed like a warm river over her exhausted body.

She was half-asleep when she heard the door to the room open.

"I came as soon as I heard," Algar told the midwife. He came toward the bed.

Maida looked up at him. She held the baby tightly to her.

"The child," he said, extending his hands.

She shook her head.

"The child," he demanded loudly and reaching down, he tore the baby from her breast. He brought the squalling baby to the window and he looked hard at it. "It is Geir's bastard," he growled, "and not my son. There is nothing of me in this whelp."

"Dear God—" Maida began to cry.

Astrid drew off into a far corner of the room.

"I will tell you about God," Algar shouted. "I will tell you that He damns you and this bastard."

Maida began to sob.

"Know, Maida," Algar roared, "I do not acknowledge this boy as my own son. He is yours and the Viking's spawn. I will give him nothing. Keep him, if you will, but he will have nothing from me."

"Send me and my child back to my father," she wept.

Algar raised the child above his head and threatening to

bash its brains out, he said, "I will send you to hell before I send you back to your father."

"Give me my child!" she screamed.

"Do you acknowledge his bastardy?"

"Yes. Give him to me."

"Do you agree that he shall have nothing of mine, neither land or anything else?"

"For the love of God, yes!"

Algar drew a deep breath. "I will have it set down in writing," he said, "and you will sign it."

Maida nodded.

He came to the bed and threw the screaming child on to it. "Bear me a son," he told her, "and I will give this one a place in my stables."

"I will bear you nothing," Maida shouted at him, clutching her baby to her.

"Then I will have other women breed me sons," he answered.

"Leave me," Maida screamed. "Leave me and beget a host of devils on the bodies of your whores."

Algar's hand smashed against Maida's face.

Her head snapped back; blood streamed from her nose and mouth, but she would not give him the satisfaction of dissolving into tears. If she had learned anything from Geir, she had learned how to be strong. She looked up at Algar and waited for another blow.

"Pity you and your bastard did not die," he said in a low, angry voice.

Maida kept silent.

Algar glared at her, turned, and stomped out of the room.

XXXVII

THE TWO WHO survived with Geir were Thorkel and Einar. All of the other men who had fled from Lid's stronghold with him had either died trying to launch the ships the night Algar and Lid had attacked Njal's stronghold, or had perished at sea.

Within a few days of their capture by the Moors, Geir and his two companions were chained to their places at the oars of a large warship. Each man wore an iron shackle around his leg. Those on the left side of the vessel were chained by their right ankle, while those on the opposite side wore the chain on their left ankle.

Geir was placed at an oar on the right side of the ship. Thorkel was several benches behind him, Einar was on the left side of the vessel, but within speaking distance.

The other slaves were men from every nation in the world. Some were black, others were colored blue and came from Ireland. A few were Vikings. Many were from the land of the Franks.

Geir occupied a place next to a man named Brian from Wales. Brian was a thickset man with wispy yellow hair and sad brown eyes. His fair skin was scarred by the whip and burned red from the sun.

He told Geir he was a priest of Christ and he had been captured when the Moors swept down on his small village on the coast of Wales.

Geir answered, "I have no use for the priests of Christ; my gods do what must be done for me."

Father Brian nodded and said no more.

Geir shouted to Thorkel and to Einar to tell them who sat next to him.

"I am with a black man," Thorkel said.

"A Frank sits next to me," Einar called.

The three men laughed.

Khalid, the overseer, laid a long black whip across their backs. None of them could laugh with the whip biting at their backs.

And Brian said to Geir, "Khalid thinks you were laughing at him."

"A long time ago," Geir answered, "I learned never to laugh at a man who holds either a whip, a sword, or a battle-ax, when you yourself have no weapon to challenge him."

"Christ is my weapon," Brian answered.

"But the whip was put on your back," Geir countered.

"It has drawn blood from every man here," Brian told him.

Geir could not deny that and he kept silent.

The warship belonged to the Emir of Morocco and its captain, Hischam, was his cousin. Besides the crew of forty-eight galley slaves, the vessel carried sixty soldiers, all of whom were Moors.

Geir kept his knowledge of Arabic a secret but nothing that was spoken in his presence escaped his understanding. He learned that Hischam was considered a fierce fighter and a good captain by his men, but Geir reserved judgment. It was easy enough for any man to swoop down on some small merchant ship and capture it. Geir would wait until Hischam gave battle to someone who could fight before he came to any conclusions about the prowess of the small dark man with a drooping black moustache.

As for Khalid, the overseer, Geir hated him. But he kept

his hate to himself. He suffered the lash without ever uttering a low moan of agony.

Many, many times the dark giant of a man would stand over a slave and for the joy of seeing him in agony, he would cut his back until it was nothing but bloody skin for the flies to feast on.

Day after day the ship moved in search of prey and when it was sighted, Hischam ordered the tempo of the rowing increased. Khalid used his whip and the men at the oars would row until their minds blurred and their body felt nothing, not even the sting of the whip. Sometimes a man's heart would burst, and he would vomit blood until he died.

Geir often thought about Maida and how much he loved her. His love for her saddened him. There was no hope of his escape from the galley and no hope of him ever seeing Maida again. He had no doubt Algar had found her and had taken her back to his village with him. Whenever Geir thought about Maida with Algar's weight on her, he ground his teeth in sullen anger.

More than once the ship engaged an enemy and then the soldiers would swarm on to the other vessel shouting, "Allah Akbar!"

Sometimes the enemy would board; then many of the slaves would die chained to their oars without the chance to fight for their lives.

Weeks passed and Geir began to speak more to Brian, telling him he once had a thrall who was a Christian.

"She spent a great deal of time praying," he said with disdain.

"Prayer," the Christ-priest said, "is the only way God can know our needs and our love for Him."

"She prayed to be forgiven for the passion she felt for me," Geir boasted.

"And did you feel the same thing toward her?"

"Yes . . . yes . . . But she was a married woman—married she said in the eyes of your God forever, even though she was my thrall."

"Where is she now?"

"With her husband," Geir answered harshly.

"God moves in mysterious ways," the Christ-priest answered.

Geir looked at the man whose soft brown eyes met his hard stare without flinching. Then in a low voice, he said, "I would have married her."

"She was already married."

Geir nodded and shrugged. Despite their differences, he and the Christ-priest became friends. He soon learned that Khalid used the whip more on Brian than on any of the other men. But the Christ-priest never cried out or faltered at the oar. Geir admired the man's strength and courage.

"Christ is my strength," Brian answered, "and God is my courage."

Geir was confused; he had always thought that Christ and God were the same.

"Christ is the son of God," Brian explained one night as the ship lay off shore. "He was born of mortal woman so He might come to men to teach them the ways of God."

Geir listened to his friend but it seemed unlikely that one God could possibly be as strong as the many gods of his people, nor did it seem to make much sense to love those whom you hate.

He looked toward the platform where Hischam and Khalid slept. He could not love them as he had come to love Brian and as he had always loved Thorkel and Einar, even if he would become a Christian ten times over. But to keep from wounding his friend, he said nothing about his feelings toward the captain or the overseer.

"But tell me," Geir asked, "why would your God allow the Moors to make a galley slave out of you?"

"To bring Christ to you," Brian answered without hesitation. "Obviously your thrall was meant to accomplish the task but could not, so He chose me to do it."

"But why should He want me?" Geir questioned.

"I do not know," the Christ-priest answered. "But as I told you before, God moves in mysterious ways."

Geir did not say anything more that night. When he rested his head on his arms which were set on the oar in front of him, he did not sleep.

For a long time he listened to the breathing of the men around him and the sounds of the sea against the hull of the ship. That Christ might want him seemed exceedingly foolish, since he was nothing more than a galley slave and he was likely to remain one for the rest of his days, unless by some miracle he might gain his freedom. But even as a free man, what would Christ want with him?

Geir saw Hischam and Khalid leave their sleeping platform and walk toward the stern of the ship. He pretended to sleep.

Hischam said, "We will join with other ships until there are five of us. Then we will raid the Cornish coast. I want only strong men at the oars. Show me those that will be strong enough to withstand such a voyage."

Khalid assured the captain that every man was fit.

"Then you want none replaced?"

"None," the overseer said.

The captain nodded approvingly and complimented Khalid on the way he managed the slaves.

"With Allah's help," the overseer replied, "all is done."

The captain stopped alongside Geir and he said, "Does this one's eyes follow you as they follow me?"

"If it will please you, I will blind him," Khalid answered.

Geir held his breath.

"No," Hischam answered, after a momentary pause. "If I am still bothered by his eyes after the raiding, we can do it then."

Khalid agreed it would be best to wait.

When they moved off, Geir slowly let the air out of his lungs. He found himself wondering whether to give thanks to Thor or to Christ for having saved him from being blinded?

In the morning the ship sailed north. Three days later they joined four other ships.

For all the time Geir had been a galley slave, the sea had remained exceedingly calm. But now they were moving into the stormy waters off the Cornish coast. Summer was drawing to an end, and already the nights were cold enough to make the men shiver.

Geir realized it was Hischam's plan to strike at the villages along the coast at harvest time. Had he been captain of the ship, he would have done the same. That way not only would Hischam manage to get gold and silver, but he would also collect a good supply of grain and possibly some livestock.

From the way two of the other ships rode in the water, Geir knew that they were not defended by soldiers but were there to carry away the booty after the raids.

When Geir mentioned to Brian they were going to the Cornish coast, the Christ-priest gave him a strange look and asked how he had come to learn that.

"I understand their language," he said.

"And you have not said anything about it all this time?" Brian questioned.

"I saw no reason—"

"It might have spared me the bite of the lash," the Christ-priest told him, obviously angry he had not been told.

And Geir reminded him, "Christ would not have lost His temper, if He had been chained beside me."

"Ah," the Christ-priest cried, "but I fall short of our Lord; I am just a humble priest."

But there was laughter in Brian's eyes and Geir knew that his friend was no longer angry with him.

The skies grayed and the sea became the color of the sky. Soon the wind came from the north and began to build, with long feathery spume blowing from their tops. The men at the oars struggled to keep steerage way and Khalid used his whip to keep them from resting, even for a moment.

At night the sea became so wild that several of the soldiers were swept overboard. One of them was thrown on top of Geir, and before the sea wrenched him from the ship, Geir slipped the man's knife from its sheath.

The next soldier who happened by suddenly stopped short and dropped to the deck. Geir pulled the knife out of the man's stomach and took his knife, too. He killed another soldier in the same way.

By morning, Geir had three knives and had managed to pass one of them to Thorkel and the other to Einar.

"If Khalid finds you or your friends with a knife," Brian warned, "he will tie you to the mast and use his whip to skin you alive."

"God provides," Geir answered with a smile.

The Christ-priest looked at him with an expression of surprise on his long face and then said, "Perhaps . . . perhaps."

The storm passed and the officer of the troops reported to the captain they had lost six men overboard.

"Too bad," Geir whispered, "I could have gotten three more knives. I might have given you one."

With a vigorous shake of his head, Brian told him, "I

was a soldier once and killed many men. But when I became a priest, I put all that behind me. I will not kill again."

"Even if it meant you could be free?" Geir questioned.

"Even then," the Christ-priest said, "I would not kill."

Geir shrugged and told the priest he had no such qualms.

"Then God meant it to be that way," the Christ-priest told him.

Geir had no idea whether he would ever get to use the knife, but he felt much better for having it than he had without it. Since that night when he had been spared being blinded, he did not spend much time looking at either Hischam or Khalid, but they were never out of his thoughts for very long.

It gave him pleasure to know that when they were close to him, he had the power to strike them dead. But he also knew their deaths would cost him his own life. And he was not such a fool to cheaply trade his life away for theirs.

Despite the warm days, the nights were so cold that Khalid gave each of the men a blanket to wrap around their shivering bodies. The black men suffered the most of the cold, and many became ill with the coughing sickness.

One afternoon, as they came around a headland, the lookout on the mast cried out, "Sails . . . sails off to the left."

Hischam looked seaward. "Vikings . . . Vikings . . . Vikings."

The troops immediately took up their positions.

Hischam gave orders to turn.

"They are going to try and fight them," Geir said.

Khalid let his whip sing through the air as he laid it on the backs of the men. He moved up and down the wooden walkway between the rows of slaves.

270

The men pulled on the oars with all of their strength. The ship responded and rushed toward the Viking vessels.

Geir could see the dragon heads on their bows. There were two ships and they were bearing down very fast.

"Now we will see how these Moors fight," he said between gasps of air to Brian.

The Christ-priest could not muster enough strength to answer.

Geir shouted to Thorkel and Einar, telling them to be ready to use their knives.

Khalid whirled around and set the whip to Geir's back, shouting at him that his mother was a whore and his father was a dog.

Geir took the flogging and clamped his teeth together to stop from crying out. The whip against his back was a blade of fire that drew blood.

Hischam called out for the slaves to row faster.

Khalid stopped whipping Geir. He moved along the walkway to let the whip loose on every man in the crew.

Geir's back was red with blood but he kept pulling at his oar and he watched the two Viking ships approach. They came with the wind behind them and the men pulling strongly at the oars.

Two of the black men began to vomit blood. One of them dropped over his oar.

Khalid came running back. With the aid of a soldier, he used a hammer and chisel to break the shackle on the dead man's foot. Then he and the soldier lifted the body over the side. It splashed into the water and immediately vanished from sight.

The Viking ships were very, very close. Suddenly their sails came down.

The next instant the ships came together. Oars splintered and the Moors, shouting, "Allah Akbar!" swarmed over the sides of the Viking ship.

271

But their shouts were met by the Vikings, "Odin . . . Odin . . . Odin . . ."

The crash of sword against sword was loud and clear in the quiet of the afternoon.

Geir shouted for Khalid.

The man turned and ran for the stern.

Geir waited until he was almost past him before he swung his hand up and he drove the blade into the man's stomach.

Khalid looked surprised. Then he dropped to the deck.

Geir pulled the dead man's sword from sheath. He waited until one of the soldiers came racing down to find out what happened to the overseer. When the man was within striking distance, Geir ran the sword into his chest.

The Moors were leaping back onto their own ship.

The Vikings followed them.

The fighting surged around the bow and now was moving amidships. Hischam was felled by a blow from a battle-ax.

The Vikings put their shields together and from behind a moving wall, they drove the Moors back to the stern. The Moors were no match for the Vikings.

Then suddenly the Moors dropped their weapons and falling on their knees pleaded for mercy.

Geir called out to the leader of the Vikings, telling him he and his friends, as well as several other members of the crew, were Norsemen.

Within minutes all of the slaves were freed and Geir approached the leader.

"I am Geir," he said. "And that is Thorkel and the young one is Einar."

"My name is Sven," the leader said. He was a tall dark-haired man with gray eyes.

Geir looked back to the Christ-priest; then suddenly he

272

turned and ran to where Brian sat. A splintered oar had gone through the man's stomach.

The Christ-priest tried to talk but could not. He died clutching Geir's hand, but there was no fear in his eyes or on his face.

Geir sat him gently down on the deck and returning to Sven, he said, "He was a Christ-priest, but he was brave and a good man."

"I have known some like that myself," Sven said.

"Though you have captured the ship," Geir said, "I ask you for it and I ask you to consider these men free."

"You ask a lot," Sven replied, realizing the man who spoke and the others with him would not hesitate to fight for what they wanted.

Geir nodded, and he said, "I have something that must be done. If I am alive after I do it, I will return the ship to wherever your stronghold is."

"And the men?"

"They will be free," Geir told him in a flat hard voice. "Those who wish to sail with me will be welcomed; those who wish to be put ashore will be put ashore."

Every one of the men shouted they would sail with him.

"So you have a crew and a ship," Sven told him with a smile. "Is there anything else you would have from me?"

"Only your friendship," Geir said, extending his hand. "And the name of the place where I must go to return this ship once I am done."

Sven grasped his hand and he told him. "Come to Trellborg in Denmark."

"I will come," Geir said, "You have my word."

XXXVIII

GIER AND THORKEL stood on the bow, looking through the early-morning mist at Algar's castle. All of what they had destroyed during their raid had been rebuilt.

"I think you should take either me or Einar," Thorkel said.

Geir shook his head and told his friend, "What I must do, I must do alone."

More of the mist burned off and all of the village was revealed. Nothing as yet was stirring but the crowing of several cocks carried over the booming sound of the surf to where the ship was.

Geir ordered Einar to turn the ship about and bring it to the beach where almost a year before, he had fought and been captured by Algar. Geir moved back to the stern and Thorkel followed him.

"If you took one of us," Thorkel pressed, "you would stand some chance of coming out alive."

"If I am not back to the ship by high noon," Geir told him, "you take command and sail the ship to Trellborg."

"I will attack—"

"No," Geir said. "Keep my word and return the ship to Sven." He motioned to the crew and commented, "Though most of them are not Vikings, they are all good men."

"Vikings never came in such dark shades," Thorkel responded.

274

With a laugh, Geir said, "Then perhaps it is about time to put some color into our fair skins."

"I have no doubt the women in Trellborg will see to that," Thorkel answered.

"Now listen carefully to what I want you to do while I am away," Geir said. He told Thorkel to sail the ship back and forth in front of the cove several times. "I want Algar to think that there are many ships outside." Geir explained. He will rush down to the beach to prevent them from entering the cove, and while he is at that I will be at my work."

"At high noon—"

"Stand offshore always," Geir said. "If you do not see me coming, turn and head out to sea."

"Those are not the orders I like," Thorkel responded gruffly. "But I will obey them."

The ship glided into a sandy shore and Geir, dressed in a monk's robe that hid his sword, warmly embraced Thorkel and Einar before he went over the side of the vessel. Quickly he waded ashore and without looking back at the ship, he vanished in the heavily wooded area just beyond the beach. There he paused and turned to watch the ship pull into deep water.

As soon as the vessel was working its way north, Geir plunged into the woods. He made his way to the road that entered the village from the west.

The sun was bright and the blue sky unmarred by a single cloud. Before long he was sweating profusely, but he dared not remove his monk's robe.

He left the woods, climbed a steep, rocky hill, crossed a field of newly mown hay that filled the air with a strong sweet smell. Then he came upon the road, which was no more than a well-used pathway, wide enough for two horses to walk abreast of one another.

There were already several people on the road. They greeted him courteously. He nodded, smiled, but said nothing, for fear they might become suspicious of his accent.

The road snaked its way between two hillocks that from the sea looked as though they were directly behind Algar's castle, when in truth they were some distance from it.

Geir had just reached the edge of the village when the morning stillness was rent with alarm horns.

Within minutes people were running in every direction and soldiers came pouring out of the barracks.

Some of the men on the watch towers near the cove were shouting, "Vikings . . . Vikings!"

Others cried, "Moors . . . Moors."

To the people it made no difference who the invaders were; their lives and possessions were imperiled by anyone with the strength of arms to take them.

Whole families were abandoning their dwellings for the safety of the hills, while many sought refuge in the walled courtyard of the castle.

Within minutes of the alarm, Geir saw Algar and his vassals gallop out of the castle yard and rush toward the beach.

A few moments later he pushed his way through the castle gate. Inside the courtyard there was as much confusion as there was outside. And taking advantage of it, Geir slipped inside the great hall, made his way up the steps.

Suddenly a soldier challenged him.

Without hesitation, Geir flung back his robe and drew his sword.

The soldier rushed at him.

Geir hurled his weapon at the man; it struck him in the chest, dropping him to his knees. He tried to pull the blade out of his body.

Geir wrenched the sword free and ran up the stone steps to the room from whose window he had first seen Maida. Without pausing, he flung the door open.

Maida screamed.

Geir stopped. Maida was seated in the corner; a child was at her breast. She tried to speak but her trembling lips would not form the words.

Geir went to her. With his free hand he picked up the child and looked at him.

"He is yours," Maida finally said.

Geir nodded. "Take your cloak." he told her. "I have a ship standing offshore—hurry!"

"I thought you were dead," she sobbed.

"Later," he told her, "later I will tell you everything."

At the door, Maida held back. "Algar will kill you if he captures you."

Geir shook his head. "We have no time for talk now," he said. "Will you come with me or must I take you as I once did?"

"No," she said with tears glistening in her eyes, "I will go with you, Geir; this time I will go with you willingly."

He took hold of her hand and quickly led her down the circular stairway. When they reached the dead man, Geir stopped, slipped the monk's robe on again, and hid his sword under it.

"You must walk with me," he told Maida, "without looking at anyone."

She nodded and held the child tightly in her arms. Just moments before Geir had burst into the room, she was thinking about him, how he, too, enjoyed mouthing the nipples of her breasts. . . .

Astride a large gray horse, Algar watched the ship. Twice it had turned and made its way past the cove but did not make any attempt to enter it.

He looked back toward the castle and then at the ship.

Suddenly he realized that the ship would never attack; it was meant to draw him away from the castle.

He wheeled his mount around and spurring it until blood flowed from its flanks he raced back to the village.

The press of people at the castle gate forced Algar to dismount. With his sword at the ready, he ran into the courtyard just as Maida and a monk were coming out of the great hall.

"Geir!" Algar shouted and rushed at him.

Geir drew his blade and pushed back the cowl of the monk's robe.

"Drop that weapon," Algar ordered, "or I will have my men cut you down."

Geir told him, "That ship out there is mine. If I am not back on it by high noon," he lied, "my men will burn this village and take everyone alive captive. Algar," he said slowly, "all of them are galley slaves; they care less about dying than my Vikings did."

Algar glanced back at the ship; it was now standing off the mouth of the cove.

"Many, many of your people will die," Geir said.

The people began to mutter.

"You can go," Algar reluctantly replied.

"I came for my woman and my child," Geir said. "I will not leave without them. The boy you know is mine; one look at him and anyone would know that. And as for the woman, she is more mine than she was ever yours."

Algar's breathing was labored and his face almost purple. Once more he looked toward the ship.

"This will be an end to it," Geir said.

Algar nodded and slowly stepped aside.

Geir took the child from Maida. He held the boy in the crook of his left arm, while in his right hand, he held his sword.

"Walk on my left," he whispered to Maida.

The three of them walked slowly out of the castle yard and across the small village square.

"My heart is pounding away," Maida said.

Geir said nothing. His eyes were on the ship; it was just off the spit of land that formed one arm of the cove. Thorkel must have seen them because he was bringing the vessel close to the beach, just inside of the cove.

From behind them, suddenly Algar shouted, "I will kill you, Geir. I will kill you!" He could not stand to have the Viking go free; he had to stop him.

The next instant, a spear thudded into Geir's left shoulder. He stumbled and handing the child up toward Maida, he said, "Hurry, run for the ship. Thorkel will keep you safe."

Maida had no time to think; the child was in her arms and she began running to the beach.

Geir reached around and pulled the bloody spearhead from his shoulder. Then, springing to his feet, he turned to face Algar.

"It will end with your head on the tip of my blade," Algar said.

Geir watched him.

The two men circled one another.

Blood streamed down Geir's left arm. There was fire in his shoulder and sweat in his eyes.

Algar slashed at him.

Geir caught the stroke at the middle of his blade. His whole arm shivered from the force of the blow. He took another blow and still another.

The two men drew close to one another; each tried desperately to push the other off balance.

Geir growled, "So you have Bluetooth, my sword."

And Algar answered, "Soon you will have him between your ribs, Viking!"

Geir lost his footing and Algar sliced down, slashing Geir across his chest before he could roll away. But an instant later, Geir was on his feet.

And once more the two men began to circle one another.

Algar lunged at him.

Geir feinted to the right; Algar moved his weapon to ward off Geir's thrust, but the attack came to the left and before he could block it, the blade was in him. He staggered and let his own weapon fall.

Geir pulled his sword free and drove it straight into Algar's chest. Then he reached down and picked up Bluetooth.

Algar fell. He looked at Geir and with blood streaming from his mouth, he shouted, "I curse you, Geir. I curse you and Maida. . . . may you rot in hell!" Then he tumbled into the dust and bled to death.

With a handful of grass, Geir wiped Bluetooth clean. Then he walked slowly down to the beach where his ship was waiting for him.

That night as Geir sat in the stern sheet with one hand on Maida's breast and the other on Bluetooth, she asked him why he came back to her.

"What else could I do, Maida?" he questioned. "I could not go on without you."

"And I found," she said, "that I was slowly dying without you; I prayed for you; I prayed that God in His mercy might find it in His heart to love you as I had come to love you."

For a while Geir did not speak. Then in a low voice, he said, "I will try your God, Maida; He seems to do more for His people than many gods of my people do for them. You will teach me His ways and I will try to follow."

"I will teach you," she whispered passionately. "I will

teach you. . . . but you must teach me once more how to love.''

"I do not think you will have much difficulty learning that," he said, gently squeezing her breast.

"No, I do not think so either," she answered, putting her hand over his.

BEST SELLERS FROM BERKLEY

AIRPORT '77   (03482-8—$1.75)
  by David Spector & Michael Scheff

THE FIRST TIME   (03152-7—$1.95)
  by Karl and Anne Taylor Fleming

GIANTS   (03271-X—$1.95)
  by Jack Ansell

THE MADONNA COMPLEX   (03528-X—$1.95)
  by Norman Bogner

ONCE AN EAGLE   (03330-9—$2.75)
  by Anton Myrer

RUDOLPH VALENTINO   (03458-5—$1.95)
  by Robert Oberfirst

THE VAMPIRE TAPES   (03508-5—$1.75)
  by Arabella Randolphe

MOSCOW FAREWELL   (03385-6—$1.95)
  by George Feifer

Send for a *free* list of all our books in print

These books are available at your local bookstore, or send
price indicated plus 30¢ per copy to cover mailing costs to
Berkley Publishing Corporation
390 Murray Hill Parkway
East Rutherford, New Jersey 07073